Praise for Jill Shalvis

"Riveting suspense laced with humor and heart is her hallmark, and Jill Shalvis always delivers."
  —Donna Kauffman, *USA Today* bestselling author of *Catch Me if You Can*

"Irresistible heroes . . . so bleeping sexy, you'll break into a sweat."
  —Stephanie Bond, author of *Whole Lotta Trouble*

"Fast, fanciful, and funny. Get ready for laughs, passion, and toe-curling romance."   —*Rendezvous*

"Jill Shalvis creates compelling romance."
  —*Romantic Times*

"Jill Shalvis. Wonderful romance, wonderful mystery. Always."   —*Affaire de Coeur*

"Sizzling passion and electric awareness."
  —wordweaving.com

"Ms. Shalvis pens a hot, steamy romance that leaves you breathless."   —Word on Romance

"Heartwarming, humorous, passionate, and sometimes profound."   —Romance Reviews Today

"Her books stir your emotions while leaving you passionately breathless."   —Writers Unlimited

"Jill Shalvis is a breath of fresh air on a hot, humid night."   —The Romance Reader's Connection

Her Sexiest Mistake

Jill Shalvis

A SIGNET ECLIPSE BOOK

SIGNET ECLIPSE
Published by New American Library, a division of
Penguin Group (USA) Inc., 375 Hudson Street,
New York, New York 10014, USA
Penguin Group (Canada), 90 Eglinton Avenue East, Suite 700, Toronto,
Ontario M4P 2Y3, Canada (a division of Pearson Penguin Canada Inc.)
Penguin Books Ltd., 80 Strand, London WC2R 0RL, England
Penguin Ireland, 25 St. Stephen's Green, Dublin 2,
Ireland (a division of Penguin Books Ltd.)
Penguin Group (Australia), 250 Camberwell Road, Camberwell, Victoria 3124,
Australia (a division of Pearson Australia Group Pty. Ltd.)
Penguin Books India Pvt. Ltd., 11 Community Centre, Panchsheel Park,
New Delhi - 110 017, India
Penguin Group (NZ), cnr Airborne and Rosedale Roads, Albany,
Auckland 1310, New Zealand (a division of Pearson New Zealand Ltd.)
Penguin Books (South Africa) (Pty.) Ltd., 24 Sturdee Avenue,
Rosebank, Johannesburg 2196, South Africa

Penguin Books Ltd., Registered Offices:
80 Strand, London WC2R 0RL, England

First published by Signet Eclipse, an imprint of New American Library,
a division of Penguin Group (USA) Inc.

First Printing, December 2005
10 9 8 7 6 5 4 3 2 1

Chapter One

Advertising executive extraordinaire, Prada shopa-holic, and all-around tough-as-steel LA Mia Appleby could put a good spin on anything, but waking up in the bed of a man when she'd only meant to admire his motorcycle wasn't one of those things.

Apparently, you could take the girl out of the trailer park, but you couldn't take the trailer park out of the girl. She hated that, but she'd long ago accepted it—in her avid appreciation of the male spe-cies, she was her mother's daughter.

Never a dip-her-head-in-the-sand type of woman, she faced the music. She opened her eyes, took in the pale pink June dawn streaking across the skylight above her, and blinked, which turned into an invol-untary squeak of surprise when the view was sud-denly hampered by a head.

A male head.

A gorgeously rumpled male head with sleepy, heavy-lidded light caramel eyes and a slow smile that had all sorts of wicked, naughty trouble in it.

God, she was a sucker for wicked, and with that bad-boy motorcycle of his and those let-me-do-you eyes, this man *so* fit the bill.

"Hey," he said in a rough morning voice that went with the dark stubbled jaw and bed hair as he slid his body over hers, pinning her to the mattress with his warm, hard torso and mile-long legs, which spread hers.

In spite of herself, her body tightened. No doubt, he was stop-the-presses hot. He had a body for sinning, of which they'd done plenty last night.

All night.

Oh, boy.

He'd moved into the neighborhood two days ago. His first night in town she'd welcomed him with a plate of cookies. The next night they'd pulled onto their street at the same time, she in her car, he on his motorcycle.

Check.

Wearing battered jeans and boots and a leather jacket.

Check!

Looking extremely tall and leanly muscled and full of mischief.

Check, check, check!

Instead of more cookies, she'd offered him a drink, which they'd shared at his place.

And then, because she'd had a shitty day, because she'd been feeling down and weak with it, because he'd looked as good as a long, tall drink of water, she'd given him a different welcome altogether: a horizontal one.

And it'd been *spectacular*.

Her job in advertising was high stress. Her *life* was high stress, and while she was very much on top of her universe, she occasionally felt the need to let go, to relax. Some people used Prozac. Mia didn't. She used other feel-good tactics, such as a good man, for instance. And sure, occasionally that meant a wild bout of mutually satisfying sex. Why not? It was immediate gratification, she enjoyed variety, and there were no calories involved.

Sure, it might have been a bad decision on her part

that this man was now a neighbor and therefore on her home turf, but she couldn't resist. Besides, she'd intended to leave his bed before midnight, telling him that while he'd been fun, there'd be no repeats.

After all, she rarely repeated.

But then he'd kissed her again, and oh, God, was he good at that. And now he was looking at her, with that two-day growth on his lean jaw, with that bed-head hair that should have been so silly but she just wanted to sink her fingers into. Those melt-me eyes seemed to see right into her, a fact that rattled her enough that she pushed at his chest. "Move," she said.

He smiled and dipped his head, taking a playful nibble out of her throat, a lovely, sexy little nibble that had her eyes rolling into the back of her head and little zaps of sexual energy zinging all her happy spots.

Of which, apparently, she had many. "Get up," she repeated.

"I *am* up." He sucked a patch of her skin into his mouth as he nudged his up part against her.

In spite of herself, she clutched at him, enjoying the feel of his hard body against hers, his rough jaw brushing her skin, the scent of him . . .

Focus, Mia. "Listen, big guy, I have to work—"

His hand stroked up her body and cupped a breast.

Her bones dissolved. "Stop that—"

His thumb rasped over her nipple. "Mmm. I love your body."

And she loved the touch. Too much. Vaulting into action, she scrambled out from beneath him, rolling off the bed. When her feet hit the floor she whirled around, looking for her clothes which had been wildly and carelessly scattered the night before. There was her tweed skirt on the floor, the matching top draped over a lamp. She stepped into the skirt, pulled on the top, slipped her feet into her heels. Her bra . . . where the hell was her bra?

"Here," he said, and she whipped around to face him.

He'd rolled onto his back and scooted up against the headboard, one arm up and behind his head. Man, oh man, she could have just looked at him all day.

Except that he was twirling her lace Wonderbra around his fingers, watching her with an expression of vast amusement.

The blankets were long gone, tumbled to the floor. The sheet, pale blue against his tanned skin, pooled low on his hips, not quite covering his EMH.

Early-Morning Hard-on.

She heard the words in Sugar's soft Southern drawl and shoved them ruthlessly to the back of her mind. After years of hard work, none of Mia's south showed, not an ounce of that trailer-trash upbringing. She'd made sure of it.

She snatched her bra from his fingers. "Thank you."

"My pleasure." His voice was still low and sleep-rough. From this close she could smell him, some uncomplicated mix of man and soap, but it was enough to have her nostrils quivering for more.

He shifted, and those six-pack abs she'd had so much fun touching last night rippled.

Oh, damn, he was something. If only the sheet wasn't tented, if only he'd show a single sign of wanting her to get out, this would be so much easier. She folded her bra and slipped it into her skirt pocket as she looked for her panties.

He let out a slow smile. "You fold your underwear?"

Forget her panties. She walked to the door.

"Hey, it's cute, that's all. A little uptight, maybe. But cute."

She reached for the handle.

"Ah, don't go. Let me get you some breakfast." He slid out of the bed and walked toward her in all his morning glory, and there was lots of glory.

"I don't eat breakfast."

"Everyone needs breakfast." His every movement was fluid and easy. Uncalculatedly sexy. Watching her thoughtfully from his deep, direct eyes, he grabbed his jeans off the floor and slid them on.

Sans underwear.

Fascinated in spite of herself, she watched. He pulled the jeans up, winced slightly, and then didn't fasten them, his wryly amused gaze meeting hers. The man was comfortable in his own skin, she'd give him that. As well he should be, because his skin, and everything beneath it, was damn fine.

She'd been with particularly fine men before, but she'd never experienced such a visceral spark. It felt different, too: close, a completely unexpected—and unwelcome—twist.

He was still watching her as he absently shoved his fingers through his short, rumpled hair. Scratched his chest.

"At least let me get you eggs, maybe some juice," he said. "Protein and sugar all in one. Breakfast of champions." He came close then, too close, lifting a hand, stroking a stray strand of hair from her face. "Last night . . ." He let out a low, rough laugh. "Pretty amazing, huh?"

Yeah, and so was he. "I've really got to go."

He cocked his head. "I thought you said you were from here. Born in LA."

She hadn't said "born here." She'd always been careful not to out-and-out lie. She'd said she *belonged* in LA. "Why?"

"Because I definitely heard a Southern drawl in that pretty voice of yours." He smiled.

She did not, because, wow, she'd stayed *waaaaay* too long if he was picking that up. How many years ago had she squashed that accent, and all that went with it, far, *far* into her past? Simply buried it beneath her carefully planned layers of college, jobs, hard work, sheer tenacity, and pure will? She was no longer poor little "Apple," a kid who had to settle, thank God, but a woman who had choices and a future that didn't include living in a crowded, broken-down mobile home full of stacks of bills that couldn't be paid. There'd been mistakes, too many to count, but she'd buried them and danced on their graves. She turned to the door.

Setting his hand on the wood above her head, he held the door closed. "Hey," he said quietly, wrapping his fingers around her arm and turning her to face him. "You okay?"

Sure. Just as soon as she got out of here and away from this man who instead of giving her a few hours of mindless oblivion made her think, made her remember where she'd come from, and she hated that. "I've really got to go."

Still looking at her, he slowly nodded. "I can see that. Mia . . ." He went to touch her again, another stroke of those fingers she knew now to be extremely talented, but this time she stepped back.

His expression as he studied her was bemused, and a little confused. As if maybe he'd never been walked away from before. And there in the swirling depths of those fathomless eyes was something else as well, something that she hadn't expected.

Affection.

Oh, no. No, no, no, no. This had to be squashed. Now. Like a bug. "Listen," she said in her cool business voice, the one meant to send him scrambling away from her. "Last night was fun, we both got off, yadda yadda. But now it's the light of day and I have work. And you have to . . ." Damn. She had no idea. "Do something, too, I'm sure. So let's just both get on with it."

He nodded, watching her thoughtfully. "And the next time we see each other, we'll just forget it ever happened. Is that it?"

Right. Except there wouldn't be a next time.

"I live here now," he said. "On your street. We're going to run into each other. What do you expect us to do, pretend we've never met?"

Hey, it was a long street.

"My God," he said with a low laugh. "That's exactly what you expect."

"Look—" She racked her brain for his name. "Uh . . ."

He stared at her in disbelief. "You don't remember my name?"

When she only winced at this, he let out a low oath, stalked away, then whipped back. "Kevin," he said, no longer looking so laid-back or sleepy-eyed. "My name is *Kevin*."

"I'm sorry. I'm not very good at this."

"No, actually." Sinking his fingers into his hair, making the short, dark silky strands stick straight up, he shook his head. "You're far better than you think."

"I meant at leaving."

"So did I." He opened the bedroom door for her, turning sideways for her to get by. The space was narrow, and her breast brushed his ribs. A shiver actually passed through her, startling her into stopping, into staring up into his eyes.

He didn't look away. Of course he didn't look away. He'd probably never run, never avoided or ducked an issue in his life. As opposed to her, who quit and ran far and fast whenever the going got tough.

His hand brushed her hip, and as her body was

inexplicably aware of each place where they'd touched, her pulse leapt.

The beat stretched into a moment, until she was forced to pull air into her lungs. It sounded like a gasp, loud in the silent room.

Again his fingers brushed her hip, this time as if trying to soothe, but this time the touch had the opposite effect because she wanted to rip her clothes off again. This was bad, very bad—not only was there the awkwardness of realizing she still wanted him, but no doubt he could *see* that want.

And yet he didn't speak, didn't move, just stood there with his fingers barely grazing her hips.

"No," she said to his unspoken question, to her need, to every damn thing, and she pushed past him. "It wasn't that good."

"Oh, come on. You can do better than that."

Already halfway down the hall, she looked back. "Excuse me?"

He stood there propping up the doorjamb with his shoulder, bare-chested, barefooted, jeans low on his hips, his expression assuring he saw right through her. "I thought maybe you'd also want to slam my character in some way to make sure that I don't call you or try to pick up where we left off."

She struggled not to wince.

"Because that's what you'd like to do, right?" he pressed. "Piss me off so there's no chance in hell I'll want to be with you again?"

She opened her mouth, then slowly closed it again.

He just waited with the patience of a saint. A rough and rumpled gorgeous saint.

Or a teacher.

Yeah, she remembered now. He'd told her he was a teacher. A teacher in a leather jacket on a motorcycle. God, her hormones hadn't had a chance.

But they had one now. "Good-bye, Kevin."

"Remember my name," he called after her. "You're going to be saying it again."

Against her better judgment, she turned back one more time. "No. I won't."

He leaned there so negligently in that deceptively lazy pose. "So you felt nothing?"

She'd felt a hell of a lot of things, mostly mind-blowing lust, but it was the light of day now and in it all she felt was a desperate need to be gone. "Absolutely nothing."

"Liar," he chided softly.

Fine. She'd just do exactly as he'd accused her: make him glad to see her go. "Last night we both agreed that this was just a scratching of an itch, a one-time thing."

"Yes," he agreed with that maddening calm. "But that was before we mutually imploded in bed."

Oh, yeah they had, but she pulled a face and put some doubt in her voice. "I'd agree it was okaaaay," she said casually.

He dropped his arms to his sides and straightened from the door, his face incredulous. "You were every bit as into it as I was, and I have the ten fingernail marks embedded in my ass to prove it. And a bite mark on my shoulder. And a—"

"I said it was *okay*," she said through her teeth. What was he doing? Why wasn't he getting mad? Why was *she* now mad?

He looked at her, his eyes suddenly narrowing in suspicion. "Why don't you tell me what part didn't work for you."

"What?"

"I can take it."

She smiled tightly because now she was going to incinerate him. "Don't say I didn't warn you."

He spread his hands out at his sides. "Give me your worst."

Walking toward him, she lifted a finger. "You have stinky feet."

Not true, but she'd wanted to list a fault. Only problem, Kevin hadn't exhibited any. Not that he didn't have them—*all* men had them—she just didn't know his yet.

And wouldn't ever know.

He laughed. "I do not have stinky—"

She put up another finger. "You have snoring issues."

"What? That's crazy. I don't—"

"And, three—"

"There's *three*?"

"Yes. Quite frankly . . ." She shrugged. "You're not that great in bed."

Again his gaze narrowed. "Not that great in bed."

She patted him on the shoulder, trying not to notice his warm skin or the hard sinew beneath. "I'm sorry to be the one to break it to you."

"Yeah. I can see you're pretty broken up about it." He scratched his chest again, looking both bewildered and a little stunned.

And sexy as hell with it.

Definitely time to go. But just as she turned away, her eyes locked on her panties lying beneath his bed. Aha! Moving back into the room, she grabbed them, folding them as she had her bra, and added them to her pocket.

Kevin was watching her, just standing there in silence. She forced a smile. "I'll just be going now." More silence.

"Yeah. So . . . thanks for—"

"For being bad in bed?" he asked silkily.

"It's nothing personal, you know. Lots of men have no idea how to please a woman."

"If I was so bad, why did you come three times?"

"I faked them."

Cost of the bottle of wine they'd shared last night:

$35. Cost of the cookies she'd bought the night before: $20. Cost of the expression on his face: *priceless*.

But he recovered quickly. "That's interesting, that faking-it business." He stalked back into the room and came close, that big, warm, strong body of his making hers yearn and burn. "Were you faking it when you begged me to—"

"Oh, no. No, no, no. I didn't beg."

"Really?"

"Really," she said to his smug and—damn it—now smiling face.

"Then what was"—and here he used a falsetto voice, mocking what she assumed was to be *her* as she'd come—"Oh, please, oh, pretty please, don't stop . . . There. God, yes, there—"

She snatched the pillow from his bed. It left her fingers and flung its way toward his smirking mug before she even became aware that she'd thrown it.

Catching it in midair, he smiled innocently. "What's the matter? Truth hurts?"

"You are impossible."

"Same goes, sweetheart."

Blind with annoyance, she whirled for the open door and plowed directly into a guy standing there.

Tall, dark-haired, and caramel-eyed, he looked like a younger version of Kevin, down to his matching mischievous come-get-me expression. Mortified at what he'd most likely just overheard, Mia didn't stick around for introductions but shoved past him and walked away.

Damn, she felt flustered. Stinky feet? Snoring? Is that the best she could do?

And as for being bad in bed . . . *Ha!* He'd been sensual, passionate, earthy . . . *amazing*. And as she let herself out his front door into the bright Southern California morning, the hazy red, smog-filled air a backdrop for the LA skyline in the valley below, she had to admit, he'd gotten to her.

Big-time. She stalked toward her house, the Glendale Hills all around her still lush and green from a late spring. Her leather T-strap Prada pumps sank into the wet grass with a little pop each step, the feeling reminding her of a very drenched Tennessee morning. Of being fourteen . . .

Even at fourteen, Mia had known her life wasn't a sitcom. People whispered about her older sister, about her momma, about their single-wide in Country Homes Trailer Estates, but mostly they whispered about her.

"Too hoity-toity."

"Thinks she's a fancy know-it-all."

Well, she had news. She *did* know it all, thank you very much. She eyed the faux Formica kitchen counter, the window lined with duct tape to keep out the mosquitoes, she listened to the *drip, drip, drip* of the kitchen sink, and she knew she was destined for better no matter what anyone—everyone—said.

While other girls her age listened to music and hung out wherever there were boys, Mia went to the library every day on her way home from school, gobbling up everything she could, much to her momma's mystified bewilderment.

There was a whole big world out there, and Mia wanted a piece of it.

Sitting at the kitchen table and fingering a crack in the veneer made when Momma's last boyfriend had thrown the iron at a cockroach, Mia dreamed about how different things would be when she grew up and left here. For one, she'd have mountains of money. She'd have a house with a tub for bathing and not for soaking clothes. She'd have walls thicker than paper-thin fake-wood paneling and a car that not only started every time but also didn't stall at stoplights. Oh, and leather seats.

She wanted real, soft, buttery leather seats.

"Apple!" This from her momma. Lynnette probably needed to be crammed, shoehorned, and zipped into her jeans for her date, a chore that Mia hated, so she pretended not to hear and instead opened her diary.

Notes for when I'm somebody, she wrote.

1. *Don't* wear do-me red lipstick (like Momma). It smears and makes you look mean even when you're not.
2. *Don't* tease your hair higher than six inches (also like Momma). It looks like you're wearing a cat on your head.
3. *Always* wear high heels, because height makes a woman smart and powerful.

Above all, Mia wanted to be smart.

"*Apple!*"

And powerful.

"Apple, baby, get your ass in here. I can't zip!"

"Coming." With a sigh, she closed the diary and hid it in the fruit drawer of the fridge, where no one but her ever looked.

She could hear her momma and sister chattering in the bedroom, and she headed that way past the tiny spot they called a living room, with worn carpet and yellowing ceilings and secondhand furniture packed into it like sardines, every inch covered with knickknacks.

The bedroom was more of the same, stuff crammed into every square inch, with white lace everywhere because her mother had a love affair with lace. Her momma had never met a garage sale she hadn't loved.

Sugar was a chip off the old block and, at eighteen, looked it. She and Mia had never gotten along, but mostly that was Sugar's doing. She didn't like to share Momma, and whenever she could get away with it, she was as mean as possible to Mia.

"Why don't you just spray-paint those jeans on?" Sugar asked Momma, who leaned into the lace-lined mirror over her dresser to admire her makeup job, which looked as if it might have been applied with a spatula.

"I would if I could. Finally, Apple," Momma said and climbed onto the bed, stretching out on her back, her pants unzipped and gaped wide.

Mia reached for the zipper, Sugar tugged the pants as closed as she could get, which still left a good two-inch gap, while Momma sucked her body in. "Zip it up," she gasped.

When Mia got it, they all sagged back, breathing heavy from the exertion. Sugar eyed Momma's hair as she popped her gum with the frequency and velocity of an M-80. "You use an entire can of hairspray on that do?"

Momma carefully patted her teased-up-and-out, bottle-processed hair, which added nearly a foot to her height. "You know it."

They grinned at each other.

Mia sighed.

Sugar shot her a dirty look. "What's the matter?"

Mia knew better than to say. That would be like poking the bear. She still had the bruise marks on her arm from the last time she'd disagreed with Sugar. "Nothing."

Sugar went back to primping. She and Momma were getting ready to go to the monthly rec center barbeque. Tonight was extra special because there was a bunch of truckers in town for some big competition, and both Momma and Sugar had their eyes on a prize.

A prize with a steady job and benefits.

Momma's smile revealed a smear of lipstick.

"Check out this color. Tastes like cherries. Somebody's going to ask me to marry him tonight."

Sugar laughed. "Looking like that, he's not going to ask you to marry him, he's going to ask you to f—"

Momma's hand slapped over Sugar's mouth. "Hey, not in front of Apple."

Sugar's mouth tightened at the reminder that there was a baby in the house that wasn't her.

Momma, oblivious, grinned at Mia. "Be good tonight, you hear? I'm going to get us a rich husband. Then you two can go to college."

Sugar laughed. "I'm going to get a rich husband of my own, thanks. Apple here, though, you might want to worry about." Sugar ran her gaze over Mia, a sneer on her painted lips. "I don't see her ever catching a man, not with that scrawny body and mousy brown hair."

"Leave her alone, Sugar," Momma said.

As for Mia, her eye began to twitch. She ignored Sugar. "I'm going to college, Momma. But on my grades. You don't need a husband."

Please don't get another husband.

Momma smiled and chucked Mia beneath the chin. "You're so sweet. How did you get so sweet? You ain't your father's child, that's for certain."

"Maybe she's the mailman's," Sugar said.

Momma smacked Sugar upside the head. Sugar rubbed the spot and said, "Jeez, just kidding. You gotta admit, she's a weirdo."

Momma stood up to primp in front of the mirror and began to sing "It's Raining Men."

Mia sighed. Momma loved men, *all* men, but mostly the kind that never stuck around—or if they did, you wished they hadn't.

Mia sank back to the bed, piled with tiaras and cheap makeup and the magazines Momma and

Sugar liked to hoard their pennies for. She ran her finger over the cover of the *Enquirer*, which had a small picture of Celine Dion in one corner. Not classically beautiful. No red lipstick or teased hair. Beautiful, but almost . . . plain.

Like Mia.

She turned her head and looked out the window. The neighbors on the left, Sally-Ann and Danny, were fighting on their front porch again, screaming and hurling insults at each other like fastballs. Their dog, Bob, was howling in tune to the screeching coming from Sally. The sound was somehow both lonely and sad, and Mia put her folded hands on the windowsill and set her chin down on them. She felt like howling, too.

On the right, Bethie and Eric, two kids in her class, were rearranging the letters on the mailboxes, probably spelling dirty words, even though Tony, the trailer park manager, had threatened to knock their heads together if he caught them again.

"Hey," Sugar complained to Momma. "You're wearing my red lace bra."

"You won't be needing it tonight." Momma waggled her eyebrows. "But I might."

Nope, Mia was going. All by herself.

Chapter Two

Kevin heard the front door slam as Mia Appleby exited his fantasy life. Sounded about right.

Now back to his regularly scheduled program—reality. Mike still stood in the doorway, hair practically singed from Mia's fiery exit. He raised a brow and a questioning shoulder at Kevin.

Kevin shook his head and looked around him. His new house was a fixer-upper, a kind term, really, given all that needed to be done to it. But the property had been just his price—cheap. He figured he could rework one room at a time, at his own pace.

There were still boxes scattered around from the move, which he was ignoring because he didn't have the time for them right now. Passing the tousled bed where he'd just had some off-the-charts, mind-blowing sex, he stripped off his jeans, then stubbed his toe on a box. "Goddamnit." In the bathroom, he cranked on the water. When he turned around, Mike was right there in his face. "Jesus, wear a bell, would ya?" He adjusted the water to his preferred temperature—scalding.

Mike merely smiled.

"I'm not kidding," Kevin said. "You ever think about knocking?"

For that, he received another shrug of the shoulder, but seeing not-so-hidden misery in his younger brother's eyes, Kevin didn't step into the water. His brother was twenty-seven, a supposed grown-up, but that didn't compute quite the same as it did with other people because Mike was different. Special.

Deaf.

What's the matter? Kevin signed with his hands instead of speaking because Mike preferred that.

Nothing, Mike signed back.

Nothing, hell, but experience had taught Kevin that pushing Mike was like pushing a brick wall.

A big fat old waste of time.

Mike was smart as hell, his IQ off the charts. But as with certain kinds of genius, it was almost too much. Like his brain couldn't handle all the extras it'd been dealt. He pretended to be normal, and for long periods pulled it off, but then those odd little self-destructive tendencies would pop out, making it impossible to keep a job, a woman, friends.

But Kevin knew the bittersweet truth: he himself had made it too easy for his brother. He'd cleaned up too many messes, made too many excuses, and now Mike was what he was. A spoiled kid in a man's body.

The babe, Mike signed. *She was a pistol.*

A spoiled kid in a man's body, with a man's appetite. *No, she was a tornado,* Kevin signed back. *Blew in and blew out.*

Mike grinned. *I like the blow part.*

Get your mind out of the gutter, you perv.

Mike waggled an eyebrow. *You had a good time.*

Yeah, but she's not my type.

Mike laughed, a low, dull-toned sound that could have been mistaken for a cough. *Could have fooled me.*

But Mia *wasn't* Kevin's usual type. He liked soft women who laughed easily and loved hard. He liked women with causes to champion, who gave their heart one-hundred-percent, every single time.

Mia Appleby didn't fit the profile. Sharp, edgy,

tough as nails, cool as cream—definitely. But soft and fast to laugh? Probably not. And he doubted she'd ever let her heart go with ease, and yet in bed . . . yeah, she'd done it for him there. But then she'd woken up, panicked that she'd stayed all night, and taken it out on him.

Bad in bed.

Bullshit. She was running scared.

Mike was still watching him. *She's pretty.*

Yeah, like a rose-with-hidden-thorns pretty. Like a sleeping-tiger-with-sharp-claws pretty. *You think they're all pretty.*

Mike agreed with a nod. *So your big dry spell's over. You finally got yourself laid again . . . and then what? Dumped? All within the same twenty-four hours. That's a record, even for you, huh?*

Kevin gave him a very universal sign that involved only his middle finger, then got into the shower. Over the roar of the water he heard Mike's toneless but unmistakable laugh.

Fine. Let him laugh. It was the truth. Between getting Mike off the streets and trying to keep the local teen center open and available for the kids who needed it, and between teaching, moving, buying this damn house, Kevin's sex life had suffered. Actually, it'd died a slow, painful death.

Mike cracked the shower door. *Can I borrow fifty?* He smiled hopefully. *You could just tack it onto what I already owe you.*

You already owe me a bazillion dollars.

Mike gave him sad puppy-dog eyes and Kevin sighed. Here was the problem. He'd established himself as the Go To. When Kevin's father had died and then his mom remarried, Mike came along pretty quickly. But when Mike's father turned out to be not just an asshole but an abusive asshole, Kevin turned into the Go To not only for his mom, but his new kid brother, too.

That he'd not been fast enough, that at age two Mike had lost his hearing due to a blow to the head by said asshole while a five-year-old Kevin watched, made it much harder to turn Mike down when he needed something. Like now. *I've got forty bucks in my wallet. Take it.*

I'm going to get that job next week, Mike signed. *You'll see.*

Kevin wouldn't be holding his breath. For the past three years, Kevin had taught high school science and coached basketball in Santa Barbara, and Mike had happily fit right in to the heavy party college scene there and found trouble nightly. When he'd slept with the much older wife of a cop and then been arrested for a bar brawl with said cop, Kevin knew it was time to leave town. Now they were back where they'd grown up, in Glendale Hills, with the first day of summer school starting in an hour. In the fall, he'd add chemistry and more coaching to the itinerary. He just hoped the familiarity would give Mike a sense of balance, of security. Mostly he hoped Mike would grow up.

Kevin took his time getting ready. The one blessing of summer school: a later start than during the regular school year. He didn't have to be in the classroom until nine forty-five.

By the time he was dressed and walked through the house, Mike was gone. More, he suspected, from the need to put distance between them so that Kevin couldn't press for details on what was wrong, rather than Mike wanting to give Kevin any privacy.

Mike had no sense of privacy. For him, everything was out there, on his sleeve, to be accepted or not, no big deal either way.

People loved that about Mike, people being women. Yeah, unbelievably, given the difficulties in communicating, Mike, the jobless, directionless, happy-go-lucky bum, was a chick magnet.

Apparently some things translated well.

It was the big joke in the house that Kevin, the brother with the job and all the responsibilities, the guy with the drive to succeed, with the need to teach and make people realize their potential, had never had half the social life of his brother.

Until last night.

Kevin shook his head at himself as he ate breakfast. He was still shaking his head as he started the one vice he allowed himself: his motorcycle. As always, riding calmed him, whether it was the balmy LA weather, the wind in his face, the speed, the sheer power of the machine beneath him . . .

On the freeway, his thoughts shifted to last night, an event he felt sure would headline his fantasies for months to come.

Bad in bed . . . *Ha!*

No way had those low, whimpery pants of hers been for show. She couldn't have faked her eyes going opaque, glazing over as he'd sent her skittering off the edge with his fingers, then his tongue.

No way.

Damn, he should have stuck to his usual evening plans. A pizza, a beer, no harm, no foul. Instead, Mia Appleby had stayed him with one glance. Maybe she wasn't classically beautiful, but she had a way of walking, of holding herself, of looking at a man that made her extremely worth a second look. And a third. There was just something about her—maybe her confidence, her no-nonsense ways, maybe her sharp mind, or maybe just the stubborn set of her chin . . .

She was a woman who knew what she wanted and went for it. She'd gone for him, and it had been quite a ride.

Until she got spooked.

She could insult him all she wanted. She could walk away—even run—but he knew better.

Last night had been more than she'd bargained for. Far more.

The roads were surprisingly clear of traffic, and he enjoyed the view of the low-riding hills on either side, still green from a late spring. The air was cool enough now but held a hint of the muggy heat yet to come once the sun got on its way. He pulled into the high school with half an hour to spare, thinking he could use the time to further prepare his new classroom.

Parking turned out to be limited due to the construction of a desperately needed new gym and cafeteria. The parking spot he'd been told to use had a Dumpster sitting on it. He eyed the next spot over, which had a sign that read RESERVED FOR PRINCIPAL.

Joe Fraser and Kevin went way back, but they hadn't exactly been friends.

In high school, Joe had been a football star and all things popular while Kevin had been backpedaling as fast as he could, surviving a broken home, dealing with Mike, etc. In fact, due to Joe's bullying and obnoxious ways, they'd hated each other.

Not much had changed there; that had been obvious during the hiring process. But Kevin got the job, with or without Joe's approval, so it was with great pleasure that he pulled into the "reserved" spot and turned off his bike.

Payback was a bitch.

The school was mostly empty. Heaven forbid anyone got here early. The halls were hot, too hot, and smelled vaguely like feet. Kevin wondered if the janitor was still Vince Wells and if he'd gotten drunk in his office again, turning on the heater instead of the AC.

Perfect. The students would all be napping at their desks by ten thirty.

Kevin passed by the front office, where Mrs. Stacy was already filing. She'd been there since the dawn of time. Not exactly the warm, fuzzy, grandma type, she stood tall and was painfully thin, with a perpetual frown on her grim face, her glasses hanging off her nose. "Yesterday when you came to set up your classroom, you left your lights on," she snapped. "Lights are expensive, Mr. McKnight. I turned them off for you."

Kevin shook his head. "I didn't—"

"Talk to the hand," she said and lifted it palm outward, an inch from his nose.

Since somewhere in the previous century she'd undoubtedly mastered the art of arguing, he only sighed and kept walking. On the walls in the hallway were posters advertising upcoming games, events, clubs. Kids were still scarce, because after all this was summer school, land of the I-don't-want-to-be-here, and they had twenty minutes until the bell.

But it turned out his classroom door was unlocked. Knowing damn well he'd locked it on his way out yesterday afternoon and that the anal Mrs. Stacy would have locked it as well, he stepped inside and staggered at the overpowering cloud of marijuana smoke. When he blinked, coughed, and waved the smoke clear, he realized the window was open, the screen still flapping.

He raced across the classroom, past the science burners lining the back, one of which was lit, and headed directly for the window.

"See?" Mrs. Stacy stood quivering righteously in his doorway, her blue hair waggling like a Dr. Seuss character. "How many times do I have to say this to you young teachers? You can't be the kids' friend. They'll walk all over you."

He didn't plan on being their friend, but he did want to make a difference. It was why he taught, he had this need to fix people.

Well aware that a shrink would have a field day with that, given that he'd never actually succeeded at fixing anyone, he stopped listening to Mrs. Stacy and stuck his head out the window.

"You have to be smarter than them," she said.

Gee, really?

But, damn, he was too late, his early-bird stoners had escaped, apparently the promise of an empty classroom too alluring to resist. Pretty ballsy to smoke right in the classroom, though. Maybe the first lesson would be going over exactly how many brain cells were lost to weed, and the long term effects.

"Mr. McKnight," she said, tapping her geriatric loafers. "I'm talking to you."

"No, you're lecturing."

"*Well.*" She said this with a sniff. "I never."

Which was probably her problem. "Did you see who came into the school this morning?"

"If I did, I'd have told you."

Yeah, that was undoubtedly true. Head still out the window, he eyed the ground. In the dirt lay a knit cap in Lakers colors, and he smiled grimly. He'd put it on his desk. Chances were, someone would want it back, and he'd be waiting.

Chapter Three

Mia walked through her quiet, peaceful, gorgeous house, with no particular destination in mind. She just loved all the big, wide, open space, the living room with views of the hills from a wall of windows, and her state-of-the-art kitchen, all meticulously and spartanly decorated by the best of the best and kept spotless by her weekly cleaning service.

No bumping elbows in the hall, no cheap paneled walls, no lingering grease smells, no cigarette-stained carpets.

But especially, no white, frothy lace.

As she moved into her sprawling earth-toned bedroom with the fabulous Century bed and dresser that had been her first splurge, she pulled the panties and bra out of her pocket and set them on her comforter. She slipped out of her skirt and top, fighting the flashback of Kevin doing the same but in a much more sensual, arousing manner.

How dare he throw her orgasms back in her face.

But man, oh man, the incredulous look on his face when she said she'd faked them, as if the thought was so beyond comprehension . . .

She laughed, even as she had to admit, with his skills in bed, it probably *was* beyond his comprehension.

Damn it.

She glanced at herself in the mirror over her dresser. Unlike her mother and Sugar, she was not blonde and luscious but brunette and average: average height, average weight, average shape, average coloring—and she'd always told herself she had no problem with that at all. When she got a new account at work or went out with a man, she knew it was because of her brains and wit, not her looks.

Still, she did have a nice rosy glow to her skin this morning. People underestimated how good sex was for their bodies. She also had stubble burn on a breast, a hip, an inner thigh . . . Warrior wounds, she thought and smiled in spite of herself.

Yeah, for last night at least, Kevin McKnight had found her beautiful. There was no doubt of that.

The knowledge was better than a spa day. She showered and then dressed to kill in a Michael Kors silk camisole, jacket, and peasant skirt. It was her own personal armor, a way to put a barrier between herself and any more altercations that might come her way that day, and when she'd slipped into her strappy Choo's wedge sandals, she looked cool and efficient. Untouchable.

You were touched plenty last night. And this morning.

That nearly put the first chink in the armor, but she successfully shoved it back. Her new neighbor, his sexy body, and his ability to fling words as fast and effectively as she could weren't worth another thought.

She left the house and got into the Audi she'd bought herself on her last birthday, the big three-oh. She was a tough cookie but not quite tough enough to avoid taking a peek down the street, where just two days ago she'd caught her first glimpse of the most incredibly sexy motorcycle she'd ever seen.

Not to mention the man straddling it. Yeah, he'd lifted off his helmet and laid his eyes right on hers, eyes that held trouble and a spark of ready mischief, and when he'd gotten off the bike and stood to his full height, Mia had thought *yum*: tall, dark, and full of attitude—just how she liked 'em.

With all sorts of wicked thoughts swimming in his gaze, he'd smiled, and she'd involuntarily put a hand to her heart as her pulse leapt.

In turn, his smile had widened and she'd melted on the spot. Clearly, he was a bit of a rebel, a bad boy, which meant he was a man after her own heart, and therein lay the problem.

She didn't like a man after her heart. She didn't like anyone to get that close, to get beneath her carefully polished façade. But truth be told, if anyone could have, it would have been one sexy, sharp, smart-mouthed Kevin McKnight.

Oh, she knew his name. First and last. And if she was being honest, she'd never forgotten it.

But this morning, only an hour after she'd left his bed, his bike was gone.

Just as well. After the things she'd said to him, he wouldn't be smiling at her again, wicked or otherwise. Stinky feet. Snoring.

God.

She'd been really frazzled to lose it so completely if that was the best she could come up with. She really wished he'd just kicked her out at two in the morning when he'd finished with her. And anyway, why hadn't he been happy she wanted to get away? Weren't men supposed to like that sort of woman, one who didn't cling and carry on about relationships?

What was wrong with him?

With a sigh, she drove the freeway with the precision of an air force bomber pilot. The skill was required in LA, especially at nine in the morning in rush-hour traffic. She thought about work and crossed her fingers for the day ahead, as she'd been working her ass off to get the new Anderson account, a hot new national beverage corporation, and she wanted it so bad she could taste it. She'd designed the campaign from start to finish, with the help of a great creative team, of course, and could already see the media and public scooping up everything she dished out.

As the air was already getting warm, she turned on the AC. She listened to traffic and news as she transitioned to the 5 south, and when she got downtown she pulled onto Sixth and into her building's parking structure.

By the time she entered the thirty-five-story glass-and-steel building that housed the advertising firm where she worked, she was ready. And when she stepped out onto the top floor, she smiled.

Oh, yeah, she had it all: a fabulous career, an office overlooking all of downtown, a beautiful house in the hills—absolutely everything she'd ever dreamed of as "Apple," sitting in a single-wide and looking out at the neighbors fighting on their porch while her mother and Sugar made plans to devour some man or another.

No one in her life from that time would recognize the woman she'd so carefully become. Sophisticated, elegant. Cool, calm ice.

Just as she'd always wanted.

Gen, the receptionist, waved at her. All around, the office buzzed. Phones rang; people moved, talked, wheeled, and dealed. Mia knew there'd been rumors of layoffs, that the powers-that-be wanted to downsize, but she loved the place this big and crazy and hoped it stayed that way. She strode toward her department. Assistant Tess Reis sat at her cubicle in front of the three offices of ad executives she worked for, her fingers pounding her keyboard, either for the slimeball Ted or the more even-keeled but insanely competitive Margot—Mia's equals.

Unlike Mia, Tess wasn't average height. Tess wasn't average anything. She was a tall, willowy, creamy-skinned twenty-seven-year-old who resembled one hell of an expensive collectable porcelain doll. She could have been a model, *should* have been a model, except for one thing.

She didn't like to be the center of attention.

What she *did* like was organization, a fact that Mia was thankful for every single day of her life since Tess had come into it.

At every turn Tess mothered, bossed, and stuck her nose where it didn't belong. "Listen," she said before Mia could even open her mouth. "It's a good news, bad news sort of day."

As they were good friends as well as coworkers, Mia trusted Tess as much as she trusted anyone. "Good first."

At that moment Margot walked up to the desk, sleek and professional in her smart black Chanel suit and blond chignon. Never one to pull punches, she eyeballed Mia while handing Tess a stack of files.

Mia lifted a brow.

"Bee-yotch," Margot said.

Adrenaline suddenly pumped through Mia. "I got the Anderson account?"

"I'm assuming so, by the huge delivery that came for you this morning." Margot shook her head. "Damn it. I'll congratulate you when I can say it without spitting."

She was so excited she couldn't hear. "Delivery?"

"A big-ass plant, which I'm sure you'll kill pronto like all the others." Turning on her heels, she walked away.

Huh. The world kept spinning on its axis. Behind them a trio of assistants, all twenty-something and young and silly, were tittering over a computer screen. Fifties jazz came out of the sound system, fitting right in with the art deco theme of the office. The office had the scent of hip success and coffee, Mia's favorite combination.

She felt like yelling *Woo hoo!* but that seemed rather high school, so she settled for a shit-eating grin instead.

Tess bent down out of sight and came back up with a huge, lush green plant in a beautifully hand-painted clay pot. "Well, now you know the good news. Do you think I should keep the plant out here? You know, to protect it?"

Yeah, yeah, so she'd killed every single plant she'd ever had, not to mention every goldfish . . .

She'd gotten the Anderson account. Everyone in the free advertising world wanted the Anderson account. She'd fought long and hard—and she'd *won*.

All around her the carefully controlled chaos continued, and though she'd have liked to burst into song and do the happy dance, she just continued to grin. "This is definitely good," she said in grand understatement.

Tess laughed and set down the plant to hug Mia.

"Does everyone know?" Mia asked.

Tess's grin widened as she pulled back. "Oh, yeah." She shifted close. "It's said that Dick actually smiled at the news that it landed in-house."

Dick Sterling was Mia's boss. "So give me the bad news," Mia told her. "Not that anything can be bad today."

Tess's smile faded. "You're not going to like it."

"Never start out with that sentence."

"Ted is waiting for you in your office."

Mia's eye twitched. "What does he want?"

"There's no telling."

"Why don't you tell him that at the moment I'm out of my mind, but he can feel free to leave a message."

Tess smiled tightly. "He says he has a beef with you, but we both know he really has a beef *for* you."

Mia wrinkled her nose. "Don't, I just ate breakfast."

"You don't eat breakfast."

"Yeah. Damn." She inhaled deeply and concentrated on the Anderson account. "All right. I can handle him."

"Like you handled—what's that guy's name on twenty-five?"

"Phil." Mia had gone out with tall and hunky Phil one night after they'd met at a mutual friend's birthday party. But he'd been a piss-poor kisser, not a promising sign. "I told you, that didn't work out."

Tess sighed. An eternal optimist always looking for "the one," she worried that Mia had commitment issues.

"Speaking of things working out. Did your sweet little old lady neighbor enjoy the cookies I baked yesterday?"

"Uh huh." Mia reached for her stack of phone messages.

Tess nabbed them first, holding them out of reach.

Mia, knowing what was coming, sighed. "What?"

"Talk to me."

"Yes, thank you, the cookies worked wonders. Look, I just got the news of the year. Trying to remain excited here."

"Do you think I can't tell when you're lying through your teeth?"

"I *am* excited."

"The cookies, Mia."

"Fine. The cookies were a huge hit," Mia said with great exaggeration, waggling her fingers for the messages.

"By—let me guess now—a *man*."

"Does it matter that they weren't for the exact neighbor you thought?"

"No, except I would have charged you double if I'd known you were going to use them as a seducing technique."

"What? *Why?*"

"Why? Because I made them thinking you were being kind to old ladies. Because I made them so you'd remember to give me a raise next month when I'm due for review. But, damn it, all that's really going on here is you're getting laid and I am not."

"I'm always kind to old ladies, and you know I'm going to recommend you for a raise. It's well deserved. Except, of course, when you hassle me. And FYI, to get laid, you have to stop waiting for your prince and date."

"Fine change of subject." Tess let out a long breath. "Just lay low on any destroying of hearts at the moment, okay? Especially with this impending Ted disaster."

"It won't be a disaster."

"Says Hurricane Heartbreaker Mia Appleby."

Unconcerned, Mia eyed her messages. "I have a creative team meeting, and then a research review for that last campaign we did for Sorvenson Foods. Busy day, as you know all too well. Can I have my messages now?"

But Tess continued to hold the messages hostage. "Was he cute?"

"Who?"

"Whoever gave you that glow."

Though Mia appreciated men, she did not sleep with them that often. She had her standards, after all, and besides, being a serial one-night-stander was simply too dangerous in this day and age. Last night had been her first . . . break, as she thought of it, in a while. "He was gorgeous." Again she reached for the messages.

"Are you going to see him again? Wait a minute, why would I ask such a stupid question?" Tess smacked her head. "Of course you're not. You don't repeat."

"Unlike some people who shall not be named. *I'm* not looking for a husband."

"Good, because you're not going to find him in the sack."

"I'll have you know, Kevin was quite amazing in the sack."

"Kevin." Tess nodded. "I'm impressed. You got his name."

Mia tried to snatch her messages, but Tess hugged them tight. "I'm just worried about you. You never attach. It's not good for you."

"I'm attached to you. Though I'd be more attached if you gave me my messages."

"I'm talking about the person you're going to grow old with. Get gray hair with. Sit on the porch swing and tell stories about the good old days with."

"I'm never going to get gray hair, thank you very much. And I don't like swings. *Messages?*"

"How could you not like swings? Tell me the truth. You're not human, right? You grew up in a pod and were placed here on earth when you were twenty-two. Fine. Take your damn messages." She slapped them into Mia's hand.

Mia looked at her, amused. "Grew up in a pod?"

"Well, that's just a guess since you won't talk about yourself before college. It's all a big mystery."

Some of her amusement vanished. "Nothing before matters."

"Mia." Now Tess gave her one of those patented maternal expressions, full of worry and concern and, damn it, affection. "Of course it matters, it—"

"Stop. Okay? Just stop. You worry far too much. Thanks for the messages." Mia grabbed the plant.

"Don't punish the poor plant!"

Mia just shook her head and headed for her office door, passing up the cubicles of the four members of her creative team, Janice, Tami, Steven, and Dillon. They were all at work on various projects, so she waved and moved on. So she didn't want to talk about her humble beginnings. So what? No reason to feel that twinge of guilt—no reason at all—just because Tess gave everything of herself, no holding back, whatever Mia needed at all times, including cookies.

Damn it, Ted Stokes *was* in her office, lounging in her chair as a matter of annoying fact, leaning back, feet up as if he owned the place. Luckily, or maybe unluckily, he'd been blessed with a face that women everywhere thought of as California beautiful. He was strong and tan, and when he smiled he flashed baby blue eyes and a dimple, melting hearts and dampening panties everywhere.

But Mia wasn't fooled by him. Beneath that fun-loving exterior beat a cold, purposeful heart. She set down the plant and gathered her bitchiness around her like a Gucci coat.

He smiled at her, that I'm-an-asshole smile, which really bit into her superiority over getting the Anderson account.

"Ah, a new plant to kill," he noted.

She smiled through her teeth. She was going to keep the damn plant alive if it was the last thing she did. "I hope you brought coffee to this unexpected party."

Ted lifted a steaming mug. His own, of course.

"What do you want, Ted?"

"Interesting question." He smiled again, batting those long lashes over his baby blues.

She did not smile back.

"You're a tough nut, Mia. I'm trying to flirt with you, in case you didn't notice. And don't say you don't flirt, because—"

"I don't flirt in the office. With coworkers."

"We could be more than coworkers. What do you say?"

"How about never? Does never work for you?"

Some of the wattage went out of his smile at that, but she didn't care. Last week in the employee break room he'd made a move on her. He'd cornered her between the sink and the refrigerator and tried to kiss her. She'd shoved him back, maybe a little harder than the situation warranted, but really, he was just lucky she'd let him keep his balls.

At the shove, he'd fallen backward into a table, spilling a glass of water, which in turn soaked into the seat of his pants. He'd made a joke of it then, apparently thinking that laughing it off would be the easiest way for his ego to handle the rejection, but she knew he'd been pissed.

"You're still upset about the kiss," he said in an annoyingly patronizing tone. "Honestly, Mia, the way you leaned into me, I thought you *wanted* me to kiss you."

"You've been fantasizing again." She liked kissing, very much. But as the queen of compartmentalizing, she'd long ago divided her needs into little groups. First and most important, job. Second, men.

Never the two shall meet.

The men in her office, and there were many, had correctly read her back-off signs. She knew they called her Ice Queen among other less flattering things, and she didn't care, because what Ted hadn't anticipated when he'd made the move on her was how he'd unwittingly put her into the position of power, a situation he greatly regretted. His eyes were no longer friendly.

"I'll get to the point of me being here," he said.

"Why don't you."

"You got the Anderson account."

The two of them might be equals on the scale when

it came to the ladder of success within this company, but that was only because he'd been here longer. Mia was better at the job. She knew it, everyone in the office knew it, and Ted knew it, too.

He just didn't like it, or her aggression in getting other—and winning—accounts. Bottom line, he was lazy. She was not.

"Yes, I got the Anderson account," she said.

"You stole it out from beneath me."

Ah. The victim angle. She should have guessed he'd go that route. She'd won the account fairly, with blood and sweat and tears. Okay, maybe not with blood or tears, but certainly with long, hard hours over the past several months. She'd put her heart and soul into it, and she wanted to hear him say it, even knowing he'd never give her that satisfaction. "I don't know what your problem is," she said quietly. "But I bet it's hard to pronounce."

His jaw ticced. "I should have gotten that account." He pushed a file across her gorgeous Baker desk. "My ideas were better."

"Now, that's just plain not nice."

"It's true."

"You're insulting my entire creative team."

"Just stating fact."

The man was impossible. She picked up his work and dropped it in the trash.

His eyes filled with anger. "Bitch."

"Oooh, ouch. You got me, Ted. Now get out."

"That account should have been mine."

"You know what? I can stand your arrogance, and maybe even stand your smugness—though it'd be easier if you weren't wearing such a tacky suit—but I won't stand being accused of stealing. *Get out.*"

"You should have to share that account with me."

"When hell freezes over." Planting her hands flat on her desk, she leaned over and looked him right in the cold eyes. "Read my lips, Ted. I don't share."

She shoved his loafers off her desk and stood her ground while he slowly, insolently rose to his feet. Never had she resented her average height more as he towered over her, leanly muscled and ticked off.

"I want that account, Mia."

"Get out. Now."

For one long beat he stood his ground, staring her down, no longer even attempting to hold the façade of friendliness.

She stared back, bitterly resenting that she had to tip her head up to do so. Tomorrow she'd wear her other Manolos, the five-inch stilettos, if it meant looking this prick right in the eyes.

Finally he slowly backed off and walked out, shutting her door too hard, rustling her new gorgeous plant. Not sure how many more people she was going to piss off today, she shifted the pot away from the door, then stood there, her heart beating just a little too hard for comfort. God, she really hated a bully, but she especially hated that he'd gotten to her and made her uneasy.

And just a tad nervous.

Refusing to let him ruin one more second of her time, she got busy, burying herself in the groundwork for her next conquest, a major athletic shoe account. She and Dick had nicknamed the file "Runner" to keep it quiet from other firms. That very secrecy and care was what had garnered her such an Ice Queen rep, but she worked hard, so what? Others could do the same; she'd only respect that.

She'd already been briefed by the Runner company on what they expected and wanted, and now it was up to her to create a campaign from scratch. Her favorite part. Most times, this involved her creative team. She loved those late-night meetings, where ideas flew freely and the creative muse took control.

But for now, with this account, she was on her own, and she worked on the research until noon.

By then she'd forgotten all about Ted, and she sat with Tess in the employee lunchroom.

"He was smiling when he left your office," Tess reported over her moo shoo. Others were around, including Margot, so she leaned in for privacy. "Smiling like a snake, too. He left for a meeting on fourth, the rat-fink bastard. I hope the layoff rumors have him worried and he's looking for a job elsewhere."

"Not likely. Don't worry, I can handle him." Mia sank her teeth into a pot sticker. She could handle anything, she thought. Suddenly the smoke alarms went off. Everyone ran into the hallway.

The thick smoke cut off Mia's air. Janice and Tami from her creative team had their laptops hugged to their breasts, but Steven and Dillon were nowhere in sight. People were already evacuating when Mia darted into her office to grab her laptop, where she found an unwelcome surprise.

The smoke came from *here*. Specifically, her trash can. *"Shit."* Grabbing the water bottle off her desk, she raced to the trash can and dumped the contents over the flames, which gave one last surge—straight upward and into her face—before dying with a hissing gasp.

"Shit," she said again, stumbling blind backward. With a gasp, she remembered her new plant. Panicked, she whirled around. It looked a little wilted but okay, and she gratefully hugged the pot close as she sank to a chair.

Margot was the first to show up, with half the building behind her. "The fire department is on its way— Ohmigod, Mia! Are you hurt?"

"No." Mia swiped her sweating forehead with her forearm, which came away black with soot. Ugh.

Tess shoved her way in, yelling, "Clear the way, let me through, damn it!" Then she skidded to a stop. "Oh, my God—"

"I'm okay," Mia said quickly.

"But honey, your eyebrow!"

Gone, Mia discovered. Just like her trash can.

But she still had the plant.

"You'd better work on that rejection policy of yours," Tess said in the employee bathroom a few hours later, after Mia refused to let the paramedics fuss over her, after everyone had been allowed back in the building and been thoroughly lectured by the fire marshal.

He'd deemed the incident "suspicious in nature," and an investigation was under way.

Mia instantly thought of Ted, but he'd been gone from the building. Which meant she had someone else after her, a fact that Tess pointed out with great worry.

"Who now?" she fretted. "Who else have you succeeded past, made look bad, or walked all over?"

She would have protested, but the truth was she hadn't made a lot of friends over the years. She stared in the mirror at her singed eyebrow. "I guess I could make a few social changes."

Tess let out a sound that said, "Ya think?"

Mia just sighed again. Maybe she could try to adopt a new kinder, gentler manner.

Oh, and a new eyebrow.

Chapter Four

Sixteen-year-old Hope Appleby was going some-where if it killed her.

And given that she'd never felt more alone, hun-gry, or desperately afraid she'd never get out of her car and into a real bed again, it just might.

She chewed on a fingernail and hummed as she drove, trying to fool herself into a lull of comfort. But she'd been driving so long now, and for so many days, the scenery blurred into itself. Tennessee to Los Angeles . . . a lot farther than it had seemed. Still, she'd always dreamed of seeing the country, and fi-nally, at sixteen years, two months, and three days old, she was seeing it plenty.

Just not quite in the style she'd imagined.

State after state passed as she headed west, Arkan-sas into Oklahoma into Texas into New Mexico. She'd been sleeping in her car to save money, trying to keep one eye open as she did because, as everyone knew, bad guys preyed on people sleeping alone in their cars.

Especially female people.

She had a flashlight, but she'd dropped it at a rest stop about five hundred miles back and couldn't get it to work after that. She'd been singing to the radio just to hear a real voice, but now she couldn't get any stations that weren't farm weather reports. Now she had nothing but herself for company, and she'd never been much good at small talk.

Not that she wanted company from strangers. No, thank you. They all looked at her funny, as though they'd never seen anyone dress goth before.

It was just black.

And a few chains.

No big deal. She'd started dressing like this only to look as different on the outside as she felt on the inside.

She'd lifted a steak knife from Denny's the day before, which was dull as a plastic butter knife but flashed fairly impressively in the light. It would be good for show, if need be, and hopefully that was all she'd need to do—even the thought of blood made her want to hurl.

She was eating as cheaply as she could and bathing in public restrooms, which were really gross. People were universal slobs, and if she had to look at *one more* slimy sink or toilet . . .

But she was in the home stretch now, nearly to her aunt Apple's in Los Angeles, and she patted the dashboard of her beat-up 1989 Dodge Diplomat. "Not much farther," she promised.

The car coughed.

Oh, God. Her biggest fear. "Don't die on me now," Hope begged it and patted the dash again. "We're going to be okay, really we are."

Or so she hoped. The problem was Apple didn't know she was coming, and Momma didn't know she'd gone.

Which left Hope in her usual spot—a big mess.

Unable to read the map and drive at the same time, she pulled off the freeway, not daring to turn off the engine for fear it would never start again. Only she didn't have much gas left . . .

"Please find it," she whispered to herself, running her finger over the foldout she'd pilfered from

a 76 station somewhere in Arizona. She'd felt a stab
of guilt until the grimy two-hundred-fifty-pound
guy behind the counter looked her over, making
her skin crawl like that time she'd gotten ants in
her bed after her momma had left out a box of
Twinkies.

When Hope had asked the guy for the key to the
restroom, he smiled (missing a front tooth!) and offered to take her himself.

Ewwww!

So she said no thanks, left with the map, and then
cursed him the whole time she was peeing in the
woods.

Now she unraveled the small scrap of paper that
had Apple's address on it. The ink had gotten
smeared. Was that 11732 High Waters Drive or
11735? Five, she decided and hoped she was right.
She searched the map for High Waters, feeling a little
frantic. "Please find it, please . . ."

There.

She wasn't too far now. Probably she could get
there by nightfall, which was good because she was
in the last of her clean clothes. She thought of how
surprised and shocked her aunt Apple was going to
be, and swallowed the niggling doubts that she
should have called ahead.

And she would have, except for two things. One,
her aunt hadn't called her. *Ever.* Though she did send
birthday cards every year, with increasingly larger
checks enclosed.

Momma said Apple never called because she'd
gotten a big head—so big Momma was surprised she
even bothered with the cards and money—but Hope
figured that Apple was *somebody* now, and somebod-
ies took care of their own, busy or not.

Hope didn't care about phone calls, or even about
Apple, really. She just needed out of town, away

from the trailer park, away from the stupid boys and mean girls, away from being a *nobody*.

Her aunt probably didn't give a rat's ass about Hope, either, but that didn't matter. Apple lived in Los Angeles, the city of angels, the city of *hope*.

Surely that was a sign, right? Hope *belonged* there. She was going to stay with Apple and become a marine biologist and swim with dolphins for the rest of her life.

And like her aunt, never look back.

She was going to get better grades, get into Stanford, and then get rich. She'd have a place by the ocean, a new car— "Sorry," she whispered to the Diplomat and stroked the dash as she sipped from the 7-Eleven Big Gulp she'd used her last bit of change for. She was going to have a *real* pool, too, not a plastic little thing where she couldn't get all wet at once. Yeah, she had big dreams, and she would live 'em, assuming she didn't run into any trouble—

A hard rap on the window jerked her so hard she nearly came out of her own skin. Soda soaked into her chest and belly and legs, her hand hit the horn— which made her jump again—and she hit her head on the visor she'd pulled down to block the lowering sun.

Heart in her throat, soda dripping off her nose, she turned and looked out her window.

And froze.

A cop stood there gesturing for her to roll down her window. Oh, God. Oh, God . . . She rolled the window down an inch. "Y-yes?"

"I need to see your driver's license and registration, please."

"Um . . . okay." She willed her heart to stop knocking into her ribs. Sticky with the soda, she fumbled through her purse, her fingers shaking like her momma's did when she needed a drink real bad.

"Are you alone?" the officer asked, leaning in slightly to search the interior of the car with those flat cop eyes.

"Yes, sir." Hope handed him her license and registration.

He eyed her for a long moment, then looked over her paperwork. "Wait here."

And then he was gone. With her license.

She counted to twenty while watching the same dark clouds move in, blocking out the sun. And then to one hundred. And then she started counting backward, and had gotten back to twelve when the cop showed up again.

He handed her the license. "Careful driving, kid. A storm is moving in."

She wasn't a kid, but she nodded obediently, and then he was gone.

And she was alone again, but that was better than being arrested for map theft. She studied the soda-soaked map, then got back onto the freeway.

Mia got home from work at six. This was early for her on an evening when she should have been out celebrating, but the fight with Ted and then the fire in her trash can had pretty much sapped her.

She figured she owed herself a quiet evening, with nothing more exciting than an extremely hot shower and a good book. Oh, and maybe a quick private little happy dance for the Anderson account. It was sweet indeed, enough to almost make her forget that she no longer had a right eyebrow.

Getting out of her car and into the sticky pre-storm humidity, she refused to crane her neck to see if there was a motorcycle parked two houses down. No need to look, because she didn't care.

Her heels clicked on the concrete walkway, but at the sound of pounding feet, a dribbling basketball, and male swearing, she pivoted the other way, to the end of the street and the basketball court there.

A competitor at heart, Mia loved a good game— of anything, but especially basketball. Something about the sweat and fast pace, not to mention the display of hard, damp, sexy bodies in shorts, called to her.

There was definitely a game in action, a vicious game of three-on-three. She moved closer to watch.

She recognized her neighbor's twin college-age sons and the fifty-something guy who lived on the next block over who'd once fixed her plumbing. There was another neighbor, frowning with concentration as he dribbled. Then the twenty-something she'd seen in Kevin's apartment.

And then, Kevin himself. Mia's gaze locked on him and held. He'd looked amazing in his jeans and leather jacket. He'd looked damn fine naked.

But on the court . . . be still her heart. He wore black basketball shorts that hung to his knees, a loose gray tank top that said *You don't have to attend every argument you're invited to.* His hair was damp, those yummy eyes following every movement of the ball with the same fierce intensity he'd used to make her come too many times to count, his long fit body primed and hard and damp with sweat.

He charged after the player with the ball, and with a hand that moved fast as lightning, he reached in and stole it. In tune to the cheers of his two teammates, he dodged free and ran down the court with lithe agility and speed, dribbling at the speed of light. Lifting his arm, he twisted in midair, performed a one-handed layup, coming down hard with a quick triumphant pump of his fist.

Someone threw the ball into play again, and Kevin caught it just as a player from the opposite team body-slammed into him.

They both crashed to the floor.

Mia held her breath. Kevin rolled to his knees and got up, offering a hand to the kid who'd knocked him on his ass.

The kid took his hand, stood.

They eyed each other.

Then grinned like idiots.

Kevin ruffled the kid's hair, then waggled a finger in his face. "Flagrant."

"Bull-fucking-shit!"

"You kiss your mother with that mouth?"

The kid grinned again. "*Not* flagrant, dude."

"I'm taking a foul shot. *Dudette.*" Dribbling, Kevin moved to the foul line.

There was just something about his easy rhythmic movements that utterly captivated Mia. He looked down at the ball, then up at the basket, a line of sweat running down his temple, his shirt sticking to him like a second skin.

He made the shot, and the roughhouse game continued.

Mia had no idea how long she stood there captivated, entranced, watching Kevin move on the court with the grace and ease of a cat, but for the life of her, she couldn't walk away. Someone blocked his next shot, but he got the rebound and went up again, taking an elbow to the cheek but making his shot. His team cheered as he came down on both feet. When the other team tossed the ball in, Kevin again snatched it away, then fired the ball to a member of his team. It was immediately passed back to him. Someone tried to take the ball away, but he simply moved faster, his face tightening into an expression that said *Back off, sucker*.

When he got into the key, he passed the ball to his brother in a bulletlike throw, and the shot was made.

"*Yeeees!*" Kevin said, looking extremely satisfied.

Whopping and high-fiving ensued, and some

manly butt-slapping, leaving Mia to assume game over, victory declared.

Kevin grabbed the ball and executed some sort of victory dance, and deep within Mia something quivered. Oh, damn. Oh, damn, this was bad, bad, bad.

Despite his easygoing demeanor, he was a fellow hard-core competitor.

How sexy was that?

Kevin swiped a towel over his face. His shirt was stuck to him, his arms and throat gleaming. He had a bruise gathering beneath one eye and a cut on his lip. And he was smiling, as if he'd just had the time of his life. His brother nudged his shoulder, and they began a conversation.

With their hands.

The brother was deaf. No big deal, but the sight of them, eloquently and easily signing, felt addicting. Even knowing she was invading their privacy, Mia stood there transfixed by their quickly moving hands, their fast smiles, the easy affection . . .

Then Kevin brushed his hand over his brother's hair, messing it up, rubbing his knuckles over his head in the affectionate age-old noogie.

The brother tossed back his head, his mouth carved in a laughing smile, then pushed away and walked off. Kevin watched him go, his smile fading, replaced by an expression of worry and concern.

Mia's smile faded, too, and she wondered what she'd missed.

Then suddenly Kevin turned his head and saw her. The hand holding the towel dropped to his side. His worry and concern faded, replaced by an expression she was fairly certain could be read as annoyance.

She would have winced, but she preferred not to show her hand, that being she felt something almost foreign—true regret at how she'd treated him this morning. But if she didn't like to repeat men, she really didn't like looking back, and so she turned away, moving up the sidewalk toward her house.

The evening had begun to cool. She couldn't believe nearly half an hour had passed since she'd parked, she'd gotten so lost in their game.

"Running. What a surprise," he said.

Slowly she turned back to face the low, husky voice she knew so intimately, thanks to last night. Kevin must have hustled to catch up with her, and yet he wasn't even breathing hard. "I'm not running," she said.

"Yeah, you are. Well, as much as you can in those ridiculous heels, anyway."

She looked down at her five-hundred-dollar Manolos. "*Ridiculous?*"

"What's the hurry? Your cookies burning?"

No, but, oddly enough, now her face was.

"You didn't really make them, did you?"

"I never claimed I did."

"It was implied. Among other things."

"Like what?"

"Like—" But suddenly his eyes narrowed and he took a step closer to her, frowning as he lifted a hand and touched her singed eyebrow. "What happened?"

She fought the urge to slap his hand away. "Nothing an eyebrow pencil won't fix." Turning away, she began to walk again, only to feel his fingers wrap around her arm and gently but firmly pull her back.

He peered into her face, so close now that she could see his eyes were more than light chocolate, but lined in dark as well, with specks of gold dancing in them. "Stop staring," she said and lifted a hand to cover her brow.

He simply took her wrist in his hand and held it out. "You're burned. What did you do, catch yourself with a whatcha-call-it, a curling iron?"

"It's nothing."

His other hand came up and gently probed at the

sensitive skin, making her hiss. His eyes cut to hers. "Nothing, huh?"

Her belly quivered. Hunger, she decided, but, damn it, deep down she knew it was his touch. He was waking up her body again, making it remember how wonderful and amazing and shockingly perfect last night had been. Trying to cover this unwelcome reaction to him, she shoved his hand away. "Just a . . . work incident." No big deal. She'd laughed it off countless times today with all the others at work, despite deep down remaining off balance about the "suspicious" incident.

But having this man look at her with concern darkening his eyes had an effect she couldn't have possibly imagined: the odd urge to set her head down on someone's shoulder, someone who cared about her, someone who would tell her she was going to be okay.

Only she'd never had the luxury of someone else's shoulder in her entire life, and she wasn't going to start now.

"A work incident?" That frown still marred his lips. "I thought you were some PR wizard."

That almost made her smile. "Advertising."

"You kick some ass today, Mia Appleby, advertising exec extraordinaire?"

"You know it." She cocked her head and studied him, blackening eye, cut lip, and all. "You're looking a little worse for wear yourself."

"Nah." He pulled a face, then swore and lifted a hand to his lip. *"Shit."*

"Uh huh. You need help cleaning that up?"

He was now gingerly touching the blooming bruise, licking his cut lip. "No, thanks. I'm still bleeding from our last encounter."

"Suit yourself." She began to back away but couldn't resist running her gaze over his face one last time. *No, you can't have him again.* "You might want to give yourself a break from basketball for a day or so."

"Are you kidding?" His eyes lit. "We *won*."

Her heart squeezed with competitive spirit. With lust. And more. She'd have to make sure to avoid the basketball courts. The entire street.

And especially his bedroom.

He touched his lip again, looked at the blood on his fingers, and shook his head. "I'm losing my touch."

Now that he was most definitely *not* doing, but before her thoughts could take her there she firmly walked away.

"See ya," he said, only slightly mockingly. "Or if you get your way, not."

That's right. They would not be seeing each other. *Keep walking.* She managed it, too, and only when she'd taken the turn on the path, did she glance back.

He was gone.

Good. Perfect. Mission accomplished. She'd distanced herself from him both physically and mentally.

Only, oddly enough, the surge of victory never came.

Hope couldn't believe how insanely people drove in California, but finally she found Mia's street. The block was nice, and there was not a trailer park within miles, she'd bet.

Mia's place was Spanish style, with ceramic-tile roofs and stucco walls. It was barely dusk, but streetlights flickered on and so did some house lights around her. Even with the dark clouds overhead, the neighborhood felt warm and friendly. Pretty.

Classy, too.

There was an outdoor basketball court at the end of the street, and beyond that a small green area and tiny park with a set of swings and a slide and a few benches. And beyond that, woods, lots and lots of woods.

She got out of her car, and her heart knocking against her ribs again, she knocked.

Thunder cracked, making her jerk. She knocked again.

But no one answered, and as the sun began to dip into the sky her aloneness settled into her gut, along with the realization that she had no money and nowhere else to go.

Inside her house, Mia let out a long breath and moved through the wide space. Her own haven. In her bedroom she removed all her protective layers—her Michael Kors, her Prada, her makeup—and when she was stripped bare, she showered.

And then, not looking at her missing eyebrow or the angry red welt/burn above it, she wrapped herself in her French silk robe and padded barefoot through the living room to stand in front of her huge picture windows. The storm had moved in and rain slashed down with a soothing sound.

Her hair fell straight and wet to her shoulders, dripping into the silk and cooling her still-heated skin. Beneath her robe, her body seemed different.

Anticipatory. Hopeful. Tight and achy.

It made no sense. She'd gotten off just last night. And as Kevin knew what he was doing in that department, she'd have thought the effects would last her a while.

And yet, truthfully, it wasn't mindless sex she yearned for . . .

But familiarity. Someone who knew her. Someone to smile at her and tell her she was fine.

Since that was a discomforting thought, she moved to her liquor cabinet and poured herself a glass of wine, trying not to think about Kevin at home right now, possibly also fresh from a shower, stretched out naked on his bed, big and lean and gorgeous. Sipping her drink, she moved through her living room, enjoying the smooth, shiny hardwood floors beneath her feet, the lovely silence.

The doorbell rang, shattering that silence, making her jump and nearly spill her wine. Then, before she could recover or even react, a heavy knock followed.

"Coming," she muttered and moved toward the door. On tiptoes, she put her eye to the peephole, then went still.

Kevin stood there, his face very close to the opening as he waved.

She looked down at herself. Silk robe and nothing else. Bare feet. Wet hair.

No makeup.

She wished she'd taken a shot of whiskey instead of the glass of wine she still held, because her body wanted to let him in. *Everywhere.* Luckily, her brain held back. *Good, brain.* "I'm a little busy," she said through the door.

"This isn't about you, Mia. Open up. It's raining like a mother."

She took another peek. He'd stepped back a bit and was already drenched. He'd changed, too, into a pair of Levi's and that leather jacket, and with the porch light glaring on his face, thrusting it into bold relief, she could see he had one hell of a shiner blooming along his right eye, and that that eye was no longer looking at her with heat and lust.

He'd been riding his bike.

He wasn't alone, she saw now, but whoever was with him had their face averted.

In fact, it appeared that Kevin was gripping the back of that person's jacket, holding them against their will.

What the hell?

She opened the door. Kevin was indeed holding

on to the back of the person next to him, a small, thin teenage girl dressed in black from head to toe, with various studs and belts and chains. "What are you doing?" she asked.

"Nothing much," he said, tightening his grip when the goth girl tried to sidestep away. "Just catching snoopy intruders in my bedroom. Listen, next time you want to spy on me, do it yourself, all right? She's just a damn kid."

The "damn kid" raised her face, which was pale and streaked with anger, sullenness, and undeniable humiliation. "I wasn't spying for her!"

Mia took in more details. The teen had jet-black hair, the color that could have come only from a bottle, and a cheap one at that. It was long, hanging in her pasty white face. Her makeup consisted of thick black eyeliner and black gloss, both of which had run in the rain. She wore a myriad of silver hoops up one ear and a brow piercing. "I don't know what this is about," Mia said. "But I'm busy."

"You're going to want to hear this." Kevin gently but firmly pushed the teen inside past Mia, following uninvited into her foyer.

Kevin let go of the girl, who crossed her arms over herself and hunched her bony shoulders, the two of them dripping on her floor. "Tell her," he said to the teen, who rolled her lips inward. "Oh, now you go mum. Great. Nice." His lip was a little puffy, and there was that bruise beneath his eye, and he looked like maybe he'd come to the end of his patience. "You're done screaming holy murder then?"

"You grabbed me!"

"You were in my house. In my bedroom. Searching my drawers!"

Mia shook her head. "She was breaking and entering? Why didn't you call the cops?"

Kevin sent her a scathing look. Nope, he was *defi-*

nitely done lusting after her. "You ever been to juvy, Mia? Not a friendly place. I just want to get to the bottom of this, and I want to get there now."

"But I have no idea . . ." Mia started, breaking off when the teen let out a harsh laugh that might have doubled as a sob.

The girl stood there, skinny and scrawny and maybe all of sixteen, quivering in her black lace-up boots as the sound escaped her lips again. Confused, Mia turned to Kevin, whose eyes were downright chilly.

"Are you really *that* self-absorbed," he asked, "that you don't recognize your own niece?"

Chapter Five

Mia stared at Kevin as the words sank in, then turned back to the girl.

Much of the teen's bravado had faded away. With the heavy black of her eyeliner and mascara smudged beneath her eyes and all that stringy black hair in her face, she looked like an Addams Family reunion reject. She was nibbling on a chipped black fingernail, already chewed to the nub.

"What's your name?" Mia asked hoarsely.

The girl shrugged, and though she looked like a drowned rat, it did nothing to dispel the obvious fact that she had a major attitude.

Kevin divided a look between them, then turned to the teen. "So she didn't know? She had no idea you were in my place?"

"Of course I didn't—" Mia started, stopping in shock when he held up a hand in her face.

"I was talking to the kid," he said.

Yeah, and he'd be talking to her fist, except . . . She stared at the girl. "Your name?"

Once again the girl pressed her lips together.

"Tell her," Kevin said, nudging her, though doing so with a clear gentleness. He seemed so tall and big next to her, almost formidable, a definite contrast to the sexy lover and basketball player Mia had already seen.

The girl looked up at him, silently imploring.

"Tell her," Kevin said again in that same infinitely patient but inexorable tone.

He had a voice on him—Mia would give him that—the kind that could coax the most saintly to sin, the law-abiding to throw caution to the wind, and a woman to forget her inhibitions. She thought of him teaching, talking to teenagers, and she had to admit, he could probably sell the most boring text-book ever written.

It certainly had sold her last night. One naughty, wicked word from those lips to her ears and she'd been gone.

The girl reacted by sidling slightly closer to him as she looked at Mia. "Hope," she whispered.

Mia leaned in. "You hope what?"

A glare was her only answer.

"Her name is Hope," Kevin clarified.

And Mia froze. "Hope . . . *Appleby*?"

Her answer was the universal gaze teenagers all over the country had perfected, the one which said *Fuck off and die, but before you do, please take care of me.*

Oh, my God. *Hope.*

Sugar's daughter.

To Mia's shame, she'd never met her. Sugar had gotten pregnant the night of that long ago BBQ, and since Mia had never been back . . .

Another shame, but though she hadn't planted her-self there physically, she had done her best with let-ters and phone calls, not that that was enough.

Still, Mia had tried, sending checks, too, money that had surely gone toward barbeque wardrobes and tacky furnishings for the trailer, at least until she died five years ago in a car accident.

After that, Mia still sent money, but Sugar hadn't been as easy to keep in touch with. As she wasn't much of a letter writer, either—and let's face it, there hadn't ever been much love between them—years had gone by without a word or thank-you. The only way Mia even knew Sugar received the money Mia sent was that the checks had always been immediately cashed.

Mia had done her best not to care, sending cards and checks directly to Hope as well, even though she'd never received an acknowledgement.

If asked, Mia would have said she hadn't needed or wanted one. But to see the kid here, without warning . . . "My God. What's going on?"

Another jerk of the shoulder.

Lost, Mia looked at Kevin. He shrugged, too.

Damn, she wished she'd downed her wine. She wanted to now but felt a little self-conscious doing so in front of a minor. "Hope." Mia struggled with the words. Funny, that. She was known for being good in an emergency, for always knowing what to do or say, but for the first time in her life she felt clueless. "What are you doing here?"

Hope kicked the toe of her black-soled boot against the hardwood floor, leaving a dark scuff mark. With the smoothness of one well used to covering her tracks, she stepped on it. "I thought I'd, you know, come see LA." Her voice was soft, and thick with a Southern drawl.

Mia did not so much as glance at Kevin. She'd told no one where she was from, not even Tess, and that wouldn't change now. "Is Sugar with you?"

"No."

"Did you fly?"

"No."

"Did you take the train?"

"No."

Kevin sighed and nudged Hope again. "Listen, you got lucky. You could have pulled your little B&E session on a cop's house. Or one with a guy who might have been extremely happy to find a young girl in his bedroom. Do you know what I'm saying?"

"Yeah. You don't want to do me."

Kevin pinched the bridge of his nose. "I'm a teacher," he said. "A high school teacher. That means that I supposedly have a boatload of patience, but that's a complete crock. What I have, Hope, is an unfortunate understanding of how your mind works. We're not the bad guys here."

She said nothing, but scuffed the wood again with another kick of her foot.

Mia winced and eyed her perfect wood floor.

"Talk to us, Hope," Kevin said.

"I didn't mean to break into your house." She spoke directly to her boots. "And I wasn't stealing nothing, I swear it."

"I didn't say you were," Kevin said. "I said you were snooping."

"I was looking around. I wanted to see her stuff."

"Whose? Mia's?" He asked this in a much more patient tone than Mia could have come up with. She wanted answers, and she wanted them now, but Kevin wasn't rushing anything. In his eyes was an understanding of Hope, one that said he'd been there.

Hope nodded. Yes, she'd thought she was looking at Mia's stuff.

Mia straightened, momentarily forgetting she stood there in nothing but her robe, gripping a glass of wine. "So why were you in *Kevin's* house?"

"Because I mixed up the address."

"Keep talking," Kevin said.

"I didn't know anything about her, okay?" Hope lifted her face, bright now with embarrassment. "I wanted to see what she was like, see if I was going to want to stay, and I messed up the two and five of the address."

"So you've never been to your aunt's place?"

Mia's stomach tightened as Hope shook her head. Kevin was nodding as if he understood this crazy situation perfectly. "So you were looking in my drawers, thinking you had Mia's things in front of you?"

"Yes." Again she rolled her lips together, as if fighting with herself. "I'm sorry," she said, the words seeming to cost her. "I didn't mean to invade your privacy."

"I got that."

Hope looked at him. Her face was still mostly covered with her long, streaky black hair, but she actually made eye contact.

He smiled approvingly.

She didn't smile back, but she kept her head up.

"Now tell us what you're doing here all alone."

She kicked at the wood floor again, and Mia did her best to not yell *Stop!*

"I wanted to come to LA like Aunt Apple did," Hope said. "I wanted to get rich and live like this."

"Aunt Apple," Kevin repeated pointedly and looked at Mia, who suddenly wished she'd downed the entire *bottle* of wine.

"Yeah. I mean, look at this place," Hope said, gesturing with a jerk of her shoulder at the foyer into the large, clean, beautifully decorated living room.

Mia knew exactly what it looked like to her: a mansion.

"I want to live like this," Hope whispered in awe.

Mia went to say that it took a hell of a lot more than want, but Kevin shot her a warning glance and she slowly closed her mouth. She hated that he was running this show but admitted to herself she was so far out of her league she couldn't even *see* her league.

"How did you get here?" Kevin asked Hope.

"For my sixteenth birthday a couple months ago, she sent me money. Five hundred dollars."

Kevin let out a low whistle. "Score."

"I bought a car. An eighty-nine Dodge Diplomat.

I drove out here using the return address from the card she sent, but the ink got smeared when I got pulled over and spilled a Coke—''

"You got pulled over?" Mia asked, horrified.

"Only once," she said defensively. "I was speeding by accident."

"Oh, my God."

Kevin shot her another zip-it look. Mia just shook her head, feeling sick. The kid had driven across the country, by herself. Good God, what if it had been her *street* name that got smeared? Hope might have gotten lost entirely, and then been at someone else's mercy, someone possibly not as kind or understanding as Kevin had been to find her prowling through his things.

"I think my car died in front of your house," Hope said morosely. "It was on its last legs anyway."

Mia let out a choked laugh. The implications of it—of a young girl on her own, and all the inherent dangers she must have faced—made her nauseous. Anything could have gone wrong, and for a moment, thinking about it, she could hardly speak. "Why didn't you call me?"

"I dunno." Another kick of the wood. "You've never called me."

Over Hope's head, Kevin looked at Mia. "Never?" he repeated in an even tone that didn't need any recrimination in it because it was all in his eyes.

"Never," Hope said.

Kevin's eyes were cool now. "Huh."

Oh, yeah, he was done wanting her. She opened her mouth to defend herself, to try to explain the complicated reasons for the lack of physical contact and that she and Sugar had never been close.

It sounded like a cop-out.

It *was* a cop-out.

"Does your family know where you are?" Kevin asked.

Hope shook her head. "It's just my mom. She probably thinks I'm at a friend's house."

"For days?"

"It's only been three, but yeah." Beneath the makeup, she went red. "I—we've had some . . . problems."

"Like?"

"Um . . ." Another kick of those black boots on her wood floor. "It's complicated."

"Did it involve the police?"

"Sorta."

Oh, that was it. Mia tossed back the wine.

"All right, my little snooper," Kevin said. "Wait here." He cocked his head at Mia and offered a smile that didn't meet his eyes. "Mia? A minute?"

Both Hope and Kevin looked at her, seeing her wet hair, her lack of clothes, her tightfisted clench on the now empty wineglass.

And she'd never felt more naked, more vulnerable in her life.

Kevin's eyes didn't zero in on her body, as she'd have liked, but stayed on her face, his mouth grim. Just last night he'd had his hands and mouth and body all over hers in wild, hot, reckless abandon.

Now this. Under different circumstances, she might have relished making him feel an inch tall, but without her armor she felt helpless.

Finally, taking matters into his own hands, Kevin smiled reassuringly at Hope and pulled Mia by the arm into the kitchen.

Yanking free, Mia went directly to the counter and poured herself another glass of wine. "I can handle it from here."

He cocked a brow as he leaned his hips back against her table. An insolent, know-it-all pose. "Can you now? *Apple?*"

She looked right into his eyes wanting to kill him with one glance, but at the last minute she held back, knowing damn well if she let him know how much it bothered her, he'd love it.

"What's the matter?" he asked. "Cat got your tongue, *Apple*?"

"Call me that again and you'll be walking funny tomorrow."

He let out a slow grin, even as she silently kicked her own ass for revealing her hand. "I can handle it from here," she repeated.

"She's a runaway. A niece you don't even know, apparently."

"Oh, and you know all of *your* family?"

"You bet your sweet ass I do. They're family," he said simply.

Yeah, he was the kind of guy who attached and attached deeply. A man who liked his family, faults and all, a man who knew kids and cared about them. He'd probably give a stranger the shirt off his back, even when the economy was decent and any bum sitting on a corner begging could get a job flipping burgers if he wanted. "Look, Hope's momma and I . . . we had our problems. We're not close."

"Lots of families aren't close. They don't go sixteen years without seeing each other."

"Well, my family does."

"Where does Hope come from?" he asked. "The accent is . . . what? Alabama?"

She was already feeling stripped bare, and it had nothing to do with being nearly naked. To hell if she was going to give him *that* information.

"You know what?" he said, tossing up his hands. "Fine, don't tell me. Don't tell me anything." He strode toward the door, then at the last minute turned back. "Just don't sweep this one under the carpet, Mia."

"And what does that mean?"

"It means that this isn't like last night. You can't just get into this for the fun and the heat and then jump back out when it suits you. This time when someone gets hurt, it's going to be a kid."

"Who got hurt last night?"

He stared at her, then shook his head, mouth tight, eyes unfathomable. "Forget it. But that's one mixed-up kid out there. She's fragile. Needy."

"Are you kidding me? She's tough as nails. And she needs no one."

He just shook his head and muttered something that sounded a lot like *How can someone so smart be so stupid?*

After the day she'd had, this made her see red. "Get out."

"Yeah, I figured that one was coming." But he didn't move. "Listen, I'm going to do something I told myself I wouldn't."

"What, stop dragging your knuckles?"

"I'm trying to help."

"Well, don't."

Shaking his head, he put his hand on the door, but then once again turned back. "I realize you probably don't hear these words very often, Ms. On Top of Her World, but trust me on this one. You *are* wrong."

"I can handle this."

"This? Jesus." He shook his head. "It's not a business deal, Mia. Or a guy you're stomping the shit out of. It's not a 'this' at all. It's a girl."

"And what do you know about girls?"

She knew her mistake the minute he flashed her a quick grin, showing a glimpse of the laid-back, bad-ass biker she'd slept with last night. "I know enough."

Damn it, but her tummy fluttered. "You're acting like it's going to be hard to watch her for a night until I can get her home. I mean, honestly, how much trouble can she be?"

He stared at her, then let out a low laugh. "You're right. You handle it. Your way."

He moved through the door and she followed, getting into the hall in time to see him touch Hope's arm, leaning in to say something softly.

In turn, Hope gripped his arm. "You're leaving?"

He nodded.

"But I thought you two were . . ." Hope waggled her fingers back and forth between him and Mia. "You know, like, doing it."

Mia choked.

To Kevin's credit, he didn't react at all. "You thought wrong."

"But I want to stay with *you*," she said to Kevin.

"Uh, that's a big negative," Mia said.

Hope's bravado seemed to desert her at this unwelcome news. "Oh."

"Look, why don't we call your mom?" Kevin said quietly. "And then—"

"No." Hope shuffled her feet some, and Mia winced at the additional scuff marks. "I don't think my mom's ready to hear from me."

"I bet she is." *She would be.* Mia grabbed the portable phone off the small desk against the wall. "We'll just call—"

"I've changed my mind about staying here," Hope said stiffly.

"Good. But we're still calling. Number?"

Hope went sullenly silent, but Mia was unmoved. "The number, Hope."

Hope rolled her eyes.

"Could you stop rolling your eyes at everything I say?" Mia requested. "It just makes me want to put your eyeballs into a jar so that you can shake it every time you feel the need to roll them at me."

Kevin made a move as if to step in, but Mia put a hand to his chest and held him back, her gaze locked on Hope's.

"I know you know the number. Let's hear it." Damn difficult to be tough when she was distracted by the heat of Kevin's chest and all that easy strength beneath her palm. Not to mention knowing exactly what he could do to her with all that strength. "Speak up."

Hope looked at Kevin.

"It's going to be okay," he said very gently.

And Hope's tough-girl image seemed to fold in on itself. "Promise?" she whispered.

Kevin put a hand on her shoulder. "Family can get complicated sometimes, that's all."

"Is yours?"

He let out a low laugh. "Oh, yeah."

"Does *your* mom drive *you* crazy?"

"My mom is gone now. So's my dad. But my brother drives me crazy. Does that count?"

She let out a little smile that didn't last long before collapsing as she rattled off her mom's number to Mia without looking at her.

Mia punched it into the phone but didn't turn it on yet. "Is she going to be home?"

"Doubt it."

"I can take a look at your car," Kevin said to Hope. "If you'd like."

Looking at him as if he was Superman, she handed over her keys.

Kevin turned to Mia. "If you have any . . . issues, I teach at the high school and run the teen center next to it. We have a summer program that started up just today."

Mia nodded and waited for him to go. When he didn't, she met his gaze and felt a punch of awareness, as well as an unbidden memory of being naked in his arms. Her body actually leaned toward him for a touch, a hug . . .

Ridiculous. She didn't need those things. And yet . . . No. *No, no, no.* She shook herself, backed up, and gave him the room he needed to go.

He oozed virility as he turned to the door, but Mia

just held her breath because it really seemed as if he was waiting for something from her.

The air sort of crackled, went still, then crackled some more.

"You're supposed to kiss him," Hope said ever so helpfully. "Guys like it when you do that."

Kevin looked at Mia, and she would have sworn there was a glint of wry amusement deep in his gaze.

"Don't you?" Hope asked him.

Kevin seemed to debate with himself on whether to answer or not. "I'm not sure where you get your perception of the male species, but some guys—"

"—are from another planet," Mia interjected dryly. "Actually, all of them are."

Kevin shot her a look. Then turned back to Hope. "You don't have to do what guys like."

"Maybe I like it, too," Hope said but didn't sound convinced.

Kevin tugged on a strand of Hope's hair. "You know where to find me if you need anything." He looked at Mia. "You, too," he said.

And then he walked out into the rain.

"He's hot," Hope said, watching him go. "For an old guy."

Yeah, well, he was gone. Hot or otherwise.

Just as she'd wanted.

So she had no idea why the sound of the door closing felt so uncomfortably . . . final. With a sigh, she turned on the phone and listened to it ring in a place two thousand miles east in Tennessee, in a single-wide trailer a world away.

Chapter Six

Sugar answered the phone in her soft Southern drawl. "Hello?"

Mia took a breath and said, "Sugar. You'll never guess who I've got here."

A silence greeted this. Then, *"Are you shitting me?"*

"Nope." Mia smiled grimly at Hope and responded in the heavy Southern drawl she'd buried for sixteen years. "Not shitting ya."

"Ah, Jesus. You still all the way out there in Cali?"

"Yep."

"Well, that sucks."

"I was thinking you could come get her—"

"Oooh, no. I've got this new job, I don't have any vacation time until September, and I'm not going to make any waves here. I'll come for her then."

Mia's eyes cut to the wall calendar. "It's June."

"That's right."

"That's unacceptable."

"Hey, tell it to the girl. She's the one who ran away from home. Sixth time this year, too. Says no one understands her. Says no one cares. Well, no one understands or cares about her need to cut school or about the lipstick that just found its way off the Piggly Wiggly shelf and into her purse!"

Mia looked at Hope. "So she's in trouble then?"

Hope looked away.

Sugar sighed mightily. "Trouble is as trouble does, and that little thing is full of it, no ifs, ands, or buts."

"You have to come get her."

"Uh huh. Listen, I know we haven't exactly stayed close, but I could use an itty-bitty favor here."

Mia's jaw tightened because she could already smell the con.

"I know you don't miss us little ol' folk."

Laying it on thick. Nice touch.

"But I've been raising that child all alone, on a low, single income. It's rough, you know? I mean, I couldn't get there sooner than the weekend anyhow . . . and trust me, the girl could use a role model. Someone who got somewhere in life, someone to show her the ropes on how to succeed, how to get what she wants without stealing it, you know?"

"I work, too, Sugar."

"Right. You work your fingers to the bone, barely scraping by."

Mia turned in a slow, frustrated circle, then caught a glimpse of Hope standing there, her face tight, closed off.

No missing the resentment, the feeling that no one wanted her, not even family.

Ah, hell.

"I'm outta here," Hope said and turned to the door.

Mia reached out and wrapped her fingers around the kid's arm. God, she was thin, so very thin. And still and chilled, despite the warm air driving the wet storm. "Wait, Hope. Sugar, listen—"

"Look, the truth is, you were always so much smarter than us, we never knew what to do with you, Apple."

"*Mia.*"

Sugar laughed good and hard over that, in her craggy voice that suggested she'd been smoking her

entire life. "Fancy name or not, you're just the person
that kid needs to motivate her back into school."

"She left school?"

Next to her, Hope closed her eyes.

"Got herself kicked out," Sugar said. "And arrested. She still owes me two grand for that whole
mess."

Clearly able to hear Sugar, Hope's mouth went
grim and she tried to tug free, but Mia held on. "You
need to come and get her now," Mia said into the
phone.

"Ship her back the way she came."

Mia shook her head. "No. I won't do that. It's a
miracle she made it here in one piece."

"One week," Sugar said. "Surely you can handle
it for a week."

"Her," Mia said softly, mirroring Kevin's words,
which was how she knew she was screwed, that she
was going to do this. "It's a *her*—" But she was talking to a dial tone. "Damn it."

"She had a date," Hope said.

"How do you know?"

"Just a guess."

Probably, but the way Hope said it, as if she understood and accepted how much more important a date
would be than her . . . Mia wanted to strangle Sugar.
Instead she set down the phone and drew a deep
breath. "All right. Let's get settled until we figure
out what we're going to do."

"Hey, if you're thinking of kicking me out, just tell
me now and I'll be gone."

"Really? Where?"

Hope jerked her shoulder again. She was good at
that. "I've got plenty of places to go."

In spite of herself, Mia was fascinated by the bravado. She'd once been in Hope's shoes, or close
enough, but she'd had strong grades behind her—

not to mention no police record—and had landed a scholarship to college. "Name one."

"Hollywood is only a few hills over. I saw it on the map."

"No one's going to Hollywood tonight. I'll show you where you can sleep, and tomorrow morning we'll—"

"What, send me back then?"

"You keep saying that, and I'll think you're eager to get home." Mia smiled grimly when Hope scowled. "So sleep first. You think you can manage to do that without getting into trouble?"

"Funny."

"You hungry?"

"Always." They went into the kitchen, where Hope looked distinctly unimpressed with Mia's sparsely filled refrigerator and cabinets. Mia didn't eat here often, and when she did, it was usually something she'd picked up on the way home. Hope wrinkled her nose at the leftover Thai. "You need to go food shopping," she said.

Mia was brought back to her childhood, when they might have always struggled to get the rent paid but there'd always been plenty of fat and carbs in the fridge. "We eat differently here in California."

"Looks like you don't eat at all."

They made do with low-fat cheese and stone-wheat crackers; then Mia took Hope to one of the two spare bedrooms, which was decorated with a dresser, nightstand, and four-poster bed she'd gotten in San Francisco, and pale silk linens from Brunschwig & Fils. The two Pacific Ocean prints on the walls added serenity and beauty to the space.

Hope stood in the doorway looking staggered. "Wow. Sugar likes white, too."

Mia resisted telling her the difference between her linens and Sugar's linens was at least a thousand thread count. "That door leads to your bathroom."

"My own?" the girl asked in hushed awe.

Something deep in Mia's belly tightened. "Yes. Your own."

"This room is as huge as our whole trailer."

Mia remembered with painful clarity the life Hope had run from, the desperation, the despair, the need to get the hell out no matter that there was nowhere to go. "Look, about the fact that we've never talked before . . ."

Hope looked at her.

"I'm sorry. Just because Sugar and I aren't close is no excuse. I should have called you. Checked in."

Hope lifted a shoulder. No biggie. "How did you do it?" The kid walked the length of the room, reverently touching the polished dresser, the tray on top of it that held five white candles. "How did you get all of this?"

"Well, I didn't get myself arrested, for one. And I stayed in school, for another." Mia looked over the girl with her ragged black pants, black tank top, large black overshirt, black boots, and the studded belt and bracelet that looked dangerous to her health. "And I was far too busy planning my escape to be worried about goth getup."

Hope fingered her pierced brow, her expression closed, and Mia sighed. "Look, just get some sleep, okay?" When she got no response, Mia moved to the door.

"Were you like me?" Hope whispered. "At all?"

She turned back and searched the girl's face. The too-black hair, lank from bad products. The black lipstick that made her look so pasty. The brow piercing. Beneath the veneer stood a painfully thin young girl, lost and achingly alone. Mia could read the fear as if it was her own, the knowledge that life wouldn't just be accepted, that there was more and she wanted a piece of it.

Were they alike at all? "I don't know," Mia answered honestly. "But it looks like we're going to find out."

By the time Kevin entered his house again, he was drenched to the skin and a jackhammer had begun to go off at the base of his skull. A helluva day. His first summer science class had been like teaching Greek to preschoolers. Nor had he found his pot smoker, but he'd caught hell from Joe.

Mrs. Stacy had tattled on him to the principal.

Joe had taken great pleasure in reading him the riot act, *not* for wasting electricity or having kids smoke weed in his classroom, but for Kevin taking his parking spot.

Then had come far more troublesome news. The teen center, housed next to the high school in a building loaned to the rec center, had gone up for sale.

Unfortunately for Kevin, the owner happened to be Beth Moore, his ex, and she hadn't been happy with him in years. She didn't care that the town couldn't buy the building and that her selling would probably mean closing the teen center, which in turn would leave lots of kids with no supervised, safe place to hang out.

And speaking of safety, or lack of, he'd had three kids sneak off into the woods this afternoon. Two boys and a girl who'd come from a broken home and had no self-esteem, which made her easy prey. Thankfully, Kevin had found them before they'd talked the girl out of her clothes, but they'd all been drinking.

Damn it. Could no one make a good decision?

Then he'd come home and found yet another teen, dressed in wannabe goth, poking in his drawers. Mia's niece. And then there'd been Mia herself, eyes cool, body hot . . .

His entire world had turned into one big Peyton Place.

Mike came into the living room, dressed for clubbing in all black, hair artfully styled to look like he'd just gotten out of bed, eyes sparkling with trouble. And he'd find it, too, then be worthless for the job interview he'd set up through Monster.com for tomorrow. This was usually the portion of the evening where Kevin gave the whole be-good spiel—don't go slutting around; you need to find a woman to love you, not fuck you; etc. etc.—but, damn, he was fresh out of pep talk tonight.

Mike stopped in the doorway as they passed each other, and looked at Kevin questioningly. *What's your problem?*

I don't have one. Nope, he had about fifty. He tried to go around, but Mike stepped in his way.

It's the hot babe, isn't it?

Of course not. He had all these other things going on, things that were important— Ah, hell. It *was* the hot babe. *I'm fine. Try to stay out of trouble tonight.* Which was like telling a bull in a china shop to be careful.

She doesn't want round two, huh?

Kevin hadn't wanted his brain to go there, but it was too late now. He pictured Mia in her robe, gripping a glass of wine as if it was a lifeline, looking pale and shaken and off her axis . . . and, damn, if that hadn't reached out and grabbed him by the throat.

Then she'd kicked him out. *I think it's safe to say there'll be no round two*, he signed.

Damn shame.

Actually, it was the smart thing. Mia had the same attitude toward sex that Mike did, and while Kevin couldn't fault her for that, he didn't have the gene that allowed him to sleep with someone and then move on in a blink. *Go*, Kevin gestured. *Just don't be stupid.*

Mike grinned. *Don't worry, Mom.*

I mean it. I don't have bail money this time.
Don't wait up.

The door shut. Kevin shook it off. He couldn't keep agonizing over every single person in his life, over their inability to make good decisions. It was too tiring. So he showered until the scalding water ran out, then pulled on a pair of sweats and wandered through his dark house toward the kitchen. The refrigerator wasn't promising. It held leftover pizza of questionable quality, a soggy-looking apple, and a beer, which he grabbed. Yeah, he was a party animal all right.

A hollow, empty-feeling one.

Just as he took a long pull from the bottle, someone knocked on his front door. Probably Mike, who'd forgotten something. Flipping on the porch light, he pulled the door open in one movement, then went still in surprise.

Mia.

She was beautiful. Maybe even crazy beautiful. And wickedly dangerous to his mental health.

Blinking from the sudden glare, she wore only that creamy, elegant robe, a pissed-off, hungry expression, and nothing else. He knew this because the light cast her in bold relief, cutting through that thin, drenched silk and highlighting her gorgeous body.

It was still raining. Her limbs glistened, her skin glowed damply. And everything within him tightened in anticipation. "What are you doing here?"

"Can you cut the light?" She lifted a hand to protect her eyes as rain dripped from her hair to the silk, plastering it to her skin, revealing that she was good and chilled.

She looked amazing, if not oddly solemn. He should send her home, for nothing else than she also looked vulnerable, and then there was that melancholy in her eyes . . .

But to hell with being the good guy, to being the

guy everyone came to when they needed something. He needed, too, goddamnit. And what he needed in this moment was to look at her.

"The light?" she said again.

"I don't think so." He drank in his fill. *Just look, don't touch.* "You never know who could be prowling around late at night."

"Funny." She drank her fill as well, her gaze lingering on his bare chest, wet now from the rain blowing at him. "You going to let me in?"

Her cool, icy voice was back, overriding any vulnerability he'd caught a glimpse of. Even wet and chilled, she now looked put together, in charge of herself and capabilities, and sexy as all hell.

Which meant he was in big trouble. Trying to maintain composure, he propped up the jamb with his shoulder, his beer dangling from his fingers. "Why? Need to hit me with another Mack truck?"

Arms crossed over her chest, Mia glanced behind her, as if worried about someone seeing her. "I'm not dressed."

"I noticed." He took another long pull of his beer, letting his gaze soak her up, all that long, still-damp chestnut hair tumbling just past her shoulders. Her eyes flashed her frustration louder than a shout, that compact, neat, tight, toned body quivering with God knew what beneath that silk. All he knew for sure was that her nipples were still poking against the material, her softly rounded belly rising and falling with her every breath. And those legs. He needed a good long time to sigh over those legs. "Where's Hope?"

"Fast asleep, and snoring like a buzz saw."

"You've got a real thing about snoring."

"Move," she said and went to brush past him, only he straightened, trapping her between his body and the jamb.

She let out a sound that spoke volumes of how frustrated she was, and glared up at him.

God, she was something, all shimmering with pent-up aggression and a barely repressed excitement, and he felt a glimmer of his own excitement, which made him a very sick man, he decided. "Do you ever say please?" he asked.

Her mouth tightened. "Fine. Will you pretty *please* let me inside so you can do me?"

He let out a surprised laugh. "What, is it my birthday?"

"Yep, and I brought you just what you wished for," she said with just a slight hint of that Southern drawl in her voice now, a sound that gave him back some of his power. He took one last breath as a smart man and stepped back. "Do you want something to drink?"

"No."

"How about—"

She kicked the door shut behind them, then slid her hands up his bare chest into his hair and tugged his head to hers.

"Okay, no drink, no talk," he said as she bit his lower lip, just sunk her teeth right into his flesh and tugged, whipping his blood into an instant froth, from cool to boiling in just under two-point-zero seconds. "Jesus."

He was already off balance, so when she gave him a light shove he fell back against the wall. Her scent surrounded him, some complicated mixture of exotic perfume and woman as she sandwiched him there with her body, taking her hot, greedy mouth on a tour along his jaw, exhaling slowly in his ear, making him groan as his hands gripped her hips hard for balance in a spinning world.

Then she slithered out of his hold and dropped to her knees.

Jesus. "Mia—"

"Right here." She yanked his sweats down, baring his ass to the cold wall behind him, and everything else to her gaze. She whispered his name then, or what might have been his name, on a sigh so soft it drifted like silk over his heated, hard flesh as she took him in her hands and stroked.

He sucked in a breath. His knees buckled, and he hit the ground hard. Had it been only a minute ago he'd been feeling hollow and empty? Because, he didn't know how, but she was changing that for him, filling him, making him feel whole.

It wasn't real. Hell, *she* wasn't real, but the warm, silk-clad body against him said otherwise, and he couldn't pull away to save himself the grief that would come later—not when his brain, hungry and awakened and desperate for release, had clocked out. She was touching him, making him smolder, then flame, and then she dragged him all the way down to the floor and straddled him.

With a slow, achingly sensual smile, she pulled a condom out of her pocket, untied her robe, and shrugged it off her shoulders.

Her breasts gleamed pale and full in the foyer light, swaying when she leaned over him and took his mouth with hers. He was lost then; but as she stoked the condom down his length, then lifted up and took him deep inside her body, he was found.

Simple and unbelievable as that. Having had enough of her being in control, he surged up and tucked her beneath him now. She tried to rear up, but he entwined their fingers, holding her hands on either side of her head as he thrust into her again and again until she cried out, shuddering as she came with a soft, gasping cry. Burying his face in her hair, he followed her over.

It took him a while to gain his breath, though he did manage to roll off her so he didn't crush her farther into the hard floor. Then he lay there gaping like a beached fish, thinking, so much for basketball keeping him in shape.

She shifted, and he was reminded of her last, hasty exit. Reaching out to pull her into him, he put his mouth to her throat, running his hand up her warm curves.

She put her hand over his, squeezed, but then scooted away and stood up.

Smiling up at her beautiful naked body, the one he wanted to put his mouth all over, every inch, he wiggled his fingers at her to come back.

Slowly she shook her head and reached for her robe.

And his smile faded. "Ah, hell. Not again."

"It's late. I've got a teenager in the house. God. *A teenager.*" She shook her head as if she still couldn't believe it. Then she glanced down at him, at his expression. She let out a sound. "You're not going to make this complicated, are you?"

Still flat on the floor,, still twitching from the aftermath of great sex, he let out a low laugh and managed to shake his head. "No, no complication." Gathering his strength, he staggered to his feet and snagged her hand, tugging her close, trying one more time to reach her. "You came over here just for this then."

She stiffened up on him and blinked warily. His little Ice Queen. "Yes."

"Well, then, I'm going to ask you to take back what you said this morning."

She didn't pretend not to know what he meant. "Fine." Her lips quirked. "You don't have—what was it—stinky feet."

Ah, wasn't she funny. "Mia."

"And you don't snore."

"*And . . .*"

"And . . ." She smiled as she belted her robe. "And maybe next time we'll get to a bed to see about that other thing."

His poor heart gave a quick kick. "Next time?"

The flicker of unease across her face fascinated him. She hadn't meant to say those words, and he knew why. She didn't like to repeat. And not only had she repeated with him, she'd just admitted she wanted to repeat again. Unable to hold it back, he smiled.

She let out a frustrated sound. "There will *not* be a next time." She flung open the front door, braved the rain. "Good night."

When it shut rather hard, he stood there, still staggered, still half aroused, feeling as if he'd been hit by the Mack truck all over again.

She was bad for him. Bad, bad, bad. Next time she came knocking, even if she wasn't wearing a damn *stitch*, he wouldn't sleep with her. He would not make the mistake a third time. "Better keep telling yourself that," he muttered and managed to find the energy to pull his sweats back up. He went to the fridge, but no food fairy had appeared, so he headed for some mindless TV.

A few hours later, the front door opened and Mike stood there, eyes glossy, crooked smile in place. He gave an exaggerated wave.

You're drunk, Kevin signed.

Nah. Just a little looped. When he signed the *looped* part, he nearly took out his own eye.

Tell me you didn't drive.

Nope. Got a ride. Mike blinked exaggeratedly and eyed Kevin. *You look like hell. What hit you?*

A Mack truck.

Was her name Mia Appleby? Mike laughed at the thought, but when Kevin didn't, Mike shook his head. *Ah, Christ. She got you again, huh?*

I don't want to talk about it. Kevin went to the kitchen, hunting through the cabinets until he found a bag of chips. He turned around to find Mike watching him. *You going to do that interview tomorrow? The one you got from Monster.com? What was it, a data inputting thing?*

Mike shrugged. *Haven't decided. Sounds boring.*

Ah, hell. Here they came, the excuses. *Maybe boring is what you need right now.*

What I need right now is another drink.

Kevin watched him stalk out the door again and felt that same ache he felt whenever he looked at the troubled kids in his classes. He couldn't fix them any more than he could fix Mike, and it killed him.

In fact, he couldn't fix any damn thing. Pushing away from the counter, he groaned at his own aching muscles, particularly the ones in his thighs. Apparently Miss Hotshot Mia Appleby was going to kill him as well.

Chapter Seven

One would think being thrown to the floor and ravished within three steps of his front door would have a man sleeping like a baby.

But Kevin slept like shit, and then was interrupted by a four a.m. text message from Mike.

Remember when you said stay out of trouble? Tried. Failed. I'm at county. Bring cash.

Kevin groaned and didn't move. No. He wasn't going to do this again, damn it. Mike's ass could just sit in jail this time.

But as he lay there in his cozy bed, he began to imagine all the things that could be happening to his brother. "Fuck." Tossing aside the covers, he got up. "Idiot," he muttered and headed for his bike, not knowing which of them he was talking about.

Public intoxication. For the second time this year. Fuming, Kevin threw the spare helmet at Mike, who caught it at his chest. *It's four in the morning.*

Not to mention he'd been forced to max out his credit card for bail.

But Mike was uncharacteristically out of charm, and looking a little green, he dutifully put on the helmet and got on the bike behind Kevin.

They made it home before Mike slid weakly off the bike and got sick in the gutter, then lay there on the sidewalk and smiled shakily up at Kevin. *Ah, admit it. What fun would your life be without me?*

Kevin could think of lots of ways, starting with having more money and ending with having more peace, but saying it wouldn't matter. *This is the last time.*

To which Mike grinned. He didn't believe it, of course, and Kevin couldn't blame him, not when he'd always come through. It was what he did, who he was.

The Go To.

One would think he must also love banging his head against the wall. *I mean it, Mike.*

No you don't. Mom told you to take care of me for the rest of my life, and you feel just guilty enough to do it. Mike lay there, getting his color back by the second, looking cocky again. *You love me, man.*

Disgusted with the both of them, Kevin shook his head and walked into the house, leaving Mike to crawl inside.

You feel guilty enough to do it.

Wasn't that the sorry truth. If he closed his eyes, he could still see his stepfather coming toward the pesky toddler Mike, could still see himself not getting to Mike in time to protect him from the blow—

From below, he heard the front door slam. Apparently, Mike had gotten inside. Guess there were some things he could do for himself, after all.

Now if only Kevin believed it.

Mia woke up three minutes before her alarm went off. Stretching, she felt a vague tightness in her muscles and let out a very satisfied smile.

Thank you, Kevin McKnight.

The guy had a mouthwatering body and knew exactly what to do with it.

Her morning ritual was to pad down the hallway to flip on the coffeemaker, and then hit the shower. She was halfway to the kitchen when she remembered.

Hope.

The guest bedroom door was cracked, and she peeked in. The kid lay flat on her back, mouth open, a soft breath emitting at regular intervals. Well, look at that. Unlike every potted plant or goldfish Mia had ever attempted to keep, she hadn't killed the kid overnight. Hope didn't even looked wilted.

Hope snuffled in her sleep, then rubbed her face and tucked her hand beneath her cheek. And just like that, void of makeup and her tough veneer, she looked all of ten years old, soft and sweet.

Ha! Sweet like poison maybe. Mia supposed this was why the gods made kids so cute when they slept: because it kept parents from murdering their young.

Then a long, shuddery sigh escaped Hope's chest, the kind one let out after a long sob-fest.

Uh oh. Mia looked closer and her stomach sank. Yep, all the telltale signs were there: the puffy eyes, the tear streaks on the silk pillowcase . . .

Suddenly Hope's eyes opened, and though they widened at the sight of Mia, she played it cool. "Whatcha looking at?"

Mia played it even cooler. "You. You look pretty like that. Without all that horrid, cheap black makeup."

Hope snorted.

"I mean it. You have beautiful blue eyes and an extremely nice mouth. Why do you do yourself up like the living dead?"

"You wouldn't understand."

"Try me."

Hope laughed. "Yeah, right. Adults don't understand sixteen-year-olds. I'd be wasting my breath."

Mia laughed, too. She laughed good and long, and ended up having to sit down right there at the foot of the bed because, damn, if she hadn't once thought the very same thing.

"Whatever," Hope muttered, looking miffed.

Mia just laughed harder; she couldn't help it. "Yeah, I know nothing about being sixteen. Nothing at all, because I went from fifteen straight to seventeen without passing go." She swiped her eyes. "Ah, hell, that was fun. Thanks."

Hope rolled her eyes.

The girl didn't appear to have much of a sense of humor. Mia blamed Sugar for that, because Mia's momma, faults and all, had at least been able to laugh at herself. "You know what? You're right. I wouldn't understand. I was never desperate to get away. Desperate to find something new, a place where I could grab my future."

Hope blinked. "You . . . really felt that way?"

"Every. Single. Day."

"Desperate to get out?" Hope pressed. "Like . . . like you were going to die if you didn't?"

Humor gone now, Mia nodded.

Hope just stared at her. "So . . ."

"Yeah."

They actually had something in common. Neither of them said it out loud, though. Nope, the Appleby women had pride in spades, so much so they often couldn't get out of their own way.

Hope busied herself playing with the blanket over her legs. Clearly she wanted to say something, probably how eternally grateful she was that Mia had taken her in, that she hadn't been shipped back immediately.

"So what's wrong with your eyebrow? I mean, it looks pretty stupid."

Honestly, the love in the room was simply overwhelming. Mia put a finger to the singed spot and sighed. "Long story."

"I have some black eyebrow pencil."

Yeah, that would fix it. "Thanks, but I'll manage. So. A week in California."

"You've got the most God-awful traffic here."

"Oh, trust me, you've seen nothing yet. You'll get a good glimpse of it this morning, though."

"Why?"

"Because I have to go to work. We're going to have to find somewhere for you to go for the day. Kevin said something about a teen center next to the high school. I think they do day trips—you should get to see something fun today."

Hope looked horrified at the thought. "A teen center?"

"Well, I can't just leave you here."

"What's the matter Apple Pie, you don't trust me with the family china?" she drawled.

"Or the silverware," Mia drawled right back.

When Hope just exuded hostility, Mia smiled. "If you don't like being treated like a thief, first order of business—stop stealing. And don't ever call me that again, by the way."

"I didn't take that lipstick."

"Whatever, Sticky Fingers." Mia stood up. "Fact remains, I can't leave you here to terrorize my neighbors."

"Yeah, Sexy Old Guy looked real scared of me."

"If you're referring to Kevin, he's only thirty-something."

"Like I said, old."

Mia's jaw tightened. "Get dressed. Do you have anything that's not black?"

"No."

"We'll go shopping after I get off work."

"On your dime?"

"Would that make you move faster? Fifteen minutes."

"I need more like thirty. And can we go to the grocery store and get some food, too? Or do you plan to starve me?"

"Tell you what. I'll give you fifteen minutes now, and fifteen more tomorrow morning. And if you pull it off, yeah, we'll hit the grocery store and load up on any and all the disgusting food your heart desires. Get going."

Hope buried her head beneath her pillow, but when Mia pulled the door shut behind her, she heard the rustling of the covers, signifying she was at least moving.

Kevin woke up with the alarm at what felt like only five seconds after he'd laid his head down, having dreamed of Mia in that damn wet silk, the material clinging to every inch of her, the look on her face as he nudged her over the edge, the way his name sounded on her lips.

A scalding shower might help marginally, he decided. Walking by Mike's bedroom, he heard the snores emitting and, not feeling kind, made the house shake when he slammed the bathroom door. It brought a sliver of grim satisfaction.

The hot shower did not, as it brought more thoughts of Mia.

Next time she came knocking, wearing only thin silk, dripping wet, eyes large and luminous, mouth full and wanting his, he wouldn't open the door.

Yeah, right.

But he sure as hell wouldn't dream about her all night. He had other things to be thinking about. Such as his job and how he'd been given every troubled kid in the entire school because he was the new guy. But he'd deal with that, *and* his resident pot smoker. He'd deal with a boneheaded principal who only cared about the bottom line and not which kids were slipping through the cracks.

And he'd deal with his brother, who was too old to still be slipping. He'd deal with all of it and be fine, like always.

He turned off the water only when it ran out of hot. *Deal with that, Mike.* He'd just reached for his towel when he heard it. Or felt it, rather. The heavy, rhythmic boom of a low bass so loud it hit in tune with his every heartbeat.

This street was mostly fancy white-bread, so the music, sounding like rap now that he opened his bathroom window and stuck his head out, wasn't the typical music for the crowd that lived here.

Interesting.

More interesting, the music came from the direction of Mia's house. He pulled on his clothes and walked into the kitchen.

Mike had gotten up and sat at the table with a pad of paper and a pencil. Shocking, as Mike didn't usually rise before noon. His back to Kevin, he was hunched over the paper, erasing something and making a low-pitched sound that from a hearing person would have been frustrated muttering.

Kevin peeked over his shoulder.

To do, Mike had written.

Whatever he'd written beneath that he was now desperately erasing. The page ripped and he growled, tearing the piece of paper off the pad, crumpling it up, and tossing it in the corner with a grand gesture.

When he saw Kevin, he went still for a startled beat, then put on a lazy smile. *Morning.*

What was that? You making a to-do list?

Mike's smile faded. *So?*

So you've never been organized before. What was on it?

A reminder to pick up your no-more-nosy pills.

Funny. Kevin went for the piece of paper, but Mike

shoved him back, hard enough that he plowed into the refrigerator. The bag of potato chips on top of it hit him in the head, raining chips all over him.

Mike smirked.

Kevin smirked back, then dove for the paper.

Mike dove, too, and they landed in a heap on the floor, crunching chips into dust beneath them.

Specifically beneath Kevin, who was on the bottom, damn it. "Get off, you lug—*oomph*," he said, seeing stars when Mike landed his elbow in his ribs.

Taking advantage of Kevin's pain, Mike grabbed for the paper, but Kevin flipped him, then inched forward for the paper just out of reach.

Mike put a knee in his back, let out a huff that Kevin knew was a laugh, and while Kevin gaped for air like a fish, Mike snatched the paper, tearing it into little bits.

They both got to their knees, breathing like lunatics, crumbs of chips falling off of Kevin.

You still fight dirty, Kevin signed, then brushed himself off.

Mike grinned. *Thank you.*

Kevin shook his head, disgusted with the both of them. *What the hell is wrong with you?*

Mike looked at him but ultimately shook his head and turned away.

Kevin pulled him back around, half braced for another wrestle session.

Mike tried a smile, but it failed to reach any real wattage. *You ever get tired of rescuing me?*

Hell, yes!

So why do you?

Well, if that wasn't the question of the hour. He'd been doing it for so long it had become second nature, ever since that terrifying morning when their mother had gone out shopping and said to Kevin, "Watch over Mikey." Kevin would never forget standing there in the ER waiting room, just a little kid himself, his mother sobbing as she yelled at him, "You were supposed to watch Mikey!"

No sane person would blame the kid, but sometimes guilt had nothing to do with being sane.

Now Mike was waiting for an answer, and the only one Kevin had couldn't be uttered. So he shrugged. *Don't make me look at that too closely or I'll remember how pissed off I am at you.*

Mike looked at his feet, huffed out a breath, then looked up again. *I don't want to be this guy anymore.*

What guy?

The happy-go-lucky fucking loser.

Kevin's heart squeezed, and he shook his head. *You're not a loser.*

I don't have any money, I mooch off my brother for a place to live, and I don't have a job.

You're going to get that job you interviewed for.

I didn't get the fucking job, all right? They cancelled the interview. They went with someone with a better resume, someone who's kept a job longer than a week.

Ah, hell. *I'm sorry.*

Yeah, and I was looking so forward to sitting at a computer for ten hours a day typing my fingers to the bone entering data processing info. He moved toward the door.

Kevin had promised himself no more interfering, no more rescuing. And yet he still rushed to get in front of his brother, putting his back to the door so Mike couldn't slam out. *I've been thinking.*

Mike lifted a brow. *Don't hurt yourself.*

Shut up and listen. I need help at the teen center.

Mike's eyes narrowed suspiciously. *I thought the teen center's up for sale, and that once the building sells, the teen center is goners.*

Right. But until that happens, I need someone.

I don't want a pity job.

Ah, come on. You know damn well there's no such thing as a "pity" job. A pity fuck, maybe, but not a pity job.

Mike wouldn't take the job. He wouldn't, because deep down, Kevin was convinced, Mike liked being unemployed, liked the handouts, the free ride.

The pity.

But it was just as hard to turn his back on the guy now as it had been when Mike was a little kid, not hearing the shouted warning of some danger coming from behind . . .

I have no experience, Mike pointed out.

It's organizing sports and events. Easy stuff.

Mike let out a snort that didn't have any humor in it and shoved his fingers through his hair.

Kevin waited.

When Mike finally nodded, he looked extremely defenseless.

So you'll do it? You'll interview?

I'll think about it. Mike pushed Kevin clear of the front door and opened it.

Kevin held him back. *You'll interview?* he repeated.

Jesus, you don't need to shout. Mike smiled at his own joke, showing a shadow of his old self. *I said I'll think about it.*

Four o'clock. I'll have the board members come. Be there.

Nodding, he turned to the door, then looked back. *You have a potato chip in your ear.*

And then he was gone.

Kevin shook his head and more chips fell. He gathered his keys and helmet and headed out, too.

The rap was still booming. The house immediately to his left was Mr. and Mrs. Dickenson. They were a couple in their fifties who enjoyed cruises to Mexico, morning walks through the hills, and opera. Not rap.

"Turn that crap down!" boomed a female voice through the morning air.

He felt the grin split his face, and he eyed the *second* house on his left.

Mia's.

Seems she and Hope were at least communicating. He headed down the walk toward his bike, then stopped when he heard the *click-click-clicking* of heels. This was accompanied by a low grumbling in one Mia Appleby's soft, silky voice as she walked to her car.

More like strutted. She was dressed to the hilt in some soft blue silky business suit and do-me heels, muttering, "I'm going to kill myself if I have to listen to that track one more time." At the sight of him, she stopped.

Before his eyes, she drew herself up to her full height, summoning a smile that didn't come even close to her eyes. "Hey."

"Wow," he said. "I've now seen more fake smiles this morning than I have all week long."

Her smile congealed, then vanished altogether. She pressed a finger to her eye. "Twitching again. Damn it."

"Going well in there, huh?" He nodded back toward her house, from which the ear-splitting rap still came.

"Define 'well.' "

"In this case, I'd say that it meant no one had been murdered."

"Well, then, yes, it's going well. Have you ever actually lived with a teenager? They're like—"

"Aliens?" he suggested helpfully, thinking of his brother.

"Exactly." She opened her car door, tossed in her briefcase, then glanced back at the house.

The music still blared from the cracks.

With a gritting of her teeth, she stalked halfway back up the walk, put her hands around her mouth, and yelled, "Your two minutes are gone! Now get your—"

The music shut off.

Mia huffed and adjusted her jacket. In her gravity-defying, towering heels, she whirled back to her car. "Have a good day," she said tightly and got behind the wheel, sliding on mirrored sunglasses that looked as expensive as the rest of her.

"You, too," he said to one of the biggest mistakes he'd ever made, straddling his bike, not missing the fact that she watched him do so.

He drove off, still feeling her gaze on him. He wasn't sure what to do with that, or with the fact that it turned him on, though his erection shriveled quick enough when he got to the school and Mrs. Stacy looked at him over her spectacles as if he was a bug on her windshield.

"You have a visitor," she said in her snooty, holier-than-thou voice. "A . . ." She consulted the sign-in-clipboard. "A Beth Moore."

Ah, hell. Just what he didn't need, Beth chewing him out this early in the morning. They'd been married once, for a whole week, and he still cringed when he thought of it. Maybe it wasn't too late to sneak out, maybe—

"Kevin," Beth said behind him.

With a grimace, he turned and faced another of his biggest mistakes.

Chapter Eight

"You always keep your clients waiting?" Beth asked coolly as she followed Kevin out of the school to the teen center, where he'd left his lesson plan for the day.

"Clients?" He shook his head. "You're not my client."

"My daughter is."

"Amber's a kid, Beth. And, no, I don't keep the kids waiting."

She followed him into his office, which was the size of a postage stamp and held a beat-up old desk and a file cabinet with drawers that didn't shut all the way.

Beth tapped her foot, dressed to kill in a bloodred suit that showed off her assets, which had only improved with time and her surgeon's help. Deciding to display those assets, she perched prettily on the corner of his desk, crossing her legs to optimize the effect of their length.

Once upon a time he'd loved those legs, but he was eighteen and extremely stupid. "What do you need?" he asked.

"Amber's going to be here for a few weeks." She patted her perfectly coiffed blond hair and pulled out a small compact from her pocket to check her makeup, also perfect. But Kevin knew beneath that cool exterior beat a self-aware, needy, high-maintenance heart.

"God knows why, but the girl loves you," she said, sounding a little baffled.

Amber was Beth's daughter from her third—or was it fourth?—marriage. A Beth clone, Amber often found trouble simply because she felt lost in the shuffle.

"Just a warning—keep her away from the boys. She's smitten."

"By who?"

"By all of them." Beth pushed away from the desk and sauntered close, running a finger over a pec. "You're looking good, Kevin. Why is it men age so fine and women sag?"

He wasn't going to touch that with a ten-foot pole. "Want to come over tonight?"

"So you can have my ass kicked again?"

"Oh, honestly." She huffed out a breath and waved a hand. "You've got to let bygones be bygones. I no longer have Daddy's bodyguards looking for your blood. I fight my own battles now."

"Uh huh." He rubbed the phantom ache in his ribs from that long-ago beating. "You got a cool mil out of husband number two, right? Or was that husband number three?"

"It was four, if you're counting." She batted her lashes at him.

"Then don't sell the teen center."

"It's too much trouble."

"What trouble?"

"The pipes are failing."

"I'll fix the pipes, I'll—"

"Oh, no," she said with a low laugh. "If you want to discuss it, come over." She smiled. "For old times' sake."

"Old times' sake." He put his hands on her arms and held her back from him. "Would that have been when you married me simply to piss off your father, or when you took what little savings I had and ran off to Paris for a shopping trip with your sister?"

At that moment Mike poked his head in the door. When he saw Beth, his eyes went flat.

"Well, look at you," Beth purred at him, cocking her head. "Haven't seen you in years."

Mike smiled grimly, relating in that one small movement gesture how well he read lips. *It's been a pleasure to go so long without seeing you,* he signed.

Beth shrugged and looked away, the ultimate rude gesture to the hearing-challenged. "Sorry, *no comprendo.*"

Mike waited until she looked at him again, and then gave her a sign no one could misunderstand.

Beth's eyes went to ice as she stepped toward him.

Kevin quickly stepped between them. "Stop."

Beth laughed. "Still protecting him from the real world?"

"You've dropped Amber off, now go."

Yeah, go back to the rock you crawled out from beneath, Mike signed.

Unable to catch the meaning, Beth narrowed her eyes. "What are you doing here anyway? You need more money from your brother? Or is it just that it's too early to be hitting the bars and you're wasting the time checking out cute underage girls?"

Kevin had to plant a hand in the middle of Mike's chest to hold him back. He wrapped his other hand around Beth's upper arm and escorted her to the door. "If you're late to pick up Amber, I'm going to charge you by the minute."

"Oooh." She shivered, making sure to brush up against him. "You know I love it when you talk tough." Before he knew what she meant to do, she slid her fingers in his hair, tugged his face forward, and planted her lips on his. "Mmm," she purred when he jerked free. She licked her lips slowly and suggestively. "Still know how to kiss. Come on, have a drink with me tonight. For old times'."

He'd rather plow his bike into a cement freeway divider. "Six o'clock."

"Is that a yes?"

"Actually, it's a hell no."

"Fine." Her eyes frosted over. "You're still impossible." She straightened her purse on her shoulder, gave one last glare to Mike, who rolled his eyes, and stalked out.

What the fuck? Mike signed.

Ignore her.

I mean you. Why didn't you kick her ass out of here? Were you not watching? That's what I just did.

Mike shook his head. *You kept Amber for her.*

Amber is a kid dealt a crappy set of parents. I'm not going to penalize her for her mother being the queen of bitches.

Mike looked at him, shook his head, but let out a low sound that was meant to be a laugh. *Whatever.*

Why are you here this early? Kevin signed.

Thought I'd check things out. See how things run.

You've given the job a lot of thought then. Kevin felt a surge of hope. Dealing with Mike was tricky, like dealing with his teens. If Kevin appeared too eager, Mike would blow him off.

But Mike surprised him. *Yeah, and you'd better get to it before I wise up to the low pay and nonexistent benefits and get the hell out of here.*

Kevin bit back his impatient reply. That Mike was here was good. It showed promise. He needed to leave it at that.

But, damn, he was getting really tired of coercing the people in his life to live up to their potential.

Hope resented like hell being treated like a stupid little kid. Granted, she'd acted the part earlier, cranking the stereo to headbanging rap for the pleasure of watching Aunt Apple's blood boil. She'd kept the music cranked as she applied her black eyeliner and lipstick. She'd actually not worn makeup until this year, when her best friend Amy-Ann dumped her for Sally, and then she was accused of stealing that lip gloss she hadn't stolen, and then her mother started acting like she was such a burden . . .

Everyone treated her as the black sheep. So she'd decided to dress the part.

Mia balked at the makeup. "Whatever look you were going for," she'd said earlier, "you missed."

"If you're worried I'm going to embarrass you," Hope had responded, "I could just stay here."

"I don't think so."

That burned, Hope admitted. Yet again being treated like a piranha or, worse, a common thief.

But truth was truth. She wasn't wanted here any more than she'd been wanted anywhere else. The thought brought a heavy weight to her shoulders and a despair that might have been assuaged by chocolate donuts, but there weren't any. There wasn't any breakfast at all except coffee and dry toast—*ick*—but Aunt Apple had promised to buy her whatever she wanted at the grocery store, and Hope was going to hold her to that.

They passed by the Diplomat, and Hope gave a tire a kick. It wouldn't start, but Kevin was going to look at it. She hoped he meant it.

She slid into Mia's fancy car, then struggled to act cool when she nearly drooled. The leather seats were soft, squishy, *wonderful*. They made an expensive-sounding noise, and she tried not to gawk over how great they felt compared to her own ripped seats, which scratched her skin.

Mia pulled out. Hope felt her glancing over, and finally she rolled her eyes. "*What?* Am I breathing wrong or something?"

"I thought teenagers were supposed to talk nonstop."

"And I thought adults weren't."

Mia sighed and slid on her fancy sunglasses, and they drove in silence until they pulled up to the biggest high school Hope had ever seen. The teen center was next to it, a building that looked like a fast-food joint without any signs.

"It used to be a drive-through burger place," Mia said. "Then an icecream shop. But the students kept ripping the place off, and both folded. It's a teen center now, at least until the building sells again."

They got out of the car. Hope suddenly felt like dragging her feet. It was one thing to go to her school and stick out like a sore thumb. Another entirely to do it in front of countless strangers.

"What's the matter?" Mia asked.

What if the kids didn't like her here either?

"Nothing."

"Well, then pick it up. I'm late— Damn it!" One of her fancy high heels got caught on the asphalt and she nearly fell on her ass.

Hope's mouth twitched.

Mia straightened and glared at her. "I'm ruining my Manolos."

Hope glanced down at the admittedly gorgeous four-inch, strappy, satin-cork wedges and secretly drooled. "I'd be more worried about your ankles." Someday she was going to wear shoes just like that, in black, ankles be damned.

"I've been walking in heels for years, my ankles are—*Argh!*" She nearly went down again, but this time when she straightened she was lopsided.

She'd broken off the heel. "*Shit.*"

"I hope you got those on sale," Hope said.

"*Now* what am I supposed to do?"

Hope lifted her heavy-soled black boots. "Payless specials, $15.99," she said, but truthfully they didn't look anywhere as sweet as the Manolos. "Want to borrow 'em?"

"No, thank you." Mia grated her teeth and hobbled into the building.

Hope followed more reluctantly. The inside of the building had been painted a different primary color on each wall, each with tons of Polaroids of the kids tacked up. In the front room, clearly once a dining area, were two huge L-shaped couches, a Ping-Pong table, and a TV with PlayStation 2 running.

There was an older girl, maybe a college student, running the show, checking kids in, assigning them to stations like Ping-Pong, PlayStation, basketball, etc. It must have been someone's birthday, because there was a balloon bouquet on the counter and confetti everywhere.

Watching Apple limp up to the sign-in area was fun. There was something to be said for Aunt Mia's confidence. Her shoulders never slumped, her chin was always high, and her clothes screamed *I paid a fortune so back off, sucker*.

Hope wanted to be just like her when she grew up.

The girl at the counter was reading an *Us Weekly* magazine with Paris Hilton on the cover, who wore some silly pink froufrou dress and was hoisting up her tiny little dog, who wore a matching outfit. The girl didn't even look at Mia.

"Excuse me," Mia said.

The girl kept reading but lifted a sign that said FULL TODAY.

"I'd like to get my niece into the program for this week," Mia said.

Still reading, the girl shook her head. "Sorry." She waved the sign. "Full today. It's horseback riding day, and we fill up fast."

Hope had no problem missing the horseback riding.

Mia opened her mouth, probably to blast the girl,

but Hope tapped her aunt on the shoulder. "Um, I can go with you to work."

"No." Still looking cool as rain despite the early-morning heat and the fact that she'd broken her sandal, Mia shook her head. "You cannot come with me to work. Listen," she said to the college girl. "Where's Kevin McKnight?"

"He's in his office, but—"

"Great. I'll talk to him."

"He's getting ready to head over to the high school. He's teaching—"

Mia simply walked around the counter, pulling Hope along with her.

"Hey," the girl called. "You can't—"

"Watch me," Mia muttered.

Hope sure did. She watched Mia look like a woman on a mission, watched the younger woman cave, watched Mia get what she wanted.

God, to be like that.

They entered a hallway. There was a huge kitchen on the right, empty. The first door on the left opened wide and a woman sauntered out. She had perfect hair, perfect makeup, a perfect bright red suit and looked like she belonged on TV with a microphone, talking about an incoming tornado or something. Hope stared at her thinking *Wow, a Mia double,* except Mia was prettier and had nicer makeup. Were all the women in California totally put together and perfect?

And where did she sign up for being-perfect lessons?

The woman narrowed her eyes at Hope. "Didn't your mother ever teach you it's rude to stare?"

Mia stopped on the spot, one heel and all, drawing herself up even taller as she put her hand on Hope's arm. "And didn't your momma ever teach you it's rude to talk to a kid that way?"

Hope stopped staring at Barbie Doll and looked in

shock at Mia. Had she just heard that right? Had Mia just . . . *stood up for her?*

Blondie looked Mia up and down, clearly assessing the clothes, the shoes, the one heel. A smirk crossed her face, but before she could put words with it, the office door opened again and out poked a head. Dark hair, matching dark eyes.

He looked just like Kevin.

He immediately turned to someone behind him and made a series of motions with his hands in an oddly graceful, beautiful way, signifying he was deaf.

Before Hope could digest that, Kevin appeared. Apparently possessing that adult ability to take in an entire situation with one glance, he sighed the sigh of a man greatly vexed. "Perfect," she thought she heard him mutter.

In Hope's world, a tense man meant things were going to start flying, so she took a big step back.

The Kevin look-alike joined them all in the hallway, smiling, though Hope had no idea what was so funny.

"If you charged all the people in designer clothes extra to babysit their brats," Blondie said to Kevin, "you'd be able to buy this place yourself."

"Six o'clock," Kevin said to her.

"Yeah, yeah." Blondie moved off, brushing her shoulder against Hope's as she went, knocking her back a few feet.

Mia reached for her and pulled her forward. "Forget her."

Hope wasn't worried about Blondie—she could have taken that skinny know-it-all—but Mia's concern did something odd: it sort of *warmed* her.

"Look," Mia said to Kevin. "I need to get Hope into your program today."

Kevin stood back and held open his office door for them to enter.

Mia hobbled past him, growling when Kevin took in her missing heel with a smile. "Zip it," she warned.

"I didn't say a word." The office was the size of Hope's car, but Kevin had a cool beanbag chair in the corner, red with white polka dots, and Hope sank into it. Next to her was a low shelving unit filled with books that had been on her high school reading list. Between two books was a jar filled with mini chocolate bars.

Her mouth watered. *Just as good as donuts . . .*

Her stomach rumbled hopefully. A quick glance at Kevin and Mia assured her they were still busy with their standoff. Jeez, those two needed to just knock it out or something, she thought. Anyway, she let her hand run over the books.

Then the jar.

She palmed two chocolate bars, and had already popped one into her mouth—*heaven*—when she felt someone's eyes on her. *Shit.* She turned her head and met Kevin's brother's steady gaze, and suddenly the chocolate tasted like sand.

She tightened her palm around the one chocolate she hadn't yet eaten and tried to pretend she didn't have anything in her mouth.

He lifted a brow.

She turned away and began to frantically chew so that she could swallow, but it wouldn't go down. Now everyone would really think she was a thief.

She'd deny it. And to that end, she slipped the second candy bar into her pocket and hoped it didn't melt, but since she was already sweating, that seemed unlikely. She looked anywhere else but at the brother: at Mia and Kevin arguing, at the ceiling and the two spitballs on the light box, then at the floor and the stacks of files next to Kevin's desk. She looked at . . . oh, God. There was nothing else.

Slowly, inevitably, her gaze was drawn back to the dark eyes.

He reached out.

She shrank back.

His smile faded and he slowly opened his palm, showing her another chocolate. Offering it.

He knew. She shook her head.

He arched a brow that said *I know you want it.*

Again she vehemently shook her head. No. Don't look at me. She closed her eyes. When she finally got up the nerve to look at him again, he was moving toward the door.

Mia stopped arguing with Kevin.

Kevin's brother signed something, and Hope's chest went tight. *He was telling on her.*

Indeed Kevin turned his head and looked right at her, then at the candy jar.

Hope stopped breathing.

Kevin nodded, and his brother walked out the door.

Kevin watched him go as if maybe he really wanted to say something else, but he didn't.

Instead he once again looked at Hope. A trickle of sweat ran between the breasts she'd just gotten last year, but Kevin smiled. He smiled like he really meant it, and Hope let out a helpless one in return, hoping she didn't have chocolate on her teeth.

Whatever he'd been mad at, it hadn't been her. She didn't know why she cared really, except for that she did. A lot. "So how are you doing this morning, Hope?" he asked.

Hope knew most people asked that as a matter of greeting, not really caring about the answer, but he sounded like he really wanted to know.

How was she doing? Actually, she hadn't given a lot of thought to that, as she'd been quite busy just surviving. Then she'd woken up in a bed, a huge, comfy, expensive bed, instead of her car. She wasn't on the road—hallelujah!—and the realization had been a little unsettling. Nice, but unsettling. Cranking the music to cover that unease had been fun, and it had the added benefit of annoying Mia. That was nice, too. And the ride over here in the Audi . . . *wow*. The navigation system alone could have kept her entertained for another cross-country drive—not that she wanted to *ever* make that drive again. "Fine."

His smile felt genuine. "I'm glad to hear it." He turned back to Mia. "You know, your accent matches Mia's."

Mia seemed to grind her teeth at this. "I do not have an accent."

"Right," he said and laughed. "Well, I'm sorry. The teen center is truly full today. I can get her in tomorrow—"

"I need her in today."

Leaning back against the wall, he crossed his arms and feet casually, lifting a brow. "Maybe you could take her sightseeing today, get to know her, and then tomorrow—"

"I have to get into work." Mia glanced at her fancy-smancy watch that Hope was betting was not a Kmart special. "I'm already running late. I need you to take her."

"Hmm."

"And what does *that* mean?"

"It means you have a real thing about getting your way," Kevin said lightly.

This seemed to make Mia's eyes nearly bug out of her head. She looked pretty good today, Hope had to admit, even with one of her sandals broken. Her skirt was a pale blue and floated on air when she moved, and her jacket revealed a lacy thing beneath, both of which hugged her body. It was a sexy, elegant look that Hope could never pull off in a million years, even if she *wanted* to wear colors again.

"Can you, or can you not, take Hope?" Mia said in a quiet but scary voice that made Hope's spine itch.

Hope would have sworn Kevin's smile changed now that it was aimed at Mia. It wasn't kind anymore, but filled with mischief, revenge, and . . . heat. Yowza, lots of heat.

"*Not*," he said firmly in an apologetic tone that didn't match his expression. "We're full up. Unless . . ."

Mia gritted her teeth. She was going to grind them to powder if she didn't watch it. "Unless what?"

"You say please." Kevin's smile widened. "You do know the word, right?"

Mia let out a low growl that sounded a bit rabid as she turned to Hope. "We're outta here."

Hope was surprised, because if you asked her, these two had some unfinished business. Their mouths were arguing, but the rest of them were not. "We are?"

"You're coming into work with me."

Hope didn't know if she was excited or wary but settled for somewhere in between because it beat the hell out of riding a horse.

Or being on a bus heading back to Tennessee.

They left Kevin's office and walked back into the bright morning sunlight. With each hobbling step Mia appeared to become more and more uptight. "Here," she said to Hope when they got outside and handed her the keys. "Start the car. I'll be right there. I need to talk to Kevin for a sec. In private."

Hmm. Hope supposed that was code for getting a quickie or something, but she stared down at the keys in her hand, then lifted her head, trying to hide her elation. "You trust me with your car?"

Mia narrowed her eyes.

"I mean, it's good," she said quickly. "I'm, like, totally trustworthy." She began to walk away, but Mia snagged her by the scruff of the neck and pulled her back.

"Let me just add that if anything happens to my car I'll personally deliver you to Tennessee right this very minute."

Hope didn't dare smile. No way was Mia going back to Tennessee to bring her home, this minute or otherwise.

"Are we clear?" Mia asked.

Hope pretended not to care less, even lifting an insolent shoulder, but inside she was jumping.

She had the keys to the Audi! And Mia hadn't said don't drive it, she'd just said not to let anything happen to it. Biting her lip to keep her smile in, she nodded. "Take your time."

Chapter Nine

Mia walked—limped—back inside the teen center, ready to kick some ass, but it was hard to remain self-righteous with only one heel.

She caught Kevin just as he came out his office door, looking clean and dangerous and sexy. He'd removed his leather jacket. His leanly muscled shoulders pushed at the limits of his dark blue T-shirt, which was loosely stuck into a pair of low-slung Levi's. His shirt read ALWAYS FINISH WHAT YOU STA—. He wore his boots, both only half laced, and had a leather saddlebag slung over his shoulder and chest. Then there were those see-all eyes, steady as the earth beneath her feet. Admittedly, she didn't know him thoroughly, but she knew enough to understand that everything about him was steady, from his rock-solid strength to the way he saw things. The man lived worlds away from hers, and yet he seemed firmly rooted, maybe more so than anyone she'd ever met.

But she was pissed and he was going to hear it, no matter how fine he looked this early in the morning.

Or naked. "Hang on," she said and pushed him back inside his office.

"Well now, darlin'," he murmured, his voice like

smooth velvet, glancing at his watch. "I'm afraid I don't have time to scratch your itch right now."

"As if I'd have you right now."

He stared at her, his eyes a warm, swirling caramel. "Did you know that the madder you get, the more your accent matches Hope's? I never did quite catch where you're both from."

"I'm from right here, right now. And I don't appreciate what you're doing," she said.

His mouth quirked. "And what's that? Breathing?"

"You turned Hope down to spite me."

"You ought to spend time with the kid before you dump her. I get the feeling she's been dumped enough."

"So this was a lesson for me?"

He smiled. "Did you need a lesson?"

"Do you ever answer a question without another question?"

"Well, if questions annoy you, brace yourself, because I have one more." He took a step toward her, and, damn it, she took an automatic one back, nearly tripping over her one good heel, coming up against his desk.

"Have you asked yourself why you're really here?" he wondered. "In my office? Growling at me, with steam coming out your pretty ears, while your even prettier eyes are saying something else entirely?"

"*What?* You're crazy."

"Admit it," he said very softly, taking the last step, bringing them toe-to-toe. His hand came up, and he glided the backs of his fingers along her jaw. "You came here this morning, *twice*, and you know what I think? I think you can't keep your eyes—"

He broke off with a raised brow when she lifted her hands and fisted them in his shirt. To shove him away, she told herself, but she didn't.

"—or your hands, off me," he finished.

Her fingers sank into the material of his shirt, feeling the heat, the strength of him beneath. "I want to—"

"Yeah . . . ?"

"Kick your ass."

He let out a soft laugh. "Bring it on, *Apple*."

She felt herself stiffen. "Oh, I'll bring it on, I'll—"

"What?"

She tipped her head up to his, saw the heat and intent in his eyes a beat before he murmured "Shh" and lowered his face, taking her mouth with his and beginning a slow simmer inside her.

The kiss started out sweet, soft, but cranked to intense quickly, a hot, deep, wet connection that reminded her that their bodies knew each other, craved each other like air, and that being this close was inviting the inexplicable maelstrom that occurred every time she let him put his hands on her. She stopped thinking then, just let herself feel, starting with the pure sensation of his solid, hard-muscled body against hers and ending with the heat of his mouth as he deepened the kiss.

He put his hands on her now, in her hair, holding her face, then with a groan glided them down her body, touching everything he could as he trapped her between the hard desk and his tough body. He stroked her breasts, then slid his hands beneath her clothes to warm her flesh with his hands, and the simmer burst into flames.

When he finally pulled back, she was grateful to have the desk behind her holding her up, because he'd just decimated her, burst right through her every single defense with one simple kiss.

Simple? Ha! She'd never been kissed so thoroughly, so deliberately, so absolutely fully.

He staggered back a step himself, looking surprised and just as shaky. "There," he said in a voice low and ragged and satisfyingly hoarse. "You're finally speechless. I like you that way."

She stared at him, let out a sound of disgust, and pushed past him to the door. "You're an ass."

"And bad in bed," he reminded her. "Don't forget that part."

She slammed the door behind her, a gaffe that surely announced in a scream how he affected her, but she couldn't seem to help it. *No more,* she told herself. *No more.* She was Mia Appleby, ad exec, queen of her world, and no one made her crazy. She kept her cool at all times.

She stalked past the front door, which was now filling up with teenagers in various states of summer dress and insolence, though she didn't see a single goth teen. A small part of her wondered how the hell the Southern, small-town Hope was going to fit in here with all these sophisticated big-city kids.

When she stepped out into the sunlight, her heart was still pounding, her nipples hard, her thighs quivering, and she stopped worrying about Hope entirely.

Because her car was gone.

After that steamy kiss, and then Mia's furious escape, Kevin let his wobbly knees collapse, and he slid weakly into his chair.

"Mr. McKnight?" Sara, the college student who supervised the kids for the morning hours at the center, stood in his doorway. "You okay?"

"Yes, of course."

"You didn't answer my knock—"

"Sorry." Sex on the brain. "What can I do for you?"

"You've got to get to the high school, right?"

Ah, shit. "Yeah." He stood up again, locked his knees in place, and hoped he didn't have *Sucker-Kissed* written all over his face. "Thanks."

She smiled at him, then vanished.

Kevin did his best to shake off the sensual languor sapping his strength and headed toward the door. What had he told himself?

No more, Mia, that's what.

And what had he done the second she'd touched him?

He'd been all over her.

But telling himself no more and actually following through were two different things. She was a puzzle, and he liked puzzles. She presented herself as a sophisticated, elegant businesswoman without an inch of softness or weakness, but he'd seen flashes of both now. Oh, yeah, she was a mystery, one he'd enjoy unwrapping if he didn't suspect it came packed with deadly explosives.

As he left out the back way of the teen center, cutting across the football field toward the high school, he wondered if she'd come knocking tonight.

But all fanciful wondering ceased abruptly when he caught sight of his classroom, one window open, the screen flapping in the breeze, and an Audi in the middle of the field.

Mia stood on the sidewalk staring at the spot where her car had been. Then she whipped out her cell phone to call Tess.

"Did you get a good eyebrow pencil?" her assistant asked sweetly in lieu of a greeting. "Or did you just plan on losing your other one today?"

"Ha ha."

"Good, you're going to need a sense of humor today. Layoffs are imminent."

"Damn it. Who?"

"Don't know." Tess sounded a little stressed. "But I can bet you it's at my level, not yours."

"Shit."

"It's okay. I'm too good to be fired."

"Well, that's the truth. I'd die without you there.

Speaking of there, and getting there . . . I have a little
car issue."

"No. No, no, no. You have the Anderson people
due here in . . . Ohmigod, twenty minutes. Mia—"

"I'll be there, but if I'm a few minutes late, ply
them with coffee and donuts." She snapped the cell
phone shut. She was going to kill Hope.

Turning in a slow circle of frustration, she stopped
halfway, staring in shock at the football field between
the school and the teen center.

There was a car in the middle of it. Some idiot had
parked on the grass and—

She shielded her eyes from the sun so she could
see more than just the outline of the car and felt a
fresh onslaught of temper.

Her car.

Her car was parked in the middle of the field. And
sitting on the hood was her soon-to-be dead niece,
and a—oh, hell no, a *boy*. Next to them stood a man,
who even from here she recognized. She had a feeling she'd recognize that body from a hundred miles,
much less a hundred yards.

"Save me from idiots," Mia muttered and stepped
onto the grass, her one good heel sinking in. Perfect.

Kevin turned and watched her hobble toward him,
and if she wasn't mistaken, his mouth curved.

When she got close enough, she spoke directly to
Hope. "What the hell is wrong with you? You looking to get arrested in this state, too? I nearly called
the police and reported the car missing!"

Hope opened her mouth but Mia lifted up her
hand. "No. No excuses. Get off the hood, get the *hell*
off my *hood*—" She spared a scathing glare at the
teenage boy sitting next to Hope, and then started
around the car for the driver's door.

Kevin shifted, and as a result she bumped right
into him. "Out of my way, Ace."

He didn't, just studied her while he rubbed his

jaw. The at least two-day growth there rasped in the morning air and scraped low at her belly.

She knew what that growth felt like against her jaw, her breasts . . . between her thighs.

"Sometimes things aren't as they seem," he said quietly, for her ears only. "And yelling isn't going to get you anywhere. Patience—"

"Do I look like I have an ounce of patience?"

Instead of answering that, he lifted a hand toward her face.

She pulled back.

"You have a—" He waggled a finger at her cheek.

She put her hand there. "What?"

"Here." His warm fingers brushed her skin and her nipples reacted again. *Very* annoying.

Then she realized he was showing her what he had. A piece of confetti. "Go ahead," he said. "You can finish blistering my hide now."

She was certain steam was coming out of her ears as she pushed past him and got into the car. Hope had already gotten into the passenger seat and was staring sullenly straight ahead.

Kevin poked his head in the driver's side, his face incredibly close to hers.

Again her body reacted.

Bad body.

"Hope," he said, looking past Mia to the girl. "It was nice that you stopped and talked to Cole. I think he needed a friend."

Hope nodded, and Kevin smiled again and said, "See you tomorrow." Then he pulled back and, without so much as even glancing at Mia, turned to the presumed Cole. He put a hand on the boy's shoulder, guiding him across the field toward the school.

Mia turned to Hope. "Well?"

Hope slid farther into her seat.

"Nothing? Really? Not even an 'I'm sorry, Mia'? An 'I screwed up, Mia'?"

"You said don't let anything happen to the Audi. And nothing did."

Mia felt her mouth fall open. "You're kidding me, right?"

Hope crossed her arms over her skinny chest and turned forward, going the silent route.

Mia shook her head. She couldn't believe it, but Hope was seething with resentment and hurt when *Mia* was the injured party here! "I don't have time for this." She threw the car into gear and drove them off the field and onto the street, heading toward the freeway as fast as she could without running anything over. The entire drive from Glendale Hills into the LA forest of high-rises, Hope stared out the window, her eyes full of antagonism. She kept her silence until they pulled into the parking structure of Mia's downtown building.

"You were gone more than a minute."

Mia looked over at her. "What?"

"You were gone like ten minutes. You get a quickie in his office or something?"

"No, I didn't get a— You know what?" She shook her head. Forced a laugh. "You are not going to make this my fault. You came to me, Hope. I let you stay in my house, eat my food—"

"You don't have any food."

"—rattle my windows, and then I ask you for one thing. To wait in the car for a minute—"

"Ten."

Mia could actually feel brain cells exploding. She glanced at the teen, with her stringy black hair, black gloss, black eyeliner that looked painted on, and still had no trouble reading loud and clear the antipathy coming off her in waves. Nothing was going to be enough to break that, or her years of pent-up anger.

Just as nothing was going to cut through the years

it had taken Mia to put a shine and polish on her lowly early existence.

There was no middle ground here.

She turned off the engine and got out of the car, walking to her trunk where she kept a spare pair of shoes. Teardrop Jimmy Choo slides, and though the color was just a little off for her outfit, that was the least of her worries. "Remember, this is a professional place of business," she told Hope. "No funny stuff, no loud music, and especially no sticky fingers."

"Gee, Aunt Apple Pie," Hope said in a slow, exaggerated drawl, cocking her head slightly to the side as if maybe she wasn't the sharpest crayon in the box. "Whatever will I do with myself if I can't square dance or steal stuff?"

Mia stopped short and turned to face her. "And don't even think about calling me that again."

"Ma'am, yes, ma'am." She snapped to attention, mockingly saluting her.

Oh, yeah. It was going to be a helluva day.

They entered the building. Mia had long ago stopped gawking at the gorgeous architecture of the glass and steel all around her, at the shiny marble flooring of the foyer bigger than her entire hometown. There was a flower cart, a donut shop where she bought Hope breakfast, an expensive jewelry shop, the glass elevators that rose so high into the sky they practically vanished, all surrounded by lush green tropical plant life cultivated throughout the bottom floor.

Hope hadn't even seen anything like it before, and she totally gawked, her hard, cynical face softening as it tipped back to catch all that she could.

"Pretty amazing, huh?" Mia showed her badge to the doorman to get into the elevators.

Hope closed her mouth and her expression and lifted that careless shoulder. "It's okay."

Mia shook her head, and they took the elevator in silence, even when the high-speed electronics whirled them up at a dizzying speed.

Hope merely clutched at the handrail, her face practically glued to the glass.

On Mia's floor, they entered a set of brass and glass double doors and stepped into the organized chaos that was Mia's entire world. Phones rang, well-dressed people hurried back and forth carrying files and laptops, talking, laughing, more talking . . .

Gen, behind the huge reception desk, covered the mic near her mouth and said to Mia, "They just got here."

Mia nodded and pulled Hope around a corner, where Tess sat at her large L-shaped desk. She also wore a headset and was talking into it. "No, that's unacceptable. That's right, but we're nothing if not flexible. How 'bout we meet you halfway?" She began handing over a stack of phone messages and another stack of files to Mia while she continued her phone conversation. "That's great, uh huh, gotcha. Buh-bye now." She looked at Mia. "I've given them coffee and donuts and set them up in the conference room. You've also got that Danville account meeting right after this one, and they've called to confirm. Steven, Dillon, Janice, and Tami are all planning on being there with the artwork and presentation. And later the fire marshal is coming back to interview. Oh, and then a staff meeting where you-know-who is going to be hailing you with questions, so I've made a list—"

"Tess." Mia put her hand on Tess's arm. "You stopped breathing. You know what the doctor said about that."

"Ha ha. If I'm anal, it's your fault. You're a slave driver." But Tess let out a long breath, then drew another, pressing a hand to her belly. "This is all giving me ulcers. Did I tell you I put the Anderson people in conference room three because your office still reeks of smoke from yesterday, speaking of which, nice makeup job on the brow." Taking another breath, she blinked at Hope, who stood off a little to the side, chewing on her black fingernails, looking more than a little out of place.

"Hello," Tess said.

"This is Hope," Mia said. "She's my . . ." She broke off, because, damn, this was going to bring up a whole host of questions she didn't want to answer.

"Long-lost daughter," Hope interjected in the thickest Southern voice Mia had ever heard. She held out a hand. "Yeah. My momma here gave me up at birth. Left me in the Piggly Wiggly Dumpster, actually, but don't judge her, she's served her time."

Tess's mouth fell open.

Mia resisted banging her head down on Tess's desk. "Funny, Hope. Tess, this is my niece, car thief and wannabe comedian."

Hope rolled her eyes.

"She's going to need something to do," Mia decided aloud. "Just keep her away from your car keys."

Hope rolled her eyes again.

"What did I tell you about that?" Mia asked her. "I'm going to get a jar—"

"Yeah, yeah, so I can just shake my eyeballs instead of roll 'em. I remember."

Tess smiled warmly at Hope. "Oh, my goodness. You're just like her!"

Both Hope and Mia gaped at her. *"What?"*

Tess came around her desk to hug Hope tight. "I love your aunt dearly, and I've been dying to meet some of her family. The two of you are two peas in a pod."

Over her head Hope stared in shock at Mia.

And if Mia hadn't felt that same shock, she'd have laughed at the look of horror on Hope's face.

Alike?

"You really need to lay off that morning crack pipe," Mia muttered to Tess. "Now let go of the girl and give her some slave labor filing or something. You do know your alphabet, right?" she asked Hope.

Hope started to roll her eyes, then stopped. "I know that my favorite Aunt Apple—"

Mia bared her teeth and Hope stopped talking, but her eyes were still lit with more than her fair share of trouble.

Damn it. Mia took an exaggerated deep breath. "Just try to be good until I can come for you."

Hope smiled sweetly. "You know it, my very dearest, *dearest* aunt."

What could she do? Child services would frown on locking the kid in the closet, so with no other choice she went off to her meeting and worked on forgetting it all. Ted, and the upcoming meetings. Tess, and the questions in her eyes. The impossible, Tums-inducing Hope. The irritating, infuriating Kevin McKnight.

Okay, make that sexy as hell Kevin McKnight.

Especially if he wasn't talking. My God, when that man wasn't intent on making her brain explode with frustration, he could really turn her on.

She grabbed some things from her office to take into the meeting, then did a double take at her plant.

Its leaves were dragging on the floor and no longer quite green. "Damn it, if you die, I'll kill you." She hurried out and stopped outside the conference room. Pasting a smile on her face, she entered.

And an hour later she was in the midst of outlining her plans for the creative personnel, production department, media planners and buyers, and the goals and objectives of the campaign. When she needed access to another file, she picked up the phone in the middle of the big conference table and dialed Tess's extension.

"Danny's Dunkin' Donuts," boomed a voice in her ear. "What's your pleasure this morning?"

Mia stared at the phone. "Sorry, Danny. Somehow I got the wrong number." She hung up. Ignoring the bad feeling sinking like a pit in her belly, she tried again.

"Danny's Dunkin' Donuts."

Mia blinked. "Uh . . ." She hung up and glanced at her clients. "Could you excuse me a minute?" Then she walked out to the main floor. Anyone and everyone at a desk was standing up, phone to their ear, looking confused. Margot and Ted came out of their offices. So did Dick.

Tess frantically waved Mia over. "Someone's re-routed all our phone lines to Danny's shop downstairs," she said quietly. "Danny's getting a kick out of it, but he doesn't know how it happened."

"Where's Hope?"

"Filing."

"Uh huh." Mia went to the filing room. No Hope. Damn it. Mia searched the floor and finally found the kid in the women's bathroom, sitting on the counter, back to the mirror, head tipped up as she smoked a cigarette, blowing lazy smoke rings into the air.

"Jesus!" Mia snatched the cigarette from her black lips and stuck it under the tap. "You can't smoke in here, the alarm'll go off!"

"Nah, it hasn't been reset since your fire adventure yesterday." Hope smiled. "Gossip train is running full steam ahead in this joint. Did you know no one but Tess likes you?"

Mia pinched the bridge of her nose. "You haven't been doing anything but filing and smoking, right?"

"In any of our conversations, did I ever mention I'm an electronics wizard? No?" She smiled. "Oh, probably because, like, we've never really had any conversations."

"Goddamnit, it *was* you."

"Well, I don't like to toot my own horn, but—"

"Did you fuck with the phones, Hope?"

"Wow, do they let you say fuck here at work? Cool."

Mia could feel each and every individual hair on her head going gray, especially when Hope let out a little smirk as if to say *Chaos, panic, and disorder, my work here is done.* Mia drew a purposeful breath. "Fix it. Now!" She twirled on her heels and started to leave the bathroom, then whirled back, snatching Hope's pack of cigarettes and lighter.

"Hey!"

"You can thank me when you're old and still have your lungs." She stalked back into the conference room, pasting a smile on her face as she did. "Well," she said to her waiting clients. "Where were we?"

They dug right back into media development and strategy for presenting their campaign until an hour later. Without warning, the speakers went from discreet soft jazz to off-the-charts, earsplitting . . . *hip-hop*?

Two of the reps from the Anderson company jerked, spilling their coffee over some of the files. Two others put their hands to their chest as if having a heart attack.

Everyone jumped up and started talking at once.

Not that anyone could hear a word over the unbelievable noise coming from the speakers.

Mia tried to tell everyone to relax, but no one could hear her. Finally she just lifted a finger, signaling she'd be right back, and hurried out into the hall.

Like this morning's donut/phone incident, people were standing there in various stages of shock. Mia headed directly to Tess. "Where's Hope?"

"She's safe!" Tess yelled. "And, ohmigod, she's just the sweetest thing ever! Did you know she helped fix the phones? Also, she helped Dick with his computer—"

Mia shook her head. "*Where* is she?"

"I gave her a break! She's in the lounge!"

Which was next to the janitor's closet, which was next to the sound system closet.

Shit.

Mia went running. The sound system closet was open, all the equipment in it blinking like mad. Hands over her ears, she searched, searched . . . and finally found the POWER button and hit it.

Blessed silence.

Mia slumped against the door, exhausted. When Dick popped his head in and saw her, he frowned. "Where the hell is your niece?"

God, could it get any worse? Remembering the threat of layoffs, she decided it was never too late to do a little senior butt-kissing, so she smiled. "Working somewhere, you know, helping out. Why?"

"Because I think she's lifted my wallet."

Chapter Ten

After summer school ended, Kevin walked across the field toward the teen center, hoping against hope Mike would be there for his interview with the board members.

Unfortunately, Mike had a bad habit of "forgetting" appointments like this, even though Kevin knew that was just a self-defense mechanism. People could say they were politically correct all they wanted, but most had a problem hiring a handicapped man.

Mike knew this all too well; he'd lived it. And Kevin had lived it with him.

The day was a hot one, and Kevin swiped his forehead with his arm. He'd spent the morning teaching science to himself. The kids had been there plenty, but as a group of teens required to take this class to make up for a failing grade, not one of them had showed signs of life. He might as well have taught How to Scratch Your Ass Effectively, because no one gave a shit.

Science fascinated him, and he'd hoped to fascinate the kids. Turns out only his classroom did that, because as he'd discovered, thanks to the science burners lining the back of his classroom, it was the most popular place on campus for smoking weed.

When he'd caught Cole climbing out the window

this morning, he had to admit he'd assumed the worst. He'd studied the files of the kids he had, so he knew Cole had a crappy home life, with no father and a mother who worked nights and slept days, paying her son less attention than she did the family cat. He knew that Cole had been beat up several times by the mother's boyfriend and that when he graduated next year he planned on entering the military in order to get far, far away.

If he graduated.

He was in danger of failing several classes, hence the summer school program.

But he also knew that despite Cole's rough home life and somber attitude, the kid had brains. He just didn't know anyone cared. He was in need, and Kevin knew all too well what happened to kids who went unheard, and he didn't intend to let that happen to Cole. He'd reach him. Somehow.

He entered his office. His empty office.

He tunneled his fingers through his hair. He couldn't save the world, he knew that. But neither, apparently, could he stop trying.

By the time Mia drove them home, she had a pounding headache and not a little bit of indigestion. It hadn't been anything she'd eaten. She tossed a glare in Hope's direction.

The kid was hunched in the passenger seat, chewing on a black thumbnail, staring gloomily out the window.

They stopped at the cell phone shop, where Mia bought a cell phone for Hope so that the next time the little thief stole her car she'd be able to call her. They'd also gone to the grocery store because Mia had promised, and though they hadn't spoken, Hope filled a cart with a bunch of crap like white bread, eggs, bacon, real butter . . .

Cholesterol City.

"So that was a fun day, huh?" Mia asked as she pulled onto her street. "We'll have to do it again sometime."

Hope stared straight ahead. "You want me to go home."

"Honey, that would be my fondest wish," Mia said fervently.

Hope slumped farther into the seat.

"But you're not driving yourself across the country again."

"My car doesn't work."

"And I'm not putting you on a plane across the country all alone."

"Ah, how sweet," Hope said. "You're worried about me."

"I'm worried about the other passengers. Who knows what you'd come up with or where you'd decide to get off. Nope, we're stuck together until Sugar comes this weekend." Mia turned off the engine and got out of her car, stole a peek to the right—

And watched as Kevin pulled up, riding that bike. God, she loved the sleek, sexy lines . . . and the bike wasn't bad, either. She locked gazes with him as he reached up and pulled off his helmet. He got off the bike, the material of his shirt stretching across his shoulders and back as he tucked the helmet beneath his arm. Looking just a little hot and a little bothered, he shoved his sunglasses to the top of his head and raised a brow.

Feeling a little hot, a little bothered herself, she raised one back.

Hope got out of the car, slammed the door, and headed up the walk. Halfway there, she whirled back and held out her hand. "Keys?"

"You've got to be kidding me."

Hope sighed. "I can't drive off with your house."

"You'd find a way," Mia muttered and tossed the

keys, managing to spill her Chanel silk clutch purse to the ground as she did.

Contents spilled: Lancôme lipstick, gold fountain pen, her Sidekick, a tampon, and . . . three condoms.

Hope looked at them and smirked. "So people your age actually do it."

"*Go.*"

Hope grabbed the groceries she was carrying and headed toward the house.

Mia began to pick up her things, wondering how much damage Hope could do.

"I take it the two of you had a great day." Kevin hunkered down at her side. He picked up the condoms and looked at her in a way that made her feel . . . hungry. He dropped the cordless back in her purse and let out a low laugh, which upped her status from hungry to starving. "For what it's worth," he said, "I'm glad people our age actually 'do' it."

"You're impossible."

"Yeah, my ex-wife told me the same thing just today."

She stared at him.

He shrugged. "Old news. I was very young and stupid when she broke my heart."

"I didn't ask."

"But you wanted to."

Damn it, she *had* wanted to. "If you know you're impossible, maybe you should do something about it."

"Nah, it's part of my charm." He handed over her pen. "I was only eighteen, the same age when she divorced me for not kissing her ass enough."

"I didn't ask that, either."

"You were wondering."

She looked at him and he laughed softly, a sound she was beginning to react to like Pavlov's dog.

Drool, drool.

"What about you? Ever been married?" he asked.

Now *she* laughed. "Do I look like the marrying type?"

His gaze ran over her face, her body, heating every single inch. "You look like the type to do whatever she pleases."

"Yeah, well, it's never pleased me to be married." Because that seemed incredibly revealing, she distanced herself. "I've got to go check on the crazy kid."

"Crazy?"

"Trust me." She stood up. "*Crazy.*" She soaked in his extremely pleasing-on-the-eyes face. "See you?"

"See me, or do me?"

She laughed.

He didn't.

And she sighed. "Right." He didn't want just sex, he liked more, and she didn't. "*Bye.*" Feeling a little like Alice down the rabbit hole, she grabbed the last bag of groceries and went into the house.

Hope was heading for the stairs.

"We have to talk," Mia said.

Hope slowly turned back, her eyes filled with misery.

Ah, hell. She was waiting to be rejected, sent away, and much of Mia's anger melted away in spite of herself.

The girl had been made to feel unimportant for most of her life, and Mia knew that feeling all too well. Damn if she'd add to it.

So how to do this? Right up front, she decided. She might be a bitch in her world, but she wouldn't be one in Hope's. "Don't look at me like that. It's just talk."

"No good ever came out of talking," Hope said. "Trust me, I know. My mom does that. 'We have to talk, Hope.'" She said this in a perfect imitation of Sugar. "'About your attitude toward the men I date.

About your grades. About your stealing.' " The kid put her hands on her hips. "Well, the men she dates are assholes, the teachers all hate me because she slept with the principal, and then his wife found out and he quit. Some jerk took his place and he's awful, but that's not my fault. And I don't steal!"

Mia stared at the kid's stiff spine, her shoulders thin and narrow and seemingly weighted with the world. Mia's early fury was still firmly in place, but now it was mixed with something that felt like sorrow and guilt and regret, and, damn it, she hated when something got in the way of her righteous anger. "Hope—"

"Look, I'm sorry I screwed up your day, okay? I know I'm going home. I'll go pack."

And with that, she took her heavy-soled boots up the stairs, probably leaving scuff marks with each step.

"Hope, wait."

Hope stopped but didn't turn around.

Fine. She'd talk to the girl's back. "I know what it's like to grow up feeling as if you don't matter. As if nothing you do or say makes any difference in this world. I know what it's like to have hopes and dreams and be afraid you won't get a chance to live them. I know, Hope."

Slowly the girl turned around.

"I'm sorry you were dealt those cards, that you had to run far and fast to get what you think you want. I, more than anyone else, understand. But you have to understand me in return. I don't know anything about raising a teenager, about being a role model, about making your world right for you. Nothing." She drew a deep breath. "But I'm willing to see this through until the end of the week if you are."

"Why?"

"Because you're so sweet and kind?"

Hope smiled. *Smiled.*

Mia covered up the unexpected emotion eased by that and pointed a finger in Hope's face. "But no more joyriding in my car."

Hope shook her head.

"No more messing with my work."

Another shake of her head.

"No more cracks about me being old."

Hope smiled.

"All right then," Mia said.

"All right then," Hope repeated in the same exact tone, though Mia would have sworn there was a light of excitement and hope in her eyes that hadn't been there before as she turned and went up the stairs.

Watching her, Mia let out a slow breath, then sat on the bottom step, wondering what the hell she'd just gotten herself into.

Kevin watched Mia vanish into her house and shook his head. "Way to keep your distance there, stud," he said and, with a disgusted shake of his head, headed toward the basketball court.

Mike was already there because of course he didn't flake out on the good stuff.

Mike didn't look at Kevin, so Kevin merely walked onto the court and got in Mike's way as he came down for a warm-up layup.

And checked him.

Mike bounced back and glared at him.

"Oh, would you like to know my problem?" Kevin asked politely, forcing him to read his lips even though he knew Mike didn't like to.

Mike shook his head.

"Too bad. They would have hired you today, you dumb-ass."

Oh, so now I'm a dumb-ass?

"Hey, if the shoe fits."

Mike snatched the ball from Kevin and drove it

down the court, executing a perfect layup. He could have played basketball for college, and possibly even the pros, but not a single college would recruit him because of his handicap.

Mike landed and turned around, no triumph in his face, nothing but desolation.

All his life he'd been whispered about, pointed at, prejudiced against, and prejudged. The times were changing, and these days a deaf man had just about the same rights and expectations as anyone else, but Mike still carried the chip on his shoulder.

It was getting damned heavy.

Kevin understood it. He had been trying to hack away at it for years, but he understood it. He waited until Mike's gaze met his. *Please interview. You're a shoo-in, I swear it.*

Mike just dribbled, thinking God knows what. Then he tossed Kevin the ball, hard enough to sting. *I'll be there*, he signed.

When?

Tomorrow. Now, are you going to play or nag?

Kevin looked at him for a long moment, searching his brother's gaze, finding nothing but bare honesty. Fear, too, but Mike wouldn't want him to comment on that, so he nodded. *First to ten, loser cooks dinner.*

Mike grinned. *Get ready to cook, Mrs. McKnight.* And he came after the ball.

Thirty minutes later they were both a sweaty, exhausted mess, slumped on one of the benches on the side of the court slurping from their water bottles.

A woman pulled onto the street in a red Honda. She got out and came along on the sidewalk, and Mike stopped drinking to watch. She wore a jean skirt cut a few inches above the knees and a red tank layered over a white one. Normal summer gear, only there was nothing normal about the tall, athletically toned brunette—she was beautiful enough to grace the cover of any magazine.

Mike glanced at Kevin and waggled his eyebrows.

Kevin rolled his eyes. *Don't even think about it*, he signed. *You're cooking dinner for me tonight.*

I'm going to be cooking all right . . .

Mike— But Mike wasn't looking. Instead he'd risen off the bench and, hiding his wince from his various aches and bruises, plastered his I'm-God's-gift smile in place.

Kevin kicked his foot to get his attention. *She's out of your league.*

Yeah? Watch and learn, big guy. Watch and learn. He moved off the court and onto the sidewalk directly in front of the woman.

She stopped and smiled at him. "Hi. Haven't seen you before. Are you new around here?"

Mike nodded his head.

"Well, welcome!" She held out her hand. "I'm Tess Reis. I don't live on this street—my best friend, Mia Appleby, does—I'm just going to drop some things off at her house. Have you met her?"

Mike nodded and shook her hand, bringing his other up to cup over hers. Then he pointed to himself, and his ear, shaking his head.

"I'm sorry," she said, shaking her head. "I don't understand."

Again Mike tapped his ear and shook his head.

"You're . . . deaf?"

He smiled and nodded.

"Oh!" And as Kevin had witnessed a thousand times, maybe more, this melted her. *Women*, he thought in amazement. Always softened for the underdog, even if that underdog was really a damn wolf in sheep's clothing.

But the two of them were seemingly managing to communicate despite the handicap, and Kevin just sighed. Bending, he gathered the waters and the ball, and stuffed them into his duffle bag.

On the sidewalk, Tess laughed out loud at something Mike did. Over her shoulder, Mike turned to Kevin and winked salaciously. *I'm going to need a rain check on cooking, big brother.*

Unbelievable, Kevin thought. Just unbelievable.

Chapter Eleven

A few days later Kevin was in his kitchen, seated at his table with a beer and stacks of paperwork. A stack for the taxes he hadn't yet gotten together, a stack for ongoing fund-raising tactics for the teen center, a stack for filling out forms for grants and funding from the state. And yet another of the pop quiz he'd given in class today to see where everyone was at.

Yeah, he knew how to party.

It was late, past midnight, and he was hip deep in grading, staring down at Cole's quiz, not surprised to find the kid had answered every question correctly, even the ones Kevin hadn't expected the kids to answer at all, when there came a knock at his kitchen door. He lifted his head, figuring it was his idiot brother coming in from a date with Tess, who he'd seen three nights running now.

But Mike had a key . . . The night was dark, and Kevin couldn't see out the glass pane in the door. Tossing his pencil down, he got up and flicked on the porch light.

Mia Appleby stood there in a filmy, gauzy sundress that bared her shoulders and arms, showing off smooth, creamy skin and a body he suddenly, sharply wanted squirming beneath his. She had a hand on her hip, her mouth turned upside down in a frown, her eyes narrowed as she took in his low-slung jeans and unbuttoned shirt hanging open over his torso.

From some part of his brain, he acknowledged the hard kick to his gut. And also farther south.

He'd seen her every morning, of course, strutting her stuff in her designer wear and towering heels as she got into her Audi with Hope in tow, the girl a contrast in her stark black and shimmering metal rings and belts and earrings. Neither of them had appeared at the teen center, though he'd spoken to Hope yesterday afternoon about her car, which needed an alternator and water pump. She'd thanked him for the news and said she'd get it fixed, but he knew she probably didn't have the money for it. Kevin also knew through Mike, who'd gotten the scoop from Tess, that Hope was having fun with all things electronic in Mia's life, and it'd amused Kevin to think about Mia dealing with the teen on a daily basis.

Mia knocked again, her eyes narrowed, looking ready to chew him up and spit him out, and *still* he felt a surge of unwanted lust.

Which really proved it. His brother wasn't the idiot. *He* was. "Where's Hope?" he asked through the glass.

"Hopefully packing."

It was Thursday. He'd thought she wasn't going home until the weekend. "She's leaving? By herself?"

"Listen, that little tornado can take care of herself. Trust me."

When he just looked at her, she sighed. "I'm not letting her take off by herself. "Sugar's coming for her on Saturday. Happy now?"

Happy? Was she kidding? "What is she really doing?"

"Probably hot-wiring my car. Believe me, she's capable."

"She's a sweet kid."

Mia laughed, a low, throaty sound. "Yeah, sweet. Listen, about tomorrow. I can't have that 'sweet' kid with me at work anymore. Now, before you begin with a lecture, you should know, she wired hip-hop and rap into my building's speakers at decibels previously uncharted. She rerouted the phones through the donut shop on the lobby level. She—"

Kevin smiled. "Smart kid."

"She stole my boss's wallet."

His smile faded. "Ah, hell. Really?"

"So the story goes. So are you going to let me in or not?"

Was the Pope Catholic? Did a bear shit in the woods? He wondered what she wore beneath that dress—

"Earth to Kevin. Come in, Kevin."

"I'm thinking." He paused while she swore softly beneath her breath, some slur on his heritage, and despite himself, a smile tugged out of him. "I didn't hear a please."

"Goddamnit, let me in."

He had no idea why, but he pulled open the door, then blocked her way in with a hand on the jamb. Her middle pressed against his forearm, and despite the chill in her voice, she was warm, very warm. He knew from experience her bare skin would be even warmer, and taste like heaven. "Maybe we should set some ground rules first," he said.

She blinked once, slow as an owl. The warm beat of desire pulsed between them along with the storm. "Like?"

"Like . . ." God, she smelled amazing. Something exotic, sensual. And she looked good enough to eat right then and there. "Like no—"

She slid past him, making sure to glide that glorious body of hers all over his as she did. "No . . . what?" she murmured, spinning to face him in his own kitchen, a daring, tough, cocky, miserable light in her eyes he figured he knew all too well.

She'd had a rough day, she was hurting, and she needed oblivion.

Him.

Damn it. "No—oomph—" was all he managed as she obliterated the rules by wrapping herself around him and kissing him—and not a hello-sweetheart kind of kiss, either, but a deep, wet, hot one—and only when air was required did she pull back. "You were saying?"

"Yeah." He cleared his throat. "Um . . . no more of that, for one thing. And no touching, either. And especially no fu—"

She lifted a condom out of her pocket, brandishing it like a trophy as she shimmied out of her sundress, answering his question of what she wore beneath it.

Just a set of high-heeled sandals and bright pink toenail polish. He took in her taut, tan skin, smooth limbs, high, full breasts. Between her legs, she was freshly waxed.

Kevin heard the rough groan leave his throat, and he slammed shut his eyes. "Put that dress back on."

"Why?"

"Because we're not doing this. Damn it, we're not."

"How about *next* time we don't."

"Mia—"

"You want me."

He supposed she was referring to the hard-on currently straining his jeans. "I want a lot of things. To play for the Lakers, a Bahamas cruise, world peace—"

"Me," she said. "You want me."

"Maybe I'd like to get to know you first."

She put her hands on her hips as if this was the stupidest thing she'd ever heard. "What?"

"You heard me. Favorite color, obnoxious siblings, high school . . . I'd like to hear it."

Still naked, she stared at him. "You have got to be joking."

"Nope. Talk to me."

"You want to talk? Right now?" She spread out her arms. "While I'm naked?"

"I want to know you, Mia. *You.*"

She looked at him as if he'd grown a second head, and for some odd reason this got to him. Had no one ever said such a thing to her before? Had no one ever worked their way beneath her tough-as-shit exterior? And who was under there anyway? He knew she worked hard, that she'd let Hope stay to be kind, that she had a Southern accent when she was upset. But he wanted more.

"You really want me to talk to you," she repeated, sounding stunned.

"Yes."

"And if I talk, you'll get naked?"

"Talk, and we'll see."

She narrowed her eyes but didn't get dressed. "Okay. I'm . . . a Leo."

"Big surprise," he murmured, trying not to swallow his tongue at how magnificent she was, standing there.

She actually laughed, telling him she did have a sense of humor to go with all that sharp wit. "Yeah. Um . . . what else?"

"You tell me."

She shook her head, still baffled. "Uh . . . I like big, open, clean spaces."

"What don't you like?"

"Talking when I could be having sex."

Now he laughed. "Tell me something about your past."

She looked down at her nude body and shook her head again, displaying disbelief that he wasn't ravishing her. "I went to UCLA—"

"Before UCLA. Tell me about your parents. Your childhood."

Her face closed up. "I didn't come here for that."

No kidding. He raced for something to say rather than reach for her. "How do you even know we're alone?"

"Because your brother took out Tess. And I'll tell you right now, Ace." She pointed a finger in his face, utterly unconcerned with her nudity. "He'd better not mess with her head. She's sweet and warm and nice. Special. She falls easily and hard, and she's been hurt. There. Now I've talked." She slapped the condom on the counter, slid a hand around the nape of his neck, and pulled him down for another brain-destroying kiss, which he returned. God, the feel of her bared body against his clothed one. *Why was he wearing clothes?* "Mmm" rumbled helplessly from his chest as she spread hot open-mouthed kisses along his throat, across a pec, a nipple, which she licked, then bit.

God. He entangled his fingers in her hair. "Wait," he managed.

" 'Wait' isn't in my vocabulary." She dropped to her knees and put her mouth low on his belly while tugging on the buttons of his Levi's.

"Mia—"

Pop, pop. "Right here," she said and yanked down his jeans, leaving him dangling in the wind, so to speak. Because his knees were wobbling, he sank to them, not easy with his jeans hampering his descent. She reached for his erection.

"Stop."

"Damn it."

"Yeah, you know that word," he said grimly, and panting a little, he put his forehead to hers.

"I know you want me," she said, the proof in her hands.

"Yeah—*Jesus*," he choked out when she stroked him slow and long, exactly the way she'd already learned he liked it. "I need you to listen."

Obediently she tipped back her head and looked into his eyes.

He cupped her face. "*Really* listen."

"Go."

"I don't want another quick tumble on the floor. I want a bed. I want you to stay afterward."

"What, and cuddle?" Her laugh might have cut into him, but his brain wasn't functioning much with her hands working their magic.

"Nothing wrong with taking our time."

"I don't have time." Before he could so much as draw a trembly breath, she'd pulled them both upright, covered him with the condom, and hopped up to the counter.

"Come on home, big guy," she murmured and pulled him in.

And as always, when he sank into her body and hugged her close, he did feel like he'd come home.

Only in the dim recesses of his mind, as he began to move within her, he knew he was the only one who felt that way.

Yeah, that was just what she'd needed. Mia slipped her dress back on. Feeling incredibly good now—funny how a couple orgasms put everything into perspective—she moved toward Kevin's back door, thinking she'd leave now while Kevin was off disposing of the condom.

"Maybe I should just give you a key."

She nearly jerked out of her skin at that low, incredibly erotic voice that only a few minutes ago had been whispering hot, sexy nothings in her ear as he'd glided in and out of her body. "A key?"

He leaned against the kitchen entry, tall, dark, and

attitude-ridden. "Yeah, you know, so you don't have to sneak around."

Definitely attitude-ridden. And not nearly as friendly as he was a minute ago. He'd pulled on a pair of sweats and nothing else. His hair stood straight up—from her own fingers, no doubt. "I don't do keys," she said.

"And I don't do this—this just-sex thing."

She stared at him, her throat suddenly incredibly thick, and she had no idea why. In fact, she had no idea why she kept coming back . . .

He stepped closer, then closer still. Before she knew what he meant to do, he took her hand and brought her up against his warm, hard body.

"What are you doing?"

"Shh," he said when she tried to pull back, holding her still. "Relax, it's just a hug."

Relax? She was going to have trouble with that, eased up against him as she was. Her body gravitated toward his as if they belonged plastered together, and he held her there, his mouth nuzzling her neck, his hand stroking up and down her spine in a touch that felt so good she wanted to melt. Her heart was beating so loud she thought for sure he would say something about it, but he didn't. "See now, isn't this nice?"

She actually swayed with him and slammed her eyes tight in denial, but that didn't work, either, because with her eyes closed, her other senses took over. The scent of him, all warm male. The feel of his soft breath brushing her skin. The firmness of his body. The heat that came off him, warming her chilled limbs as his fingers stroked the small of her back. His legs brushing hers . . .

He felt so good that she couldn't move, couldn't do anything but hold on. Her hand slid up his chest and then around his neck. At that came a low rumble of approval from deep in his throat, and he tugged her a little closer still. He wanted her again, every bit as much as she wanted him, but she had a feeling his want was different than hers, and she pulled back.

His eyes were enigmatic and intelligent, the eyes of a man who cared and cared deeply about things, things like this. He was the type of man she'd always stayed away from, the type who finished what he started, the type who didn't quit at something just because it got difficult. He was strong, reliable. Solid.

Oh, no doubt, if she'd been the relationship type, she'd want him for keeps.

But she wasn't, and she couldn't be. "I've got to go," she whispered. Stepping back, she averted her face so he couldn't see the need that was surely written all over it. It embarrassed her, this knot of hunger in her belly, made her feel weak to still feel that all-consuming hunger for a man she'd just had.

"Don't do this to me again, Mia," he said quietly.

"I have to."

"Then don't come back."

At that unexpected sharp knife to the gut, she nodded and let herself out into the night.

Chapter Twelve

Kevin woke up reaching for a woman who wasn't there, and the day didn't improve much after that.

Mia arrived at the teen center with Hope, both career woman and goth kid sticking out like a sore thumb, but at least Hope smiled at him and appeared happy to see him.

He couldn't say the same about Mia, who signed Hope in, then headed back toward her car with only a single long look.

Because he'd already established he was an idiot, he followed her, then blocked her way when she would have slid into her car and driven off without a word, without a smile. Reaching out, he touched the small, nearly healed burn over her missing eyebrow.

She closed her eyes, then opened them. "Kevin—"

"Humor me. How are you doing?"

"Fine."

She certainly looked it, with her perfect makeup, her hair shiny and tamed, her suitdress cut in a way that screamed *I am woman, hear me roar*. She even let out a tight smile, though it didn't come close to reaching her eyes. See, he knew the difference now. He'd gotten a real smile last night, for instance, when he'd been buried deep within her, her legs wrapped around his waist.

"What do you want from me?" she asked, sounding genuinely confused.

"Tell you, and you'll comply?" When she only glared at him, he sighed. "All right. Let's start with a thank-you for last night."

"Thank you for the orgasm. Okay, two. Two orgasms. Thank you very much for both of those. Can I have my A plus and be excused now, Mr. McKnight?"

At her mocking tone, he scrubbed his hands over his face. "I have no idea what I was thinking coming out here after you. Forget it." He started to walk away, then whirled back. He grabbed her, just hauled her up against him and covered her mouth with his.

Oh, yeah, God bless those ridiculously sexy high-heeled sandals because they put her at a perfect height for this. He'd meant to just touch his lips to hers, but he ended up practically inhaling her whole, only vaguely hearing her keys and purse hit the ground, much more tuned to the way she twined her arms around his neck and held on.

God, the little whimper she let out when her tongue met his was the sexiest sound he'd ever heard. Then suddenly she staggered back a step, staring at him for a long beat. Blinked. And then the cool, in-charge-of-her-world Mia reappeared. "What the hell was that?" she asked.

"Stupidity at its finest." Shaking his head at himself, he bent for her keys and her purse, which she calmly took.

"Thank you," she murmured as if he was a valet and nothing more. She slipped into her car, slid her shades over her eyes, and started the engine.

Only then did she look up at him through the opened window; the only sign that they'd just kissed each other stupid was that her lip gloss was gone. Something in her eyes shifted, warmed, and she sighed. "I don't know what to say to you."

"How about whatever's on your mind."

"Okay, how's this? Seeing you makes me want to rip your clothes off again," she said tightly, looking unhappy about it. "Thinking about what you do to me when said clothes are off makes me need to sit down. And when you touch me—"

"Yeah." He closed his eyes. "You're right. Maybe we shouldn't talk."

"Tried to tell you."

"Right. Well . . . have a good day."

She put the car into gear. "You're the one who's got Hope, so I should be saying that to you."

"She's a good kid."

"Just lock up anything of value, Ace." And without another word, she drove off into the morning sun.

Kevin watched her go, then looked down at his jeans, which were straining a bit in front. "Down, boy," he murmured and headed to face his day.

School went as fine as it could possibly go for a bunch of lazy slackers, but near the end of his class, he realized the Lakers knit cap he'd found the other morning was missing from the lost-and-found box in front of his desk. A quick glance across the classroom had him groaning inwardly.

Adam had it shoved on his head. Adam was the resident jock and, now it appeared, also the resident stoner. Before he could confront that situation, he received a frantic call from Sara at the teen center. Someone had rigged the ice maker on the refrigerator to continuously make ice cubes, and by the time it was discovered the entire kitchen floor was covered with ice.

Kevin rushed over there and found everyone having an ice fight in the kitchen.

There were injuries. A freshman girl had taken an ice cube to the lip and was screaming bloody murder. A sophomore boy had slipped trying to skate on the slick linoleum floor and now had a nice bump to the head, which Kevin figured had a shot of actually knocking some sense into him.

In the middle of the chaos, Hope sat on the ratty couch in the front room, arms crossed defensively, looking straight ahead.

Kevin took one look at her and knew. "Whatcha doing?"

"Taking a time-out from the sandbox," she said stiffly. "I don't belong here."

Kevin looked around at all the kids—diversified, but all basically privileged, and spoiled. "I guess they could use a bit more black in their color scheme."

She snorted, then chewed on her lower lip. "About that ice thing. Anyone really hurt?"

"Well, Katie can't wear lipstick for a few days, which she thinks is a felony, but as for Chris, he has a hard head, thankfully. He'll live."

She studied her boots.

He crouched in front of her. "Hope."

It took her a moment to look at him. When she did, she caved like a cheap suitcase. "I'm sorry," she whispered.

"Are you really?"

"It's just that the girl told me I was stupid. And the sophomore? He thinks he's Tony Hawk. The only one who's nice to me is Adam."

Adam being the stoner, and also a first-class jerk who bed-hopped with shocking ease among the younger, easier influenced girls. If he was being nice, it was to get into her pants, but Kevin kept that to himself. "Adam is a player," he said carefully. "Know that now."

"He said you'd say that."

Kevin kept his face even. "I've been trying to get that ice machine to work forever."

"It was no sweat."

"If it was no sweat, and if you really pulled off all that stuff at Mia's work—"

"She ratted me out?"

"Nah. The grapevine." He eyed her for a moment. "Pretty impressive list of feats."

"I didn't steal the money."

"What about the other stuff? The phone rerouting, for instance?"

Hope looked away. "Maybe I did that."

"Do you want to know what I think?"

"I dunno," she said warily.

"I think you're incredibly smart and also incredibly bored, and that you should be in my summer science class."

"I failed science."

"No possible way."

"The teacher didn't like me."

"Well, I like you. Take my class, do well and pass it, and get credit for it."

"I'm getting shipped back tomorrow."

"What about your car?"

"Mia said she'd pay me what it's worth and I can buy something else back home."

"Do you want to go back?"

Another hesitation, then a lift of her shoulder.

"Think about it," he suggested.

Hope let out a laugh that sounded rusty but genuine. "Yeah. Maybe . . ."

When it came to advertising, Mia had worked her way up the old-fashioned way—from working the mail room to lowly assistant, to gofer, to creative team member, to ad exec, and she'd loved each and every job as she'd climbed the ladder.

But she especially loved where she was now, in a corner office with a glorious view of downtown LA, with accounts stacking up and a reputation for being the best of the best.

A reputation that was taking a beating within the building this week, thanks to Hurricane Hope. For three days Mia had been trying to get Sugar to nail down the plans for tomorrow because one thing Mia wouldn't do was blindly put Hope on a plane heading east.

Finally, Friday afternoon, Sugar answered her phone. "Tomorrow doesn't really work for me," she said right up front.

Mia's eye twitched. "Sunday then."

"Well . . ."

"Sugar. You *are* coming, right?"

"Actually, Apple, I need another week."

Mia thunked her head down on her desk, imagining what her hips would look like with another week of bacon and eggs for breakfast, imagining also the look on Dick's face when she continued to leave the office on time to pick up the kid. So much for senior butt-kissing . . . "Another *week*?"

"You have no idea what it's like, being in charge of a teenager."

Mia was beginning to, and she had to admit, she actually felt some sympathy for Sugar. "I'm not sure Hope wants to stay."

"She doesn't have a choice, if her car is really broken."

"It is." She sighed. *Hell.* "Promise you'll come next week then?"

"Promise."

Only problem, Sugar's promise had never been worth much.

That night Mia let Hope cook chili dogs and French fries. They had salad for "something green" as Hope said, seeming quite happy loading up her arteries with a year's worth of cholesterol.

Because the kid looked so . . . content, Mia waited until afterward to tell her the news. "I talked to your mom today."

In the act of clearing the table, Hope went still. "What time is she coming tomorrow?"

Mia stood up and took the plates from Hope's hands, setting them in the sink before turning back to Hope. "She's not."

Hope nodded, giving no sign of whether this was a good or bad thing.

"She said next week," Mia said.

Hope nodded again. "So can we have hot dogs again tomorrow?"

"Do they make them low-fat?"

Hope snorted but still didn't give any indication of how she felt about staying.

"So . . . you okay?" Mia asked.

"Peachy."

Sarcasm and wit. A mechanism Mia herself had perfected and understood all too well.

"I'm going to take a shower." Hope left the room, and Mia looked out the window, feeling . . . she didn't know. Worried. Stressed. Strung too damn tight.

Kevin's bike sat parked in front of his house, looking sleek and sexy, like the man. Mia heard the shower turn on upstairs, and then she headed for the back door.

Her sandals slapped on the concrete, the heat from the day rising up through her feet. She didn't realize she was holding her breath until Kevin opened his door.

Wearing only a pair of loose basketball shorts hanging to his knees and his chest bare, he looked better than the dessert she hadn't allowed herself.

His gaze went wary. "Mia—"

Not wanting to hear why this was a bad idea, she stepped over the threshold and into his personal space, winding her arms around his neck and sighing in pleasure even before their mouths met. "Are we alone?" she murmured.

"Yeah, but—"

She kicked the door shut, slid her hands into his hair and brought his mouth back to hers, his delicious, talented, gorgeous mouth.

Seemingly just as hungry, he lifted her up against him, his mouth trailing hot kisses down her neck, his hands snaking beneath her skirt. When his fingers found her thong, he let out a rough "Fuck" in a strained voice.

She knew she had him then, that he would take her hard and fast and help her forget.

Despite Mia's intentions of making sure the next week was an improvement over the shockingly bad previous one, somehow the shit kept hitting the fan. She was in the middle of a handful of accounts, all in different phases but none more exciting than the highly secret Runner account. The good news: she put together a fabulous campaign.

The bad news: Tess's computer crashed and her files vanished.

All of them. Poof, gone.

It meant many hours of stress, trying to re-create everything, and as a result she felt strung tight. Making it worse, Dickhead started asking a bunch of questions about the Anderson account, about her team's creative strategies, the production of planned ads, the media blitz, and the execution of all of the above. He was suddenly extremely interested in exactly how she'd gone about getting the account, and finally admitted that Ted had complained about her.

One morning she came into her office and found a sign leaning against her potted plant that said RESCUE ME.

To top off things nicely, Sugar claimed she needed another few weeks "kid-free," leaving Mia not sure how to explain to Hope that even if she'd wanted to go home, no one wanted her.

Halfway through the week, Mia and Hope were eating bagels and bacon—Mia was going to have to pick up an extra few yoga classes every week just to keep up—when from outside came the rumbling of Kevin's motorcycle starting up. Casually, Mia moved to the window to peer out at him.

"You think he's hot." Hope came up beside her and grinned. "Admit it."

"Do not."

"Do so."

"Do not."

"Do so."

"Do—" Mia broke off and pinched the bridge of her nose. "Get ready to go."

"I am ready." Hope spread out her hands, revealing her black trousers—three sizes too big and staying in place by some random act of fate—and her black tank top, ripped in several spots and showing glimpses of a black bra. Her makeup was also black, and she'd filled in the chipped black nail polish with what smelled like a permanent Sharpie marker.

"Aren't you guys going to the movies this afternoon?" Mia asked her.

"So?"

"So I'll give you one thousand dollars to wear something bright pink today."

Hope chewed on her wad of gum, then blew a big bubble.

Pink.

Pop.

"Yeah. I was thinking something Chanel," Mia said.

For this, she got an eye roll.

After she dropped Hope off at the teen center and got to work, the fun began. Layoffs had hit close to home. Half her creative team had to go. It didn't help that Margot and Ted faced the same cuts, not when saying good-bye to Tami and Steven.

That afternoon, the Anderson people started asking her about Ted, wanting to know if he could join her in handling their account. When Mia went to Dick about it, she realized the good-old-boy network had gone into effect when she hadn't been paying attention, because he just said, "Do what you have to do to keep the Anderson people happy."

Afraid to say anything because she was *seriously* peeved, and when she was seriously peeved, her Southern accent buttered her every word, she simply bit her tongue and stalked out of the office, where she ran into Margot. Mia and Margot had never exactly been friends, but in this firm, where they were in the definite minority as far as women went, were in fact the only two females at this level, they had a silent agreement to stick together when needed.

"Layoffs," Margot said furiously. "Suck."

"*Men* suck."

Margot nodded, and in rare solidarity they smiled grimly at each other.

Mia went back to her office, going over and over the Runner stuff, wishing Tess would show up so she could get her opinion, but Tess had gone to lunch two hours ago and hadn't come back.

Then, finally, Tess reappeared. She stuck her head in Mia's office with an apologetic look on her face. "Sorry."

"Are you sick?"

"No." A flush worked its way up Tess's throat. "I, um . . ."

"Ah, hell." She scrubbed her hands over her face. "*Mike.*"

Tess sighed dreamily.

Mia searched Tess's face, found utter bliss, and let worry work its course. "It's only been a few dates. You can't engage your heart that quickly."

"It was engaged the first moment I laid eyes on him."

"Oh, Tess. Really?"

"Really." Tess's eyes wandered to her plant. "Hey, you've got to water that thing."

"I've watered it. I've *not* watered it. Nothing makes it happy and it's going to die to spite me. You're changing the subject. Tell me about him. What does he what to do with himself?"

"Well, he's between careers at the moment, but he's putting in time at the teen center every day for a while."

"Great." Mia tossed her pen aside. "Damn it, you have too big a heart, you know this. You fall too hard, and then get hurt."

"No I don't."

Mia ticked them off on her fingers. "Scott. Jon. Timothy—"

"Okay, fine. I've fallen too hard, too fast before, but not this time."

"Ha. You've already slept with him, the hurt is just around the corner."

"Shows what you know." Tess lifted her chin smugly. "I haven't sleep with him. Yet."

Mia groaned. "How do you even communicate? You don't know sign language."

"He reads lips, and that's where I was today. I started a sign language class." Another dreamy sigh escaped her. "Did I tell you? He's been making cookie dough with me at night."

Tess had a small home business called Cookie Madness. She made cookie dough for extra cash, and she was amazing at it. She sold it by the pound, mostly to two small local bakeries, and in Mia's opinion it was the best dough in the world. So many times she'd bugged Tess to get serious about the business, to let Mia market it, but Tess had resisted, enjoying the smallness of the company.

"Mia." Tess smiled at her doubt. "Stop thinking. Just be happy for me."

"If he hurts you, I hurt him."

"I'll be sure to tell him. Now prepare yourself. I have wince-inducing news."

"God." Mia pressed her fingers to her eyelids. "What now?"

"King Dickface wants to see you in his office."

"Ted says the Anderson people asked for him specifically, and that you wouldn't let him on board," Dick said without preamble.

"Ted also says he's a human being, but I have my doubts." Mia smiled.

Dick did not. "Fix this," he said and went back to his computer.

Mia moved to the door thinking, if she could only figure out how to set her cell phone to stun . . .

"Mia."

She turned back. "Yes?"

"Ted wants to fire Tess. Says she came on to him."

Mia found it difficult to speak with her jaw locked tight, but she managed. "Ted has an ego problem. Trust me, Tess wouldn't touch him with a ten-foot pole."

"We're laying off at the lower tier this week, and I'm just looking for people to give me a reason to let them go, so you might want to make sure."

What she would like to make sure of was Ted's slow, painful demise, but she merely nodded.

"How's it going with your niece? Is she in jail yet?"

"She's not a bad kid," she heard herself say and left in tune to his low laugh.

Mike showed up for work each day, a fact that quite frankly surprised Kevin. Mike even exhibited a glimmer of true interest: not just the happy-go-lucky, what-the-fuck Mike, but a man who wanted this job and who cared about making a living.

Now if Kevin could get Cole to care about his grades, convince Beth not to sell the building, get Joe off his back, get Mia to open up . . . if, if, if.

To suitably exhaust himself, he took a very long ride on the bike, after which he planned to fall into bed and not dream of Mia, or how if she knocked he hoped she was wearing that gauzy sundress again.

No. Christ, what was wrong with him? He was not going to keep sleeping with her whenever she knocked.

Yeah, but there was no sleeping involved, a little voice reminded him, while his body surged and said *Oh, pretty please, one more time.*

He parked the bike on his dark street and, in spite of himself, looked up at Mia's house. It was well lit, and from somewhere inside came the thudding beat of music. Not as loud as the previous week, which meant the two wildly opinioned, edgy, fierce females inside—so different and yet somehow so similar—had come to some sort of compromise.

Interesting.

Encouraging.

It was possible he'd never met two more incredibly stubborn women. It'd been easy to let Hope inside his heart, and he was glad she'd gotten to stay as long as she had. He'd ordered the parts for her car in case she somehow pulled off the impossible and stayed even longer. There was just something about her tough exterior and soft, vulnerable inside that melted him. He understood her. Whatever her background, it hadn't been easy, but she hadn't allowed her spirit to be taken from her.

He could identify with that.

He identified with Mia, too, whether she liked it or not. Identified, and craved.

She craved, too, or she wouldn't keep showing up on his doorstep.

From the top floor, probably her bedroom window,

Mia appeared, looking blindly out into the night, her expression one of such sadness it pulled the air right out of his lungs.

She wasn't all tough, kick-ass, coldhearted woman, any more than Hope was—not that she'd admit it. He stood there trying to talk himself into walking away instead of knocking on her door, when he heard an odd noise.

A different window, a different female standing in the window directly beneath Mia. Then the face vanished.

The screen popped out. A leg appeared, and a pale face glanced back to make sure no one was watching her escape.

Hope, on the move.

Kevin sighed. Guess he was going over there, after all.

Chapter Thirteen

Hope swung her other leg out the den window and for a moment clung to the ledge, looking down. Not so far, only eight feet or so. Not enough to break her legs.

Probably.

But the bushes planted directly below looked a little prickly and uncomfortable, topped with the now bent screen. Aunt Apple wouldn't be happy about that, but she squelched the regret because not even Mia wanted her around, not really.

And yet she didn't send you back . . .

Yeah, yeah, give the woman a medal. Hope looked down. She just wanted to go somewhere and think . . .

And smoke.

And, okay, also see Adam. He said he'd meet her by the basketball court, where they'd maybe play one-on-one for a while. At the teen center, she'd looked into his sharp blue eyes and thought *It's not a game you want.*

She wasn't stupid, she knew what boys *did* want, and wasting time on the court with a girl was not it.

But Adam was so cute, cute enough for her to pretend she liked what he liked. He'd been playing football for a few years, putting on muscle where most guys her age were still too skinny. He was big and built and all the girls wanted him, including that beautiful Amber, but Adam wanted Hope. The rush of that!

God, she wanted a smoke bad. She wasn't addicted, though. Nope, she would quit anytime. She pulled the pack out of her pocket with fingers that shook, then stared down at her hands in horror. *Shaking, like her momma's.* Maybe she should quit.

Tomorrow.

She looked down again and got dizzy. If it hadn't been for Adam, she'd have just sneaked a puff or two inside. And she'd started to, but then she looked around her at the wide-open, uncluttered, beautifully decorated house and faced the truth: she loved it here. It was clean and smelled good and so big she could be by herself whenever she wanted, without hearing another soul snore or yell. And the air conditioner, pure heaven on earth. No plastering her face to the inside of the freezer, she could get cool in any room of the house.

No, she couldn't smoke in there.

She could have just told Mia she was going outside; Mia didn't have any hold on her or anything. But it just felt good not to ask. Or tell. Or talk at all.

And that, if she was admitting stuff, was the most beautiful thing of all about this trip west. Mia, for all her faults—and there were many—didn't bother her with the little stuff, or expectations at all, for that matter.

So she straddled the ledge, looking down at the screen. Somehow she had to get it back up to the window. Closing her eyes, holding her breath, she jumped.

Luckily, the screen broke her fall. Unluckily, the screen didn't take it so well. She lay there for a moment and took stock. No pain anywhere, and she could still feel her arms and legs.

Plus her cigarette was only kinda bent.

With a wince, she stood up, then moved out of the bushes. She walked around to the side of the house where she couldn't inadvertently be seen by Mia out one of the windows, then headed toward the basketball court.

It was empty. She sat back against the steel post of the basket, then lit the cigarette. She'd just deeply inhaled when someone said, "And here all this time I thought you were so smart."

She nearly dropped the lit cigarette into her lap. *Kevin.* Shit. *Shit, shit, shit.* She clamped her mouth shut, trapping the smoke, wondering how to get rid of him before she had to breathe.

But he sat on the ground next to her, then leaned back, raising a brow, signaling that it was her turn to talk.

Hard to do with a mouthful of smoke and holding her breath. She went for a smile that she hoped didn't look like a grimace. *Look at me, I'm fine, and I'm not smoking or anything.*

Only suffocating.

"Pretty night," Kevin said casually, putting his hands behind his head, crossing his feet. He had those old boots on, laced only halfway. They looked comfortable, like the man.

Not her, though. Completely. Out. Of. Air. Turning her head away from him, she tried to let out the smoke slowly, but the problem was her lungs. They were demanding more air. Right now. So she ended up trying to drag more in before she let the smoke all the way out, and then choked for her efforts.

Coughing, eyes watering, she bent over, trying to wheeze a lungful of air in.

Anybody would have laughed at her. Anyone. After all, she was being totally stupid trying to hide the smoke.

But Kevin didn't laugh. He put a hand on her back and patted her lightly as she coughed. And coughed.

"Better?" he asked when she finally could breathe again.

She swiped at the tears streaming down her face and nodded.

He still didn't seem to expect her to make excuses, or even speak. He just waited until he was sure she wasn't going to die, and then leaned back, once again making himself perfectly at home in the dark night.

Something hooted. A light breeze blew, brushing the bushes together with a soft, wispy sound. An insect buzzed her face.

And still they sat there in shockingly companionable silence.

"Don't you love it out here?" he finally said with a sigh. "The quiet. The noise."

She couldn't stand it another second. "I was smoking."

"Yeah. You were turning an interesting shade of blue, too."

She didn't get it. "Aren't you going to, like, yell at me?"

"If you want to be stupid and kill yourself, that's your business."

"I'm quitting tomorrow," she heard herself say.

He turned his head and smiled at her. "That's good."

The warmth of his approval washed over her. They watched the night some more. "At home," she said after a few minutes, "we'd be attacked alive by the mosquitoes, and sweating like crazy."

"You should see August. Plenty of mosquitoes then."

"I'm going back."

"You know, you could always just ask to stay."

She wanted to, God she wanted to, but she just shrugged.

"Your call." Kevin went back to his easy quiet.

Then came the sound of a front door opening. And

then running footsteps. Hope straightened to see Mia flying down the sidewalk, her bathrobe swirling behind her, her fancy high-heeled mules slapping down on the concrete as she came to a skidding halt between the Diplomat and the Audi.

Uh oh.

Hope glanced at Kevin. "Maybe you should have left a note," he suggested.

Mia whipped her cell out of her pocket, her breath rasping loudly as she stood beneath the streetlight, trying to hold her robe closed while dialing at the same time.

"Mia," Kevin called out as he rose to his feet. "Over here."

Mia's head whipped toward them, but Hope could tell she couldn't see in the dark.

Mia's hair wasn't in its usual perfect state. That is, it was piled on top of her head, precariously perched there with pieces hanging down in her eyes, and it was damp as if she'd been in the bath or something. She wore no makeup, and if Hope's eyesight was correct, she wore nothing beneath the gown. Wow. Her Aunt Apple had it going on.

"Hope?" Mia squinted toward them. Breathing heavily, she put her hand to her chest. "God. I thought—" She moved on the sidewalk until she came to the gate at center court. Slipping inside she came right up to them. "I really thought—"

She broke off when her voice cracked.

Kevin reached out for her, putting his hand on her arm and squeezing, and shockingly, for a moment, Mia leaned into him.

"You thought that I'd what?" Hope asked. "Stolen your car?"

Mia grimaced. "More like rewired the thing so that when I started it the horn would go off or something. Don't even try to tell me you couldn't do that if you wanted."

Hope jerked a shoulder.

"You so belong in my science class," Kevin said with a low laugh.

Hope hugged herself. "Whatever."

"Hope, you can't just vanish on me," Mia said. "It gives me gray hair."

"You vanish, too. To go to his house." She jerked a shoulder toward Kevin. "You're totally crushing on him."

Kevin eyed Mia with interest. "Really? Crushing?"

But Mia's nostrils were wriggling. "Is that smoke— Hope, were you smoking again?"

Shit. "Yeah. But I didn't inhale."

Mia about had a coronary. "You think this is funny? Smoking *kills*, Hope."

"So does stress," Hope pointed out. "So does being a workaholic. A perfectionist—"

"Okay, great, thank you. I get the point," Mia said tightly. "Look, I thought you'd left. That's why I was upset."

Something that felt suspiciously like regret and guilt twisted through Hope. "Well, I do live to upset you."

"Hope," Kevin said quietly, "come on. Meet her halfway."

Hope sighed. "Okay, yeah. Whatever. I'm sorry, okay? I'm sorry I made you run out here without makeup and with your hair all crazy."

Mia put her hand to her hair. "Crazy?"

"Well, there's three whole hairs out of place. A crime, I know, in your perfect world."

"Is that what you think?" Mia asked, shocked. "That my world is perfect? Listen, you need a serious reality check if you really think my life is perfect."

Hope shrugged. "You have a hotshot car, a hotshot job, a hot boyfriend, and your house is—"

"Yeah, hot. I get it," Mia muttered, not looking at Kevin. "Look, we can analyze me later. This is about you, and the scare you gave me. I'm responsible for you while you're here, damn it. And in case you're still not clear on this, I freaked when I thought you'd left. I didn't want you to go. And when I thought you had, I—"

"Wanted to celebrate?"

"No."

"I know I'm a pain. I know you're not interested in family, my momma said."

She made a sorrowful noise. "Hope, I've wanted to say this for a while. Your momma and I . . . we weren't close growing up. It doesn't matter now why, it's just how it was. But it is my fault that I never pushed past that to get to know you, and I am sorry for that, sorrier than I can say."

Hope looked at her, feeling her throat tighten. "Really?"

"Really." Mia glanced at Kevin, as if seeking help. In response, he ran his hand up her arm again in a sweet, united gesture, which was strange—the last time Hope had looked, the two of them generated heat and lots of sparks, but she'd missed this other, deeper bond.

In a shocking move, Mia reached for Hope's hand, bringing Hope into the circle, and for a moment Hope couldn't even breathe for fear Mia would pull away.

"We have definitely gotten off on the wrong foot here," Mia said softly. "Maybe we could start over."

"Why?" Hope asked warily.

"Hell, I don't know, maybe I want to get to know your sunny and gentle disposition."

Kevin choked out a laugh. "Sorry," he said when they both looked over at him. "I was just thinking how special it is that the sweet and gentle disposition runs in the family."

"I'll have you know, we're as different as night and day," Mia said.

Well duh, Hope thought.

"Although, I'll give you that we might both be a little stubborn," Mia said.

Well, at least one of them was, Hope thought, but it wasn't her.

Kevin just grinned.

Mia shook her head and said an extremely off-color word that made Kevin's grin spread.

Mia rolled her eyes, and right then and there Hope felt something new bloom in her chest, something she'd never expected.

Affection. Not wanting to be moved, wanting to soak in her self-righteous pity a bit longer, she bit it back. "Starting over . . . What does that mean exactly?"

"It means we wipe the slate clean. I pretend you just drove up." Mia thrust out her hand. "Nice to meet you, Hope. Maybe you can stay until the weekend."

Right. In three days her mother was supposedly coming for her, for real this time. Hope stared at the proffered hand and then shook it as she met Mia's eyes. "It's nice to meet you, long-lost Aunt Apple— *Mia*," she corrected quickly when Mia's smile slipped.

"I don't know, I kind of like Aunt Apple," Kevin said.

Footsteps sounded on the walk behind them, coming closer. Adam came into view, and when he saw the two adults with Hope, he slowed his steps. "Uh . . . hi."

Hope's heart started pounding. God, he was cute. That thought warred with another. Only three more days . . .

Kevin nodded to Adam. "What's up?"

Adam slid his hands into his pocket. "Just hanging."

Mia looked Adam over, too, taking in the baggy T-shirt, the loose pants that sagged past his butt, revealing black boxers, and the surfer shoes. She sighed. "Just don't get into any trouble."

Adam shot her his charm-the-stupid-adult smile. "No trouble."

Mia and Kevin exchanged a long look, but finally Mia shook her head. "Be in by eleven, Hope. That's half an hour from now." Then she and Kevin walked toward their houses.

Kevin turned back. "Adam?"

"Yeah?"

"If you give her alcohol or pot, I'll castrate you."

Adam swallowed hard. "No alcohol. No pot."

"Good."

Hope watched Kevin catch up with Mia, feeling oddly warm and fuzzy. And cared for. Mia had freaked when she'd thought Hope had left, and yet she was still sending her home in a matter of days . . . *Sucked*.

Adam smiled at Hope, his eyes sleepy and sexy as he stepped close. "Hey."

He was seriously in her personal space, looking at her with those eyes, and she tried to relax. "Hey back atcha."

Adam craned his neck to make sure they were all alone. When he saw that they were, he pulled her into the trees beyond the basketball court.

"Uh—"

"You look pretty," he said huskily and touched her cheek.

"I . . . do?"

He slid an arm around her, tugging her close, burying his face in her neck. "And you smell *yum*. Let's hang here," he murmured and kissed her throat.

"M—maybe for a minute."

"You have thirty," he reminded her.

Suddenly that seemed like a very long time. *What the hell had Mia been thinking?*

Adam kissed her then, sticking his tongue in her mouth and a hand up her shirt. His other hand slid into the back of her pants, startling her. "Wait," she gasped.

He pulled back a fraction.

"I have my period," she said brilliantly.

Adam sighed and stepped free. "Damn."

"Yeah. Sorry," she said, breathing a huge sigh of relief. "Want to smoke?"

"Sure. What the hell."

Mia rushed toward her house without looking back, inexplicably close to losing it in a big way. She needed to be alone, to think, to process. God. When she thought Hope had left, she panicked. And then when she leaned on Kevin, as if it was the most natural thing in the world . . . She went around to the back of her house, slipping into her dark kitchen—

"Ow," Kevin said, rubbing his forehead where the door hit him.

She looked at him and felt an odd ache in her chest to go with her tight throat and burning eyes. She was holding on by a thread here. "Go home."

Instead he shut the door behind him and looked at her from those dark, sexy eyes that never failed to melt her into a pool of longing.

Damn, it was ridiculous how she responded to him. Ridiculous, and just a little humiliating. "I have nothing to say to you."

"Not even about your crush on me?"

"Ha ha." She stalked over to her table and put her hands flat on the wood, gulping in air. Hope was okay. She hadn't run off to do anything stupid.

And the man behind her . . . Well, things weren't

so black-and-white with him. The way he looked standing there on the court with Hope: big, bad, tough, and so unexpectedly sweet she almost hadn't been able to breathe when she'd looked into his eyes.

Damn it, what was it about him? He made her think, laugh, yearn . . .

"Is it true?" he asked.

His hands came up, gripped the table at either side of her hips, putting them extremely close and in an unexpectedly intimate position. "Mia," he said very softly, tipping his head so that his breath brushed her jaw, her ear, making her feel touched by him, when in truth not an inch of him touched her at all.

"I read between the lines when you were talking about your sister. She was pretty rough on you, wasn't she?"

Mia lifted a shoulder. "All that's in the past now."

"Yeah. But I'm sorry I judged you for not being closer to your family. I had no right," he said quietly. "I think you were great tonight. I think you reached her." He sprawled his hands wide so that his thumbs just lightly skimmed over her hips. He was tall, hard with muscle from all his days playing basketball, and she felt trapped by him, petite and extremely feminine. Beneath the flimsy robe, her body reacted predictably.

"Is what true?" She had to clear her rough throat. "That I have a crush on you? Don't be ridiculous."

Leaning in, he let his mouth just barely brush her throat.

The hollow at the base of her neck.

And then her collarbone.

Oh, God. She had to lock her knees. She had no idea what to do with her hands, so they helped themselves to his shirt, fisting comfortably over his pecs, which were warm and solid. Real.

At her touch, he let out a low groan and stepped back, letting out a sound of disbelief. "How the hell did I end up here again?"

"I—" She was about to say it was because their bodies seemed to have a thing for each other, but she looked into his eyes—eyes the color of the Caribbean Sea, eyes that weren't holding anything back— and she lost the glib words. Instead she sank her hands into his hair and dragged his mouth to hers.

Chapter Fourteen

Mia sank into the kiss, thrilling to the way he touched her. "God," he murmured, taking another hot little love bite out of her throat. "Why couldn't you be wearing a suit of armor?"

Her head fell back. The man could take her from zero to sixty with a single touch. For someone so laid-back and casual, he had a real edgy thing going when he concentrated, and when it came to her, he usually concentrated extremely well. His hair was tousled, and a lock of it fell over his knotted brow; his eyes were dark and sleepy and filled with an intense heat.

It was silly how strongly he affected her, but just looking at him, she felt her pulse skip. Her amusement at herself for that vanished in a flash when his fingers pulled open her robe. His low, throaty groan was heady stuff. He lifted her up onto the table, put his hands on her thighs, and pushed them open. "Look at you," he murmured. "You're already wet for me." With a light touch that sent her pulse skittering, he stroked her, outlined her, then slowly pushed two fingers into her.

His grip on her was presumptuous, familiar, and just a little rough, and she should have kicked his ass for it. Instead, she fought to see past the sexual haze and tried to rip his clothes off. She shoved up his shirt and had his jeans half undone when he shook his head as if trying to clear it and stepped free. "Mia. We have to stop." ·

"Damn it, I hate that word."

He let out a low, groaning laugh and touched his forehead to hers, squeezing her hips gently. "Hope. Remember Hope. I know you gave her a half hour, but she could come in the door anytime."

"Oh, God." She blinked, and wanted to cry. "There are teenagers around. Does that mean we can't have sex? I really need to have sex, Kevin. Right now."

He glanced over her shoulder at her pantry closet, and she wasn't so far gone that she couldn't laugh breathlessly. "Not there. Come on." She hopped off the table, grabbed his hand, and tugged him out of the kitchen, down the hall past the living room and up the stairs, her robe billowing behind her. Just outside her bedroom door he pulled her around, backing her to the wall, holding her there while he dropped to his knees.

"What about the kid?"

"We'll hear her." Then he opened her robe and her thighs and glided his thumb deliberately over her.

She gasped. Shivered. By the time he leaned in and replaced his thumb with his tongue, she was already halfway gone. Gripping his head, she let him take her the rest of the way to an explosive climax. When she stopped shuddering, he sat back on his heels and looked up at her from heavy-lidded eyes.

"Come up here," she managed.

He straightened to his full height, and she hopped up and wrapped her legs around his hips, making him groan, and turned, trapping her between his body and the wall. One of her Prada mules fell to the floor with a thud.

He cupped her face and looked deep into her eyes as he slowly pushed his hips into hers, making it abundantly clear that he was hard as the wall at her back, and he said, "We really need to talk, about why, if I'm so awful in bed, you keep wanting me so bad."

She closed her eyes, her own little cheap escape, and arched against his erection, making him hiss again as he staggered with her into her bedroom. One moment she was holding on to his tense shoulders, and the next she was flying through the air, then bouncing on her bed.

He locked the door, then came to the mattress, tucking her beneath him, holding her down as he crawled up her body, his eyes dark and determined, his body hot and taut. "Now. I figure we still have a few minutes. About that talk . . ."

As if it could be as simple for her as it was for him. He gave all, and expected the same in return. No hesitation, no second-guessing, no pretense, and sure as hell no wondering what anyone thought of him.

It was his sexiest, most arousing trait.

He didn't care about impressing her, or even being impressed by her. He just cared about her.

And he wanted her to care back.

So simple, so terrifying.

"Later," she murmured, and because he held her hands down on either side of her head, she arched her body into his.

He made short work of losing her robe, then his shirt and pants, stopping only to fish something from the pocket.

In the dark, the condom packet seemed to glimmer.

Her entire body quivered, the searing reaction startling her. "A well prepared man," she murmured. "I like that. Let me—"

He lifted it out of reach, smiling down at her in a way that wasn't entirely friendly. "Not until you talk to me—"

"Please," she said softly. "Just love me."

He looked down at her for a long beat, clearly torn. She knew what he wanted. He wanted the words, he wanted her to tell him how much she needed this. Him.

But holding that back was her last weapon, her last line of defense against him, and she wouldn't.

Couldn't.

How about that? The fearless Mia Appleby, scared spitless by a silly little emotion which she couldn't even begin to name. Because that irritated her, she surged up, snatched the condom away from him, and tore it open. With her teeth. She knew he was watching her, felt him reining himself in. With a sexy smile, she pushed him flat to the mattress, straddled him, and protected them both. "This'll have to be quick—*Hey!*"

She was flat on her back.

Pinned by his big, tough body.

Unable to move an inch.

"I know you're in a damn hurry." He danced his fingers up her side, then down. "Always are."

"Seriously. We have like three minutes left."

His fingers glided over her hips, between her legs, and she jumped as if shot.

"I can make you come in three," he murmured.

Damn it, that was true, but she didn't like that he knew it. "Prove it, big guy."

"Hang on then."

She slid her hands down the sleek, hard, contoured muscles of his back and cupped his ass. Squeezed. "I'm hanging on."

"Good." He nipped at her chin, her lip, and when she opened to him, he slid his tongue possessively to hers at the same moment he plunged inside her, filled her.

"Oh, my God," she panted in tune to his roughly uttered "Oh, yeah." His hands fastened on her hips as he rode her just the way she wanted, hard and fast and well, his eyes locked on hers; and in that beat of time something happened, something deep and unexplainable, and when she came, exploded really, his name tumbled from her lips as she fell.

And fell.

She felt him tremble as he pressed his face into her hair and followed her over, and for the first time in recent memory, for the first time maybe ever, she clung to him hard, not in a hurry to do anything but be right here where she was.

With him.

Kevin was happily floating, his toes slowly uncurling, when he felt Mia sat up beside him.

"Yeah," she said. "Sorry. But you're still no good at that."

Sprawled facedown on her bed, he didn't bother to move a single muscle. "You are such a little liar."

"Get up."

"Already was," he muttered into her pillow. It smelled like her, which he liked. Too much. "But give me a minute and maybe—"

"I meant up off the bed." She added a playful slap on his ass.

He cracked open an eye and leveled it on her. "You're playing with trouble, woman."

She laughed, and in one smooth motion he sat up, snagged her around the waist, then put her over his knees, smiling down at the view.

"You wouldn't dare," she said with a shocked laugh, struggling to get up, wriggling all over the place, giving him more of the enticing, tantalizing peep show every time she scissored her legs.

He clamped his hand down over her bare ass and squeezed.

"Let me up," she said on a laugh. "Right this minute."

"Or . . . ?"

"Or I'm going to kick your ass—"

He brought his hand down, not exactly lightly, then traced the outline of his nice red handprint while she squirmed. "You're going to kick my ass? Really?"

"Yes, I'm—" This broke off on a moan when he took his fingers on a tour between her thighs now.

"Oh, my God," she gasped and opened her legs farther.

He dipped in, played for a moment, then sighed. "We don't have time."

She sat up. "I knew that."

He watched as she slipped her amazing body into her robe. "You know what I think? You're crazy about me."

She snorted, and he grinned.

"Yeah, that's right," he continued. "You're so crazy about me you need me to get the hell out of here before you admit the rest—that not only am I *not* bad in bed, I'm the best you've ever had."

Tossing back her head, she laughed, a full-belly gut laugh that stopped his heart.

She bent to pick up his clothes. Reflexes a bit slow from the mind-blowing orgasm, he didn't manage to catch his shirt before it hit him in the face. He was still pulling the material from his mouth when his pants hit him next.

"Hurry," she said, belting her robe. She tossed back her hair and smoothed it down with her fingers, the mass obediently falling into place as if she'd spent hours on it. She slid one foot into a high-heeled mule, then looked around for the other.

Kevin slid his legs into his pants and kept watching her. He couldn't help himself: she moved in quick, economical movements, always the fastest, bestest way from point A to point B—even in bed.

It fascinated him, but he wanted to see what happened when she let go of that amazing control. He wanted to cause it.

Clearly, he was insane.

He'd promised himself he wouldn't do this again with her, and here he was. "Hallway," he said.

She had bent over to see beneath the bed, giving him a very fine view of her very fine ass. He wondered if his handprint was still on it. "Excuse me?"

"Your shoe. Hallway. We left it there when—"

"Oh, yeah." When she would have brushed past him, he caught her arm, pulled her back around. "So," he said. "That was pretty nice back there—"

"Yeah, yeah. It was nice. It was great. Now we don't have time for the cuddle stuff, move it!"

He laughed. What else could he do? "There's always time for the cuddle stuff," he murmured and took the time to pull her in closer and kiss her softly. He could feel her jolt of surprise at the tender touch, the way her breath hitched.

She kissed him back, then stepped clear, licking her lips as if wanting to get every last taste. "You have to go," she said and shoved his shoes against his chest. "They can't catch us—it'll give them ideas."

He dropped his boots and stepped into them without bothering to lace them up. "I think they've already got ideas."

She went still and stared at him. "You think they're having sex? My God, why didn't you tell me? We have to stop them."

"I just meant that they're thinking about it. It's what teenagers do. At least teenage males. They wake up thinking about it, they eat thinking about it, they sleep thinking about it."

"Don't tell me this. I don't want to have to kill that Adam kid."

"Yeah. I just wish it was a different guy. Maybe Cole, who's a little screwed up in the parental department, but a really great kid."

"No one's good enough for Hope."

Again he stepped close, putting his hand on the bedroom door when she might have shoved him out of it. "That, Mia Appleby, is the sweetest thing I've ever heard you say. I think she's growing on you."

"Maybe," she admitted. "Damn it."

"You're amazing to let her stay."

"What was I going to do, throw her out into the street?" Again, she tried to get past him.

But he held on. "Was there anyone there for you? When you ran away?"

"I didn't—" She broke off and looked away. "Look, I realize that what we've done might have given you the idea that we've got something going on here, enough to share this kind of stuff, but—"

"But we don't." He stared at her, wondering how he'd forgotten that. "Right. Sorry." And he moved out the door without looking back. Going cold turkey, or so he told himself.

No more. He'd had his fill.

Now if only he believed it.

The next morning Mia had no hot water. A certain teen had used it all. When she entered the kitchen, the same teen was at the stove.

Flipping something in the pan. "What are you doing?"

"You might have heard of it," Hope said, hair wet from all of *Mia's* hot water. "It's called cooking."

"But we just cooked yesterday."

"We? You mean me and the house in my pocket?" Hope handed her a plate filled with eggs, hash browns, and toast. "You can't always go out to eat."

"Why not?" Mia stared down at the food. Fat City. "You really made all this?"

"Funny thing, a stove. You see it actually heats up, and then—"

"Okay, smart-ass."

"Eat. It's the breakfast of champions. You'll be able to make more heads roll, you'll feel like a queen, you'll—"

"I get it." Mia took a bite, and then another.

Hope had her hands on her hips, looking a little like . . . *Oh, God.* Without her black makeup, she looked like . . . Mia swallowed hard. She looked like Mia herself. She swallowed the bite that had suddenly congealed in her mouth and stared, stunned at the realization.

"Is it good?"

"Yeah," she whispered.

Hope nodded, satisfied to have gotten her way, and went off to get dressed and paint herself up. And when she reappeared, she had her attitude and toughness firmly in place and looked nothing like Mia at all.

Mia sighed in relief and glanced at the calendar by the refrigerator. Two more days.

On the way to work, she cranked the air to combat the already warm day and accessed her messages. There was a client questioning the research budget for their company, another calling for trafficking reports, which would have been ready if she hadn't lost half her creative team. Then Tess's voice came on. "I want to trade this job for what's behind door number one. Seriously, Mia, why didn't you tell me Dickhead told you I'd come on to Ted? You'd best get in before you have to bail me out for murder."

Mia shook her head and wondered what the hell Ted was up to now, and drove faster.

"Look at that," Hope commented dryly from the passenger seat. "Your breakfast is working. You have the energy this morning to kick ass from the car. Usually it takes three lattes."

"Hope?"

"Yes?" the girl asked sweetly.

"New rule. No baiting me before ten o'clock." In the rearview mirror she checked the placement of the collar of her Michael Kors silk top, which was up to help cover the beard rash she'd gotten the night before from Kevin.

Then she noticed Hope was wearing a black T-shirt with a mock turtleneck beneath it. Also black. "Are you crazy? You're going to melt."

Hope fiddled with the neckline but said nothing.

Suspicion filled Mia, and reaching out, she peeled the neck of the material away from the kid.

"Hey!" She slapped Mia's hand away, but not before Mia saw the evidence.

"Damn it, you have a hickey!"

Hope crossed her arms over her chest and slunk into the seat. "So?"

Mia pulled up to the teen center and turned to Hope. "So sex can be as bad for your health as cigarettes."

"Jeez, I'm not having sex!"

"You're not?"

"No, Aunt Apple, that would be *you*." She flicked at Mia's collar, revealing Kevin's whisker burns.

They stared at each other, Hope's gaze filling with a slow, seething resentment.

"Okay," Mia said, fixing her collar again. "Okay, listen. Maybe we both need to slow down a little."

"I'm not the one with the false accusations, thank you very much."

"I mean in general. Maybe try to be less . . . worldly, and more . . . tolerant of each other."

Hope arched a brow. "*You're* going to be more tolerant?"

"Hey, I will if you will."

Hope's nose nearly hit the top of the Audi. "I'm perfectly tolerant."

"Then what's with all the screwing with the music,

the phones lines, the ice makers of the world? You're practically shouting *Look at me, I need attention!*"

Hope rolled her eyes. "Fine. Maybe I could be slightly more tolerant of your life."

That seemed too easy, and Mia eyed her a moment. "So you're going to stay out of trouble today?"

"Yeah." Hope was staring at the high school. "I wish I could take summer school."

"You'll be home this weekend. By Monday you can be signed up—"

"Here. I want to take the science class here. With Kevin. He said I could add it—"

"Hold on." Mia removed her seat belt and turned in her seat to face Hope. "You talked to Kevin about this?"

"Well, yeah. He said it was no big deal to add—"

No big deal? Jesus. What did he know of her life? Or the additional stress this would cause? "Hope," she said gently. "You're going home this weekend."

"Right." Hope looked down at her clenched hands. "Because you hate having me here."

"Now, listen—"

"No, I get it. Loud and clear. Nice tolerance, Aunt Apple." She opened the passenger door and sprinted out toward the teen center.

"Hope!"

But the kid didn't stop.

Mia watched her go, thinking she was getting good at alienating people. Real good.

•

Chapter Fifteen

At the teen center, Kevin paced his office and looked at his watch. Again. There was a staff meeting this morning with a couple members of the board, who were in the kitchen getting their coffee, waiting for Kevin. And Mike. In less than sixty seconds, Mike was going to be late. Damn it, he'd woken him up with plenty of time to get here, and now—

The door opened. Mike poked his head in. Smiled, though it didn't quite meet his eyes.

Kevin let out the breath he'd been holding and pointed to his watch.

Mike lifted his wrist. *Sorry, no watch.*

Kevin shook his head. *You've got to get it together.*

Mike's not-quite-real smile faded entirely. *Gee, Mom, relax.*

You were nearly late.

Nearly doesn't count except in horseshoes and hand grenades.

Yeah, yeah, let's go. He moved to the door but then hesitated, fighting the urge to give Mike a list. Remember to look into their eyes. Remember to keep your cool. Remember . . .

But determination and pride blazed from Mike's eyes, and Kevin didn't sign a word except *It's going to be fine.*

Mike stared at him, then let some of the smile come back. *Always is.*

Hope tried to not seethe with resentment watching Adam play Ping-Pong with Amber, a popular girl with perfect hair, perfect makeup, and a perfect body clad in bright sunshine yellow. Hope needed sunglasses just to look at her.

Feeling someone's eyes on her, she looked up and found Cole watching her. She hadn't talked to him since that day she'd seen him go out Kevin's classroom window and had driven the Audi over the field to give him a ride—or would have given him a ride if Kevin hadn't stopped them.

She hadn't avoided him on purpose—well, maybe she had a little. It was just that he was no more popular than she was, and she'd wanted something different here.

Not that *that* had materialized for her.

Cole smiled. Embarrassed to have been caught staring at Adam, she looked away. Her metal belt cut into her hips, her stud bracelets clanked together noisily as she walked to the electronic dartboard on the wall, and suddenly she wished she wasn't wearing any of it.

There was a game in progress, with a group of middle schoolers. These kids were younger and actually seemed to like her, so she stayed, regaling them with her stories, all of which were made up, of course. She had an entire background fabricated: she was the lone daughter of a wealthy couple who were older and traveled to places like the Greek islands and east Africa. At the moment, they were on a world cruise and she was stuck here with Mia against her will because her nanny had run off with their chef. In fact, her aunt hated having her here, hated it so much that she threatened to beat Hope every single night if Hope didn't perform a long list of chores like she was Cinderella or something.

Just yesterday Adam had been totally impressed by the story, but today he was busy with Amber.

It was because she hadn't put out the other night, she knew it. He'd been into her then. She should have just done it, gotten it over with.

Cole gestured to the darts. "Can I play?"

"All yours," Hope said and handed the darts over without looking at him. Undoing the top two buttons of her top, she headed for Adam.

He looked up when she got closer, and then took a second look at the visible mark he'd put on her neck.

Next to him, Amber frowned.

"Coming over tonight?" Hope murmured to Adam.

His gaze dropped to her breasts. "I don't know."

"Because I'm feeling *much* better," she assured him and absorbed his hungry smile.

Mia's day did not go as planned. She spent the morning at a client's office, and when she checked her messages, she had a cryptic "Call me" from Dick, and another, even more cryptic "Oh, boy" from Tess.

Neither answered her return call, and when she got back to her building and pushed the elevator button, the doors opened to reveal Tess.

She stepped off, holding a box with her personal items, and Mia's stomach rolled over. "What the hell?"

"Well, it's a good news, bad news sort of thing," Tess said like always, but utterly without the usual smile. In fact, her eyes were red, she wore no lip gloss, and her face was pale.

Mia's cell began to vibrate, but she ignored it, her eyes locked on Tess's face. "Bad news first."

Tess stepped off the elevator. "I quit."

"Oh, no you didn't." Mia tried to grab the box out of her hands.

Tess held firm. "Ask me for the good news."

"Tess—"

"Ask me."

"Fine. What's the good news?"

"After I quit, Dickhead fired me, so I think that means I can get unemployment."

"*What?*"

"Yeah." Tess shook her head and began to walk. "Ted is such an asshole."

"Tell me something I don't know." Mia turned and followed her through the huge lobby, with no idea where they were going.

"He got this sort of sick thrill by pushing my buttons, you know?"

Mia did know. It drove her crazy that Ted picked on Tess. But to work there without her warm, easy support . . . Damn it, Mia couldn't even imagine. "Go on," she said tightly.

"You've already heard all this. He kept giving me stuff to do that wasn't my job and wanting me to do it ahead of everyone else's stuff. It was rude, but I could have dealt with that." Tess was talking like this was no big deal, but Mia knew Tess needed this job financially.

And Mia needed her. Not financially, but in every other way. "Oh, Tess."

Tess stopped in front of the donut stand, put down her things, and bought a dozen. "He talked to me like I was an idiot, but I could handle that, too." She offered a donut to Mia, who felt like eating the whole box. "But this morning he was going through the other reps' sales files, yours included."

"*What?*"

"Yeah, looking at the trafficking reports, at your media research, all for the Anderson account. When

I caught him at it, he had the nerve to tell Dickhead
that *I* was setting him up to fail, that *I* wasn't giving
him important messages, that *I* was giving confiden-
tial information to other reps, doing everything I
could to sabotage him. And then he told Dickhead
that's how you got the Anderson account."

Mia stared at her. "This is insane. I'm going to get
your job back, Tess. I'm going to—"

Tess's eyes filled with tears, and Mia wanted to
kick something. Preferably Ted's balls.

"No," Tess said with a sniff. "Don't. Don't jeopar-
dize yourself."

"I don't care about that."

But Tess was shaking her head. "I won't come
back here."

"Tess—"

"I mean it, Mia. I won't, not even for you. I have
better things ahead for me."

"Like what?"

"Like . . . Cookie Madness."

Cookie Madness was a fun thing, a make-a-little-
extra-money thing, not a living thing. Mia put her
hands on Tess's arms, her throat tight. "Tess—"

"It's what I want."

Mia studied her best friend, felt her heart tug, and
nodded. "Then I'll help you."

"I'll count on it."

Mia ate an entire donut standing up. "What am I
going to do without you?"

"Oh, honey. You don't need me. You never have."
Leaning in, Tess kissed her on her cheek. "Your cell
is vibrating, I can hear it from here. Go on up. I'll
be okay."

"Tess—"

"Go. You have that meeting in twenty. If you lose
the Anderson account now, I'll never forgive you."

Mia's throat closed, and she watched Tess walk
away, head high. "Tess."

Tess turned back.

"You're sure?"

Tess's eyes were glittering with pride. "Very. Now go kick ass."

Oh, she intended to.

It felt so odd to be stressed about work, Mia thought on the drive home. Always she'd thrived on the intensity of it all, but suddenly it felt like too much. Tess was gone, Tami and Steven were gone, everyone else was nervous about the layoffs . . .

Well, except Margot, who, also now missing an assistant, asked Mia if she was going to walk off like Ted had, because she would like Mia's office.

Ted didn't say anything to Mia at all, but he didn't have to; his knowing smirk said it all.

And if work wasn't enough, Sugar left a message on Mia's cell saying this weekend was bad for her as well. And nothing, nothing at all, was as it should be in Mia's world.

Which reminded her, damn it, she had to pull over and do a U-turn because she'd forgotten Hope at the teen center.

Nice, Aunt Apple.

When she finally pulled up at the place, she found a car wash in action. High schoolers held up signs or directed cars toward more kids waiting with sponges and buckets.

Mia parked and got out in the blazing heat. Music boomed, and thanks to the education Hope had given her, she recognized 50 Cent rapping about all things sexual. The teens were mostly wet and soapy, having a grand old time as they washed cars for cash. In the beating-down heat, Mia searched the masses for Hope but couldn't find her.

Mike was exchanging hose warfare with two boys over a Honda; another group was doing the same over a Toyota truck. There was a gaggle of girls wriggling signs that read HELP US KEEP OUR TEEN CENTER, LET US WASH YOUR CAR, HAND WASH!!

She saw a man in front of a Jeep filling a bucket from the hose. Bent at the waist, he was shirtless, his jeans rolled up to his shins, feet bare. Kevin straightened, his torso broad and leanly muscled, his belly flat and ridged. His gaze locked right on her, hose still held loosely in his hand at his side as he smiled.

Mia got hotter, and she realized she'd smiled first, a big, fat dopey one. Good Lord, she needed to have that fixed. No smiling. Not today. Today sucked.

Dropping the hose, Kevin came toward her in that loose-limbed, easy gait he had. "Hey."

"Hey yourself. So how many more cars do you need to wash to buy the teen center?" she asked, her pulse quickening for no reason other than he looked damn good.

"Just about every single one in the state of California."

She sighed. "I'm sorry."

"Yeah. Thanks."

"Where's Hope?" She tore her gaze off him and searched the crowd. "I don't see her."

"Look again," he suggested and pointed back toward the Jeep.

Mia swiped her damp forehead and scanned the group. Just a girl in jean cutoffs and a white T-shirt working the sponge over the wet windows, her hair stuffed beneath a Dodgers baseball cap. "I don't see—" Her gaze froze, widened. "My God."

Kevin laughed.

The girl was Hope, sans black clothing, sans black makeup. "I can't believe it. Where's all the black?"

"She got wet and borrowed some clothes from another girl."

"Ah, so the change is only temporary."

Kevin shrugged. "I don't know. Maybe you should

tell her you hate it, and then she'll keep at it." At her soft agreeing laugh, he shifted a little closer and ran a finger over her cheek. "So what's up with you today?"

His voice was warm and deep, and sent a bolt of pure lust through her so that she crossed her arms over her hopeful nipples. "Nothing."

"You are such a liar. A pretty one, but a liar nonetheless." He stepped even closer.

Stressed and weak and down, she became extremely aware of his bare torso, tough with strength, a golden red from being in the sun. Broad shoulders on which to set her head. Lust she could deal with. But the yearning that followed that lust was hard to take. "Just a bad day," she finally answered. *I want to bite you and then lick you from head to toe . . .*

"Queen Mia." He let out another laugh that somehow made her want to press her face to the crook of his neck and hold on.

Hold on.

Terrifying thought. "I'm not the queen of much today," she admitted, and at his easy, thoughtful look that said *Tell me all about it*, she felt her throat tighten. "Tess got fired, my new account is being taken over by the king of all assholes, and Sugar is too busy for her own daughter."

"Been through the wringer today, have you?"

"To say the least."

"You could keep Hope."

"I can't do that."

"Why?"

"Why?" She searched for the reasons, telling herself there were just so many. "Because I have a life."

"Right. And it's full and perfect, right? No need to make any changes to it, not when you have it all."

"Don't start with me."

"Oh, that's right. I'm only good for the stress relief. The horizontal kind."

She felt a reluctant smile tug at her lips. "Horizontal? We've been vertical plenty, as I recall."

He looked at her mouth and shook his head, an unwilling smile on his own lips. "I do like the look of that smile on you."

She met his eyes, saw the flicker of heat and reluctant affection, and felt some reluctant affection of her own kick in. Damn it. "You look good all wet and soapy, Mr. McKnight."

"You trying to change the subject?"

She opened her purse and pulled out a twenty. "For the cause?"

He arched a brow. "You want me to wash your car?"

"Yep, while I watch. Unless my money isn't good here."

He snatched the twenty from her fingers, then waved at Mike, who sauntered over, dressed pretty much the same as Kevin. He took the twenty and stuck it in a cash box.

Kevin signed something, and Mike grinned as he walked away.

"What did you tell him?" Mia asked, shifting her feet on the baking asphalt.

"That I was going to give you the works."

"Hey!"

"Your car." His expression was all innocence. "I was talking about your car. Wait here. I'll call Hope over to help."

"Yeah, about that . . . " Mia winced. "That sucky day I mentioned? It also includes the disagreement we got into this morning. She's not happy with me."

"Well, it's possible her day has been worse than yours. There's apparently some question of whether Adam is going out with Hope or Amber."

Mia followed Kevin's gaze to a pretty little blonde, leading a cheer on the sidewalk to attract more cars.

She was everything Mia—and Hope—had never been. "That punk."

She swiped a hand over her hot, damp face. "He gave Hope a hickey."

"I saw."

Of course he'd seen; he didn't miss a thing. "I'm going to kill him."

"They didn't have sex," Kevin said.

"But she knows *we* did," Mia said. "And she thinks I'm the biggest hypocrite out there."

"Ah. That makes sense then."

She looked at him warily and tried not to wilt in the heat. "I'm not going to like this, am I?"

He sighed. "She's been telling stories."

"Runaway stories?"

"More like . . . lies."

"Oh, boy. What's she saying?"

"She's just talking, being a teenager, trying to fit in."

"What's she saying?"

"That she's from some rich family and they've dumped her with you for the summer and you're treating her like Cinderella before the ball. Any of that background stuff true?"

"Are you kidding me? You know it's not."

His eyes never left hers. "How would I know? You've never told me anything of your past."

"Okay, you know what? It's too hot for this. I'm just going to take her home."

Kevin splashed the hose over her feet, making her gasp with the sudden cold.

She stared down at her silky, strappy heels. "These are Jimmy Choo's," she said in shock. "You can't just—"

He did it again, splashing just a bit higher now, past her ankles nearly to her knees. Water spots appeared on the bottom of her pleasant D&G skirt. *"Hey!"*

"Oops."

Mia narrowed her eyes and took the last step between them, putting them toe-to-toe, and if she'd been a foot taller, nose-to-nose. "I'll have you know these shoes are expensive."

"And I'll have you know that haughty tone you use when you're irritated really turns me on. It's sick, I know, but true."

"You don't want to play with me. Trust me. I always win."

He flashed a slow and utterly wicked smile. "Did you know that when you're backed into a corner, your Southern accent shines right through?"

"I'm not—"

"Oh, that's right. We don't talk about that. Or your past. You don't even cop to having one."

Echoes of Tess saying the same thing went through her head. "My past is too complicated to discuss in this heat." She reached for the hose, but he evaded.

"I've got air-conditioning at home," he said.

"You said you weren't going to answer the door to me anymore." She again tried to snatch the hose from him, but he pulled back and, in the guise of pointing it at her car, missed entirely.

And nailed her legs, making her gasp again.

From behind them, the kids began to notice and let out a bunch of whistles and *woo hoos*. "Water fight!" someone yelled.

That was all they needed to hear. With shrieks of laughter and screams, the kids turned on each other.

In the midst of it all, Kevin took a step toward Mia, a wicked light of intent in his eyes.

She backed up, her butt hitting her car. "I mean it. Don't you even think about—"

The hose hit her thighs and belly, and laughing, she finally grabbed the hose and pointed it at Kevin's chest, nailing him full blast. He burst out laughing, the sound even sexier than his voice, and then just stepped through the spray toward her. Pulling a total girl, she screamed, dropped the hose, and went running around the Jeep, ducking down on the far side of it.

"Aunt Apple?"

Mia opened her eyes from her crouch by the passenger door and came face-to-face with Hope. Or at least she thought it was Hope. With a cap on and her face devoid of makeup, she looked like a different girl entirely, sweet and pretty. And fairly shocked.

"Are you . . . *squealing*?" Hope asked in a disbelieving voice.

"Apparently, yes." She would marvel over that shocking fact later. "I'll pay you twenty bucks to sidetrack Kevin so I can get him."

Hope's eyes widened. "Twenty?"

"Okay, forty."

Hope just stared at her.

"*Sixty.* Come on, Hope. Help me out here."

Hope shook her head, looking bowled over. "I'd have done it for nothing, you know."

"Have I taught you nothing? Aim higher, girl."

"Yeah." Hope touched the cap, looking a bit self-conscious. "I'm, um, sorry about this morning."

Mia blinked in surprise, but the girl was gone. She waited a minute, then, assuming Hope wanted that sixty bucks, stood up. No Kevin in sight. Perfect. She tiptoed toward a forgotten bucket filled with soapy water, her heels squishing all the way. Damn him. She took another quick look around.

Still no Kevin. This was too good to be true.

Without warning, she was grabbed from behind and pulled against an extremely wet, warm, hard chest. "Gotcha," Kevin said low and husky in her ear, tightening his arms on her as he laughed softly.

Goose bumps rose everywhere, but pride dictated that she struggle. "When I get free," she vowed, "I'm going to get you."

"Promise?"

"Let go!"

Another soft laugh. "I don't think so."

"Let go or I'll . . ." Hard enough to think when he held her like he did; harder still to maintain her righteous dignity.

"You'll what?" he goaded. "Make it good now."

"I'll get Hope to rewire your house so that every time you switch on an appliance, country music blasts at earsplitting decibels throughout your house."

"Nice one." But he still held on to her, his arms banded tight around her middle, the fingers of his left hand spread wide and nearly, just nearly, brushing her breast. "Face it, Mia. I won. And I'm going to claim my prize."

Her nipples went happy. "Dream on. There's kids watching."

He laughed again, and even though she kept squirming, he didn't let her go. "Not everything is about sex."

"Between us it is."

For a beat, he went utterly still. Then he bit lightly on her ear, making her hiss in a breath, and not in pain. "It's not *all* about sex," he repeated. "And I'm going to prove it to you. Tonight. Dinner. With me."

"As in a date?"

"Yeah."

"I don't—"

"See you at six thirty." With that, he let her go and walked away.

"I didn't say yes!" she yelled after him.

He didn't even look back, the bastard.

Well, fine. But she wasn't going. No way. Not going to get in a restaurant and stare at him over

flickering candles and wine, and talk . . . Not going
to ride on the back of that motorcycle, clinging to his
hard, warm body. Not going to go home with him
and let that body make hers sing.

Ah, hell. She was going to go.

Chapter Sixteen

Kevin came down the stairs, and Mike took his gaze off the TV long enough to sign, *Scary woman left you a text message.*

Who?

Beth. Mike used the remote to flick through the channels with a speed that suggested annoyance. The volume was earsplitting, not that he could tell, but after a minute he tossed the remote aside to sign in quick, agitated gestures. *She said to tell you she'd like a conjugal visit tonight, and bring dinner.*

Kevin laughed. *She did not say that.*

Word for word. Since when is she sniffing around you again?

Since Amber is at the teen center for the summer. Beth's under the misguided impression I'm a better catch these days.

Mike took in what Kevin was wearing and raised a brow.

Kevin looked down at himself. He'd showered and put on fresh jeans and a clean black T-shirt. Given who Mia probably usually dated—*not* high school science teachers on a budget—this was probably slumming it. The TV, still at earsplitting decibels, was driving him crazy, so he grabbed the remote. *Loud enough for you?*

Mike's face closed. *Sorry if I can't hear it.*

The old stab of guilt still brought pain. He knew it, and Mike knew it.

Sometimes he knew Mike liked knowing it. *Look, Mia and I are going to dinner. Want me to bring you something?*

So you're going to get fed before she does you this time. That's nice.

Kevin's jaw ticked. *Do you want something or not?*

I'm going to Tess's.

She might not be up to it, she—

Quit. I know, we've been text-messaging. She says she's pissed, but I think she's sad. I'm going to cheer her up.

Kevin thought of Mia, and how protective of Tess she was. If Mike fooled around with Tess, as was his custom with women, and then dumped her in about a week, also his custom, Mia would kill him. *Maybe you should call Kim. Or Carrie. Or how about—*

Tess.

Yes, but Monica called you, just this morning, said you hadn't gone out with her in weeks. I bet she'd take you clubbing.

Mike's smile faded. *Last time I went clubbing, you had to bail me out of jail. I thought you'd be thrilled I was doing this. You have a problem with Tess?*

No, I have a problem with you screwing around with her and then dumping her.

Mike stared at him. *How do you know she's not the one?*

Kevin laughed.

Mike's face tightened. *You're that sure I'm going to fuck it up?*

Kevin didn't know what to say to that without starting the fight that Mike was clearly looking for. *What's the big deal? Just find another woman to play with.*

Why don't you?

What are you talking about?

Or are you going to come home dragging your heart behind you again.

What does that mean?

Mike stood up. *It means you're one to talk. You're currently sleeping with the female equivalent of me. You ever think of that? Yet another person in your life that is broken but doesn't want to be fixed. Yet another person in your life for you to anguish over, and in this case, get screwed over.*

Kevin stared at Mike, hearing the words as if his brother had actually spoken them, feeling them settle into his chest. *I don't have time for this shit.*

Right. Because it's about you this time. Mike nodded agreeably. *You never have time to deal with yourself, only others. Go. Go get fucked tonight. Literally and figuratively, see if I care.*

Whatever. Kevin strode to the door, feeling far more suited to be heading to an aggressive basketball game than a date.

But maybe a date with Mia would be right up his alley. Maybe for once he'd do this her way. Get all his aggressions and stress out with a spectacular orgasm. And then move on.

Yeah, sounded perfect. But he slammed the door to make it even more perfect. Too bad Mike couldn't hear it.

Mia dialed Sugar's number, and while she waited impatiently someone hit the doorbell. Still waiting on Sugar to pick up the phone on her end, Mia pulled open the door, then found herself momentarily struck by the sight of Kevin standing there looking a little attitude-ridden, a little edgy, a little like he wanted to take her up against the doorjamb. Her heart kicked hard.

"Hello" came Sugar's cranky, Southern voice in

her ear, as always with perfect timing. "Who the hell is this?"

"It's Mia."

"Well, listen to you, all fancy LA voice. I've gotten your messages. I suppose you're wanting money for those plane tickets I'm not using this weekend. And maybe for taking care of Hope all this time."

"What? No, I don't want money for taking care of Hope, or the tickets. I just want to see when I can reschedule the flights. I thought—"

"I'm busy then."

Mia's eye twitched. "But I didn't say when."

"Yeah. See, the thing is, I'm having some troubles. Mental ones." Sugar's voice lowered, as if this was a state secret. "I'm having a breakdown on a account of my daughter driving me insane. There's this thirty-day recovery period, or so my doctor says."

Thirty days, her ass. "Sugar." Calm. Be calm. "You can't just desert your daughter for thirty more days."

"Oh, but see, that's the beauty of this. I'm not deserting her at all. She's with you. And you're family. I'll call you in August. Okay?"

"*August!*"

"Otherwise, I just don't know what I'll do. Please, Mia. Look, I know I've been a shit to you while she's been there—"

"How about for all my life?"

Sugar sighed. "I was kinda hoping you were over some of that early stuff."

Now Mia sighed. "I am."

"Then, please. For me."

"I'll think about it," she said, because suddenly Sugar really did sound like she was on the very edge. "But—"

But nothing. She was talking to a dial tone. "Damn it." She hit the OFF button with her thumb and tossed the phone to the couch. *"Damn it."*

"Maybe it won't be as bad as you think."

Whirling around, she focused. Gorgeous, edgy guy standing in her foyer, holding an extra helmet, which set her hormones all aquiver as if she was—"A teenager," she said. And slapped her forehead. "Oh, my God, I'm thinking like a teenager. What kind of influence can I possibly be? I can't do this. I can't." She set her fingers to her twitching eye. "I have no idea how to do this."

Kevin sighed and set the helmet down. "It's going to be okay."

"Really? How? How is it going to be okay? By August I won't have any eardrums left, or a job for that matter. Kevin, I have no idea what I'm doing here," she admitted quietly.

"It's a one-day-at-a-time thing," he assured her with a lopsided smile that seemed slightly self-mocking as he took her hand. "Trust me on this. Where's Hope now?"

"Upstairs. Tess is coming by to get her. They're going to make cookie dough. I guess your brother is joining them."

Kevin laughed. "Hope'll make a good chaperone."

"Do they need one?"

He ran his finger over the furrow between her brows. "Stop worrying."

"Easier said than done."

"Know what you need? A ride."

Her tummy quivered. "Is your house empty?"

He stared at her, then let out a low laugh. "I meant on the bike."

Damn it. "I knew that."

He shook his head and took her hand. "Let's get out of here before I forget why we have to."

"Yeah, about that . . ." She dragged her feet. "Kevin, what are we doing?"

"Getting some food, and hopefully some laughs while we're at it. Sounds like we both need it."

"I meant more generally than that."

"I know. Just come out with me tonight. Let's see where it goes. No plan, no media blitz, no campaign, no expectations."

She had to smile. "Yeah, okay."

They rode over the canyons toward the ocean, and as always the experience was both visceral and sensual, almost overwhelmingly so. Mia leaned into Kevin with every turn, her breath catching with wonder at how it felt to have such power between her legs, the utter exhilaration of being so exposed to the elements.

Not to mention the feel of the man she clung to. Every inch of her legs brushed his, his broad back making a perfect resting spot for her breasts and belly.

And, God, he smelled seriously *dee-lish.* It should be illegal to smell that good. The evening wind was warm from the long summer day, and the sound of it almost tuned out the rest of the world.

They ended up at a small outdoor café in Malibu, where they shared a finger salad and a huge club sandwich. With the ocean pounding the surf as the sun set, Mia sighed with an odd comfort. "Teaching seems like an odd vocation for a rebel," she said and picked up an olive.

"A rebel." He grinned. "You only say that because of the bike."

"Yeah, I like the bike a lot," she admitted. And the man on it . . .

He bit into his sandwich and, watching her, chewed thoughtfully. "If I'm a so-called rebel, it's only because rules don't seem to agree with me much. Or authority, for that matter."

"But to be a teacher and not respect authority . . ."

"I didn't say I didn't respect it," he said. "But I do believe in showing these kids, or people in general, that it's okay to have your own thoughts, to do things your own way. As long as it's legal," he corrected and shook his head. "We're still working on that in my classroom. And my house."

"Yeah, about your brother. You two live together. Have you always?"

"Wait." He cocked his head. "Was that . . . a personal question?"

She rolled her eyes. "Maybe. But it's for Tess, not me. Are you two close?"

He smiled. "Better be careful there, you're going to get to know me."

"Funny," she said. "Now answer the question. He's had trouble keeping jobs."

"Some."

"So you help him out."

"Yeah. People discriminate against him for his hearing loss, you know? He pretends it doesn't matter, but it does. And, yeah, I help him out."

"Does he appreciate it?"

"Sometimes." He laughed roughly. "Actually, mostly no."

"Ah. So you gather and collect the needy," she said. "Whether they like it or not. Is that it?"

"No. That's not it." He stuffed another bite in, chewed some more. "Okay, maybe," he conceded after swallowing. "Actually, we just fought about this very thing. About you, actually."

She straightened in immediate defense mode. "Me? Why?"

"Mike thinks I tend to put people in my life that need fixing. People that don't want to be fixed. Himself included."

Mia connected the dots and felt a frown gather. "Well, he's right there. I don't want to be fixed, so don't even try."

He lifted his hands as if in surrender. "Wouldn't even think of it."

"Because we're just . . . you know. Releasing steam."

"Right." He nodded sagely. "Nothing else. Not friendship, or affection, or more."

Her breath caught, jammed in her throat. "Well, maybe a little bit of that."

Leaning over, he pulled off her mirrored sunglasses.

"Hey," she protested.

"The sun is down. Your retinas are no longer in danger."

But what about her heart?

"That's the first time you've admitted we're more than bed partners. I wanted to see your eyes."

Her stomach jangled. "I said 'little' bit more. You heard that part, right?"

He laughed softly. "Were you always like this? So independent? So . . . closed off?"

"You think I'm closed off?"

"Definitely not in bed. But out of it, yeah."

She stared at him, then looked away, where the waves hit the beach with a rhythm that soothed. "I have not been plied with enough alcohol for this."

Without missing a beat, Kevin lifted a hand, gestured to the waitress for another beer.

When she brought it, Mia took a long sip and said, "I have no idea why my guard is always down around you."

He smiled, looking quite pleased with himself. "I've worn you down."

"This isn't funny. I don't like to think about my past, about where I came from."

"Why?"

"Because it reminds me that I was once nothing. Less than nothing. It makes me feel vulnerable, like in a blink of fate I could find myself there again."

"Seems to me, Mia, we make our own fate. You've

certainly made yours. You know exactly who you are. No one can take that from you."

But she didn't know. Not that she could admit that. "I'm sorry." She pushed away the beer. "I lied. I'm not ready to do this, not even with all the alcohol in the joint."

Accepting this with his usual easy grace, he easily moved the conversation on, in no time enthralling her with the antics of his students, whether it be climbing out the windows or their fondness for the burners in the back of the classroom.

"Tell me it wasn't Adam," she said of his mysterious pot smoker.

Kevin shot her a long look.

"*Shit.* Why couldn't it be someone nice and sweet lusting after Hope?"

"She's smart, she'll figure him out. There's also another kid who likes her. The one I told you about, Cole."

"Terrific."

"Cole's a good guy."

He spoke quietly and from the heart. The kids meant a lot to him, all of them, she could tell. "I bet you're amazing at what you do," she said softly.

"The best," he agreed and made her laugh. He did that a lot, she noted, and they continued to talk over ice cream, where she discovered he'd gone to UCLA as well.

"I went to junior college first," he said. "And then into UCLA poorer than dirt."

"I've been poorer than dirt," she said without thinking and then stared at him. "There I go again. What is it about you that makes my mouth run?"

He just smiled and let her think about it. Afterward he paid for the bill even though she reached for it, and then took her hand to walk through the restaurant. She excused herself to go to the restroom, and when she came out, saw him waiting for her in the reception area, which had gotten crowded. He had his back to her and was talking to a tall, willowy, gorgeous blonde. The same one who'd been at the teen center, the one who'd practically screamed *old money*. As Mia moved closer she heard the woman say, "I've changed my wicked ways. I won't leave claw marks this time, promise."

Whoa.

"Beth." Kevin let out a low laugh and shoved a hand through his hair, a gesture Mia recognized as discomfort. "I can't."

"What is it, another woman? Who could be more important than your ex-wife?"

Mia absorbed that with a little shock of jealousy, which was not only stupid, but made no sense. The ex. The one he'd married when he was eighteen. The one who'd broken his heart.

"The thing is," Kevin said. "There's an *ex* in *ex*-wife for a reason."

"Damn it," Blond Woman said. "Don't give me that. We were kids and I was stupid. I want another shot at you."

Mia would have given anything to see Kevin's face. Did he want another chance, too?

And what would she do if he did?

She didn't realize she was holding her breath until Kevin shook his head. "Beth—"

"Don't tell me no."

"I know the word is foreign to you, I know. But no. There's someone else."

"Ditch her."

"Yeah." Kevin laughed roughly. "Can't do that."

"Why not? You in love or something?"

At that, Mia laughed to herself. Love. Yeah, right. As if he'd fall in love with *her*.

But Kevin didn't laugh. "Actually," he said, his back still to Mia, "I don't know yet."

Mia gasped and Kevin whipped around to face

her, and if Mia had thought she couldn't breathe before, she was really screwed now. "I . . . have to go,"
she said brilliantly.

"Mia." He grimaced. "I—"

"No. Listen, I really have to go."

"I think it was the L-word," Beth told Kevin with
a *tsk*. "She lost all her color at that, did you notice?"

"I—I'm sorry." Mia couldn't draw air into her
taxed lungs. "I really have to go."

"Yeah, that's the classic kiss-off," Beth said to
Kevin helpfully.

"If you could just zip it for a minute," he said.

Beth shrugged. "Sure. I'll meet you in the bar
when she's done dumping you."

Kevin ignored her and looked at Mia again, who
swallowed hard.

"I'm not the falling-in-love sort of woman," she
whispered. "I don't even get close enough to have
this conversation. I don't even like to repeat."

"You repeated me."

"I know, I just don't know why."

"Don't you?"

"Look, I'm not good at sharing myself. In fact, I
don't share at all. I think I missed that day in
kindergarten."

"So what now then?" he asked. "Are you freaking
out and walking away?"

"Oh, I'm freaking out." She put a hand to her racing heart, looked at her legs. "But I don't appear to
be walking away."

He let out a breath.

"Of course I can't walk because my legs turned to
rubber and I can't feel my toes."

At that, he smiled, the one that always made her
feel everything was going to be okay, and reached
for her hand. "How about we just take it one step at
a time?"

She felt his long, strong fingers entwined with hers,

and could suddenly breathe. "As long as you're not in a hurry."

"No hurry," he promised. "Let's get out of here?"

He took her to the beach, where they kicked off their shoes and let their toes sink into the sand, still warm from the sun of the day.

With her Choo's dangling from her fingers, Mia stared out at the pounding surf. "I can feel my toes again."

He smiled.

"What?"

"Nothing. You just said that with a very Southern accent, that's all."

Mia scrubbed a hand over her face.

"I like the sound of it."

"It's Tennessee. I'm Southern white trash from a single-wide stuffed to the gills with crap."

"Tennessee is pretty. And there's nothing wrong with living in a trailer, if that's your life."

"It was," she said quietly. "For far too long. Hope feels the same. It's why she's here. I can't believe she's staying another month. God help the both of us."

"It'll be good."

"Said the man who doesn't have to listen to her music or live in fear of flipping on a light switch and having the doorbell go off instead."

"Is it that bad?" he asked quietly.

She stared at him. Shook her head. "I hate that I waited sixteen years to get to know her," she whispered. "But I wish like hell I could have eased into this instead of going from no contact to a full-time gig."

"Well, that's honest, at least."

She let out a breath. "Yeah."

"Put her in my science class. It's where she wants to be anyway."

Mia turned to him, took in the strong lines of his

body and face, and felt some of her tension release. He wasn't going to be scared off, as she might have been. He wasn't going to do anything but accept her. The realization was like a breath of fresh air. "You'll still add her?"

"I can't wait to add her. She's smart, Mia." Kevin leaned in and touched his lips to hers, and she felt the shocking urge to cling. *Cling.* "And so are you," he said. "You'll both find the happy medium. If you want it."

If she wanted it . . . If she wanted it . . .

He was still looking at her, and now he was closer than he'd been. Mia had no idea how badly she wanted his mouth on hers until he leaned in and gave her just that, put his warm, sexy lips to hers with a soft, low sound that scraped at her belly. His hands came up and cradled her face, his fingers sinking into her hair as the taste and smell of him surrounded her like the soft mist from the ocean at her back. The kiss seemed to flow all the way through her, along her veins, in time to the beat of her heart, much deeper than she'd imagined, igniting all sorts of sensations.

His fingers tightened on her, and he made a low, lost noise that had her pressing her body closer, closer still, hungry in a way she couldn't remember feeling, hungry and needy. They kissed and kissed like that, until a wave splashed over their feet, making her gasp.

He pulled back and slowly opened his eyes, as if he needed a moment, and she knew the feeling. She put a hand on his jaw, mesmerized by him, pulled in by him like the gravitational pull of the tide.

"What was that for?" she whispered, her voice a little hoarse.

"To show you the happy medium. It's right there, for the taking."

The words haunted her on the long, lovely, dark

ride home through the night while holding on to a warm, hard body she most definitely wanted next to hers.

Kevin enjoyed the ride as well, and especially the arms around him holding him tight. When he turned off the bike and pulled off his helmet, he turned to Mia. "Cold?"

"No." Mia let out a long sigh that sounded blissful, and slowly, almost reluctantly it seemed, slipped her arms from around his middle—or maybe that was just wishful yearning on his part.

But slip away she did, pulling off the helmet, tossing back her hair. "I could do that every night."

Worked for him.

"I hear you go out sometimes, you know. I lie in bed and think *Lucky bastard*."

"Join me anytime."

She handed him the helmet. "Anytime is a pretty wide-open invite."

"I mean it."

She didn't respond to that, and he knew she was considering the offer, maybe putting it up against the other things he'd said tonight.

"Let me walk you inside," he said and reached for her hand.

"Actually . . ." She met his gaze, her own steady and warming with each passing second. "I was thinking I'd walk *you* inside."

She brushed her mouth over his jaw as he unlocked his front door. Then, when she followed him in, she turned to face him and fastened her mouth to his throat. "Your bike makes me hot," she murmured between nibbles. She slid her arms around his neck and tugged his mouth to hers. "Hurry up and get your mouth on me."

He couldn't think when she looked at him like that, like she was already halfway to orgasmic bliss and only he could get her the rest of the way. To slow her down, he captured her hands and held her arms out to her sides.

"Kevin? What are you doing?"

"Looking at you." Her work clothes fascinated him, but tonight she wore tight black jeans and a long, sleeveless black-and-silvery sheer tunic sort of thing, with a black camisole beneath. He hadn't been able to take his eyes off her. He pulled off the tunic while she tugged his light jacket off his shoulders, gliding her hands beneath his shirt, shoving it up to put her mouth on his pec, making his muscles jump and quiver as she spread hot, open-mouthed kisses across his chest. "God. Why are you wearing so many clothes?"

With all the blood in his brain draining south for the cause, he couldn't talk. He reached for her instead, but his arms caught at his side, trapped in the jacket hanging at his elbows. "Damn it."

She let out a breathless laugh and popped open his Levi's. "I love your body. I could just eat you up. How did you get to be so gorgeous?"

Flapping his arms, he let the jacket fall off. Then he tore off his shirt and made the same haste with hers. One quick tug had her camisole to her waist, her breasts free. He filled his hands with them while she kicked off her heels. "My jeans," she said breathlessly. "Hurry."

In a blink, he had her jeans off, his down, and a condom on. Whipping them around, he pressed her back against the door and lifted her up, wrapping her legs around him. "Hold on," he demanded and thrust into her, her soft cry mingling with his low groan. It was all he could do to hold them upright. He had no idea how he could need her this way, crave her like water, but somehow she filled him, just as he now filled her.

As if she felt the same, she stared into his eyes as

she held on tight, allowing him to see her, the hunger, the want, the need, the affection, all of it, and it staggered him.

In that moment, something within him shifted, changed. *Fell.* It was as if he could see, for that one beat, every bit of her, all the way to her heart and soul. She was accepting him, maybe for the first time, wanting him, letting him in. He almost lost it on that alone because, though he'd wanted this very thing from her, he hadn't been sure she had it to give. Throat thick, he touched his forehead to hers.

"Please," she whispered, gliding her hands up his back.

Yeah, I'll please, he thought and began to move, thrusting in and out until she shattered in his arms, eyes glazed but open on his, mouth trembling as his name tumbled with shock from her lips. He lasted another whole big whopping two seconds before he let himself go as well. His knees buckled as he shuddered into his powerful climax, and he took them both down to the floor. "Jesus," he breathed, then murmured it again on a shaky sigh, brushing his lips over her hair. "You're going to kill me," he said.

"Mmm. But what a way to go." She looked hot and damp and extremely proud of herself. Propping a hand on his still-heaving chest, she leaned in and kissed him. "Thanks."

He blinked when she got up. *"Thanks?"*

"Yeah. I needed that." She slipped back into her jeans, then her heels. And then, while he was still trying to gather his wits, flat on his back on the floor, his pants still at his thighs, she pulled open the front door.

"No. You are not—"

But he was talking to himself because she was already gone. "—leaving."

He stared up at his ceiling, wondering if she'd thanked him for dinner, the orgasm, or for just plain being an idiot.

Chapter Seventeen

Monday morning, Hope came downstairs, groggy and sleepy and wishing mornings didn't come so early. Mia liked to get up at the crack of dawn, which proved it—they couldn't really be related.

Over the weekend, Mia had taken her shopping in Beverly Hills, where the prices had given her sticker shock.

And then Hope had taken Mia shopping in return—to Target, where Mia was coaxed into buying a pair of sweats that actually looked quite comfortable. They'd had fun, a fact that surprised both of them.

All weekend, Hope's cell phone had been vibrating with messages from Adam. She'd saved them and read every single one over and over. All she had to do was call him or text him back, but she knew what he wanted, what he expected, and though she'd thought she was ready, she wasn't.

It's just that Friday night, at Tess's, they'd watched a movie with subtitles for Mike, who Hope kept forgetting was deaf because he was so . . . normal. She'd sat in Tess's small but comfortable living room, watching Mike make Tess smile. An odd envy had twisted through her, which made no sense. She could have called Adam . . .

And maybe if he'd looked at her like Mike looked at Tess, she would have. All warm and safe.

But nothing about it seemed safe. Truthfully, being with him reminded her of being back home. Sugar's guys always made her feel a little uncomfortable, too, and a little weird. It felt disloyal to think it, and just a little mean, but she couldn't help it.

And as Sugar hadn't shown up, the feeling must be mutual. Mia had made excuses for Sugar, but Hope knew the truth. Her momma didn't want her back. With a sigh, she moved toward the kitchen, hoping there were still donuts, but she couldn't count on it since her aunt had developed a fondness for them, too.

From the kitchen came Mia's voice. "You win, Sugar," Mia said clearly on the phone. "Take your damn thirty days."

Thirty days? Hope's heart jerked with hopeful excitement. Had she heard right? She opened the kitchen door in time to hear Mia say, "But at the end, you'd better— Hey!" Her aunt pulled the phone away from her ear and stared at it. "She hung up on me. *Bitch*—" She broke off when she caught sight of Hope standing in the doorway. She let out a little smile, though it seemed a little strained.

Hope couldn't blame her, seeing as she'd just been shit on by Sugar. Hope knew the feeling well. "Hi."

"Hi back atcha. Want some breakfast? I've actually managed to boil water for oatmeal."

"No, thanks." Hope's happy little bubble had burst, leaving her feeling just a little sick. How she'd forgotten, even for a second, that Mia didn't want her, either, was beyond her. "I can walk to the teen center this morning."

"Driving you is no problem. Kevin told me he ordered the parts for your car."

This was thrown in so casually Hope blinked. "He . . . did? But I don't have the money."

"I can always give you a list of chores to do to earn it. You know, like . . . *Cinderella*."

Hope blushed. So Mia had heard the stories she'd been telling.

Mia looked at her watch. "Yikes. We have to leave, if I'm going to sign you up for Kevin's class."

Hope's heart clutched. "What? Really?"

"Really. I know you don't want me here."

Mia let out a sigh, then stood and came close. "You understand that it's your mother who drives me insane, not you, right?"

"I drive you insane, too. I make steam come out your ears. I've seen it."

Mia smiled at that. "And you enjoy that—don't pretend you don't."

"You're not who I expected." Hope hadn't meant for that to come out, but there it was.

"What'd you expect?"

"I don't know. I mean, you're beautiful and you have an amazing place, though you have flying ants in my bathroom coming out of the ceiling."

"What?"

"Yeah, and by the way, *ewwww*. But anyway, you have a kick-ass job, and your car—" She sighed. "Heaven. But it seems . . . I don't know. Not cold exactly. But emptier than I thought it would be."

Mia looked staggered. "You think my life is empty?"

"More like lonely. You don't even have a plant."

"I'm not lonely," Mia said, looking affronted. "And just so you know, I have a plant in my office. Sure, it's not looking so good right now, but I really don't get what the big deal is."

"I'm just saying I came here looking for a different life . . ."

Mia closed her eyes. "I know. I lived your life. I remember."

"And this is great. But when I'm older, I want . . .

more," Hope whispered, an odd lump in her throat. "I don't know what exactly, just *more*."

"I'm sorry, Hope." She really looked it. "But for now, you're stuck. Your mom—"

"I know."

Mia nodded. "Then let's at least get you in Kevin's class, if he'll still have you."

"I'm still going to drive you crazy." She held her breath, waiting for Mia to deny it.

"Uh huh. And I'm going to drive you crazy, too. We'll call it even."

No pat, easy answer. Just the honest truth. Hope looked at her and suddenly felt like smiling, because, after all, she was getting pretty much what she'd wanted.

"Now for the rules," Mia said.

"We already did this."

"We're going it again. Rule number one—"

"There's more than one?"

"Listen up, smart-ass, and you can tell me yours, too. First, no rattling my windows with your music."

"Fine. No making fun of my makeup."

"Ouch. I'll try. No more smoking."

"Only if you give up the God complex," Hope said.

"*What?*"

"Come on, you're always right and your opinion is the only one that matters."

Mia rolled her lips together and considered. "Overruled. I *am* God here in this house. Next rule—no sex."

"You've already mentioned this a time or two."

"You can never repeat it enough. No sex."

"You can't make a rule like that."

"I can and I am," Mia said firmly.

"I'm sixteen. Old enough."

"Not in my house, it isn't."

"How about you?"

Mia lifted her chin. "I, thankfully, *am* old enough."

"That sucks."

"Take it or leave it," Mia said.

Hope had no intention of leaving it. To give herself a second, she kicked her toe over the tile and left a mark. To her credit, Mia hardly grimaced. "I'll take it," Hope said.

On the drive to the high school, Mia pulled out her cell phone and called Tess. "I've made a bunch of calls. I have five clients who'd love to interview you."

"That's incredibly sweet," Tess said. "But I told you, I'm making a go at this cookie dough thing full-time. I mean, honestly, can you think of a better job than making cookie dough?"

Um, yes, but she'd keep that to herself.

"Oh, and remember when you said you wanted to help? Well, know any good ad execs?"

Mia grinned. "Are you kidding? I'll make you an ad campaign that makes you rich."

"Hey, if I just make a living, I'll be thrilled."

Mia would make sure of it.

"How's it going there with Hope?"

Mia looked over at her niece. The jet-black hair dye was slowly fading. She still wore black pants and black boots, but her tank was gray today. More interesting, she didn't have all the metal and steel armor on. "Hope's good. But my house has flying ants."

"Termites? Oh, no! You have to get rid of them before they eat your house. I'll call someone for you."

"Honey, that's the beauty of no longer being my assistant—you don't have to do this stuff anymore."

"You're like a lifelong habit. Let me call Buddy."

Buddy was one of Tess's ex-boyfriends. He'd been a great guy, except for his inability to date only one woman at a time. "Tell me you're not still in contact with him."

"How about we focus on your house not being destroyed," Tess said diplomatically, because of course she was still in touch with Buddy. She was still in touch with everyone she'd ever met. It was that big-heart thing again. "I'm calling him."

Imagining the termites sitting on their butts gnawing on her wood walls, Mia sighed. "Fine, thanks." She clicked off and walked Hope into the high school, feeling an unaccustomed set of nerves. She had no idea why until she stopped in the doorway to Kevin's classroom.

And then she knew exactly why.

Kevin himself. Friday night, and the wild, wonderful, amazing sex.

She'd avoided him all weekend, needing to think. *Obsess.* When they'd made love, right before she'd climaxed something had happened. Time had stopped, worlds had collided, and stars had fallen.

She still had no idea what that little beat had been about, but for that one second something had happened, something deep and connected and . . . terrifying.

And when they'd finished, she realized she lay there breathing crazily and hugging up to him like a lost little monkey, so she forced herself to get up and get out.

He was pissed, and she knew it.

But she'd had to go or lose it, and for the rest of the weekend, whenever her brain wandered from where she'd ordered it, it always took her back to that moment at the end when he'd been buried inside her, when she looked into his eyes and exploded. And then the next, which was her leaving him flat on the floor, looking hot and sated. Sexy.

Exhausted.

Hurt.

God, her heart hurt, too. She was actually having pains over this. Now the person responsible for those pains stood at the front of the room, his back to them, writing something across the board.

He turned around. He wore loose cargo jeans, those perpetually unlaced boots, and an unbuttoned long-sleeved shirt over a plain white T-shirt that read: I AM AUTHORIZED TO THINK YOU'RE STUPID, both shirts having apparently never met an iron they liked. His hair was adorably rumpled, and when he smiled at Hope, it turned Mia upside down.

Again Friday night flashed in her mind, how he looked after they'd both come so explosively all over each other. His eyes had been dark and soft, and the way he'd touched her—*God*. Something fathomless and yawning had opened up inside her, and she couldn't seem to close it again.

It was so big she couldn't face it, but she needn't have worried. He wasn't looking at her like that anymore. In fact, he wasn't even looking at her at all.

"Hey," he said to Hope, sounding extremely pleased. "Tell me you're here to add my class."

Hope nodded.

"Great! We don't start for another fifteen minutes, so let me show you what we're working on." He gestured Hope toward his desk and they put their heads together over a book.

Mia, still at the door, cleared her throat.

They both looked up.

And for the first time in her life, Mia didn't know what to say, how to charm, how to get her way. Hell, she didn't even know what her way even *was*. "Kevin."

"Thanks for letting her take the class," he said, smile cool, eyes equally cool. "Was there anything else?"

Ouch. And for no known reason, a ball of panic began to swirl deep in her gut. "Uh . . . no."

How to fix this? How?

But before she could decide, he went back to showing Hope something in the book.

And Mia, well used to alienating people and moving on, lifted her chin and walked right out of the room.

Kevin turned to watch her go, then tossed aside his dry-erase pen and shoved his fingers through his hair, swearing softly. He caught Hope's curious eye and muttered an apology.

"That's okay," Hope said, wise beyond her years as he knew her to be. "She brings out the worst in people. All us Applebys do."

Kevin stared at her. "Is that what you think?"

She lifted a shoulder. "Fact is fact."

The girl's bravado attitude matched her aunt's, and damn if he wasn't incredibly attached to both of them—prickly, grumpy, *beautiful.*

Still, Mia had hurt him, letting him feel he was nothing more than a good lay.

Or a bad one, as she'd tried to convince him so many times.

For every step they took forward, she pushed them back two. In fact, unless they were in bed—or on his foyer floor—lost in their odd and wonderful chemical attraction, she was doing her damnedest to pretend their connection didn't exist.

And if the way Hope looked at the world—that is to say suspiciously and very, very carefully—was any indication of how Mia had been as a kid, then she had been doing it for a long time.

She probably had reasons, too. Good reasons.

Not that he'd know, because she didn't talk about herself.

Well, that was the first thing that was going to change. He'd been patient; he'd been easy.

But if she wanted more, then so did he.

And he figured she owed him. Big. He was going to make her pay up, and it wouldn't be in her favored way. It would be with talking. And then and only then would he let her distract him with that gorgeous body.

The thought of it amused him.

And aroused him.

Hope was looking at him strangely. "So you really like her, huh?"

Hell if that wasn't the unfortunate truth. "Is that a problem?"

"Not for me. But for you, it might be."

Yeah. Truer words had never been spoken.

Chapter Eighteen

Work made Mia's head spin. First Ted nosed his way into another Anderson account meeting, and right there on the spot made some creative adjustments with the wording of the ad that had taken her and Dillon and Janice all week to come up with.

And because the Anderson people loved the adjustments, Mia couldn't say a word.

But it burned.

Sure, she was aggressive when it came to her work, but she never, never, horned in on others.

Then Dickhead himself couldn't find the gold pen he'd gotten for ten years of "exemplary" service, and had the nerve to ask her if Hope might have lifted it over the weekend.

Mia had to keep checking to make sure her head was still on her shoulders, that it hadn't blown off.

Without Tess handling the front desk and with no assistant yet to replace her, the phones went crazy and Mia forgot an appointment with a client.

Forgot. An. Appointment.

Oh, and her plant's leaves had stopped sagging. Now they were just falling right off. In desperation, she put the plant on her desk and pointed at the thing. "Stop dying, damn it!"

Then she went into her own files to get the artwork and ad mock-ups for tomorrow's meetings, and she found everything all jumbled up and out of order, as if someone had recently gone through and shuffled everything.

Someone with fat, nosy fingers.

Ted?

Hard to tell, but she missed Tess with all her might. Tess who would have cut off the fingers of anyone who tried to mess with her.

She realized her head hurt. Work, always her life, her joy, had given her a headache. She couldn't believe it.

Early in the afternoon, Tess called to check on her, and just her voice lifted Mia's spirits. At least until her words sank in.

"Bad news."

"Perfect, because I'm way too happy," Mia said wryly.

"Okay, let's do this another way. *Good* news. You get to take a weeklong vacation from your house, which has termites."

"Um . . . *what?*"

"The place has to be tented," Tess said apologetically. "You have to get out and stay out for five days."

"Oh, my God."

"Buddy's working you in, his schedule is crazed. If you get out by six tonight, he can do you. No pun intended."

"Oh, my God," Mia repeated.

"Is that a yes?"

"And if I say no?"

"Termites eat you out of house and home."

"Shit."

"I'll take that as a yes."

"*Shit.*"

"Honey, you're beginning to sound like a parrot. Why don't you and Hope stay with me?"

Tess had an apartment the size of a postage stamp.

Plus Mia didn't want to impose, but mostly she liked to be on her own. "Thanks, but we'll rough it at a hotel."

"You never lean on me."

"Of course I do."

"Name the time."

"Um . . ."

"Uh huh. And why did I have to find out from Mike that you were born and raised in Tennessee like Hope? I mean, I've heard the accent, which I matched to Hope's the first day I saw her, but, damn it, I wanted to hear about you from you."

So she'd fooled exactly no one.

"Honey, honestly. What is wrong with growing up from humble roots?"

Mia sighed. "Do we have to do this now?"

"As opposed to never, right? You'd prefer that."

"Look, I'm a different person now. I like people to know me as I am *now*."

"But who you *were* factors in. You're a smart woman. You know that."

Maybe. But she'd been running for so many years because she didn't *want* to face the fact that, looking around at her life right now, right this minute, she might have to admit she was far more her momma's daughter than she'd ever wanted to be. Sure, she had money and a good job, but she hadn't ever kept a man, or even a friend, for longer than it took to sneeze.

Tess being the exception somehow, but mostly that was a tribute to Tess's tenacity rather than anything Mia had done. "Look," she said. "I don't lean easily, I don't share easily, you know that. But I do both with you more than anyone else."

Tess sniffed, sounding slightly appeased. "Well, that counts for something, I suppose."

"I have to go. You wouldn't believe the crap here. So are we okay?"

"Yeah. I love you, Mia."

Mia sighed. Lots of people were throwing that word around lately. But there was leaning, and there was truth. "Damn it, I love you back." She hung up.

Then dialed a local hotel she often used for business. No availability. A few minutes later she discovered why, after calling her way through the phonebook. Thanks to some geek/tech convention that had come to town, there wasn't a single hotel worth staying in within thirty miles that had availability, and she was not going to a motel, thank you very much.

If it had been just herself, Mia might have taken her credit card and her weary soul off to the Bahamas until she could deal with her issues, but she had Hope.

And Hope had school.

Finally she escaped the building she would have sworn she loved being inside more than life itself and took her first deep breath of the day, even if it was pure smog.

She drove straight to Tess's. "I need a pound of cookie dough," she said when Tess opened her door. "And a spoon."

Mike peeked out over Tess's shoulder with a grin on his face. He smiled at Mia, kissed Tess, and then, with a wave, left.

Mia watched him go, then looked at Tess. She wore a matching grin to Mike's, flour smudged on her cheek, and sported a suspicious-looking red spot on her throat that screamed *I just had sex*. When Mia shot her a bland smile, Tess covered her red cheeks with her hands. "So I needed some cheering up."

"I didn't say a word."

"Honey, you speak volumes with the mere arch of a brow."

"Look, a good cheer-up requires chocolate, not a penis."

"Hello Mrs. Pot. Meet Kettle."

Mia let out a sigh. "I'm just worried about your tender heart getting broken."

"Well, don't." Tess's smile faded and so did some of her glow. She turned away and went into the tiny kitchen and began to measure ingredients. "I'm just having fun. I'm not going to let my heart get involved."

Mia squeezed into the kitchen and hopped up onto the counter. "That's new."

"Yeah, well, maybe things change."

"Like what things?"

"Like maybe he has a bazillion women to chose from and I'm fairly worthless at the moment," Tess said quietly, mixing dry ingredients in a bowl.

"What?" Fury rose hard and fast. "You're not worthless, and if he said—"

"No. He adores me. He's sweet and kind and sexy and funny, and makes me feel like I'm the most important thing on the planet."

"But . . . ?" Mia asked, reaching for a bowl that looked finished. She fished a wooden spoon out of the canister and dug in. "Because I'm feeling like there's a big 'but' here."

Tess shook her head. "It's nothing."

"Tell me."

"Other women text-message him, or at least one did. I read it. It said *Come do me.*"

"*What?*"

"He was so embarrassed, and deleted it right away. He told me that he's led a fairly wild past and that sometimes that past comes up and bites him on the ass, but that's he's changed. That since me, he's changed."

"And you believe him?"

Tess stared at her, then shook her head. "I want to."

"Oh, Tess."

"Look, I'm getting ready for the unemployment line, okay? I don't have a lot of time to stress about this."

A stab of guilt pierced Mia's heart. "Collect unemployment because Dickhead is an asshole, but we're going to make this cookie dough thing work. I've made a bunch of calls. I have a few clients interested in using the dough as charity fund-raisers. They're going to call you."

"Oh, Mia. Thank you—"

"I don't want your thanks. After all you've ever done for me? My God. I'd do anything."

"Stop." She began to pour the dough into the pound-size containers she sold to her customers.

Mia dug into hers and moaned out loud. White chocolate chip. "Oh, my God. That's better than sex."

Tess laughed. "No, it's not."

Mia thought of Kevin and how good he felt buried deep inside her, and felt a shiver rack her. "Okay, not quite. But close. Seriously, you're going to be the Mrs. Fields of cookie dough."

Tess grinned. "I want to be."

"You need a bigger kitchen."

"Yeah, but the start-up cost—"

"I'll lend it to you. No, don't say no yet," she said quickly when Tess opened her mouth. "Just think about it. Cookie dough in malls across the country . . . you'll make millions."

"I don't need millions," Tess said softly. "Just enough to get by on so that I could stay home with my babies."

"Babies!" Mia grabbed her shoulders. "You're not—"

"No. But someday . . ."

"You are *not* thinking of having babies with Mike." But the look on Tess's face said it all. "Shit." Mia dug for another big spoonful of dough. "That's insane." The sugar rush began, but she took yet another. "Utterly and totally insane. I mean, sure, he's cute and sexy as hell, I'll give you that. But the text messages—"

"You should have seen his face, Mia. He was horrified that I would think he was with another woman during this time he'd been with me. He wanted me to believe him."

"And you do."

She sighed. "He doesn't know it yet, but yes. I think I do. Don't say it's too soon."

"Can I just think it?"

"I have so much going on. I need you. I need your help."

Mia's gut twisted. "I'm right here. For anything. You know that."

"I know. I'm blessed, because Mike said the same thing." When she saw Mia's face, she smiled. "You know, it's okay to lean on a man once in a while."

"Why would you want to lean on anyone?" Mia asked a bit desperately, thinking of Kevin and how she'd had the urge to do just that. "And how do you really know it's okay?" she whispered.

"You have to trust." Reaching over, Tess squeezed her hand. "Let your guard down once in a while."

Mia stuffed another spoonful of dough in her mouth, then looked at her watch and groaned. "I've gotta go. I have to run a few errands, find a hotel, pick up the kid, then work some more. Damn it."

"You used to love your work."

Yeah, and wasn't that yet another worry. Something was happening to her neat and tidy world, something not so neat or tidy at all . . .

Mia raced out of Tess's place and ran her errands; the printing shop for the new Runner posters that she'd had made, the shoe-repair shop where she'd turned in the Manolos with the broken heel, the dry cleaners . . .

By the time she finished, she had five minutes to pick up Hope before the teen center closed. She had no idea what happened if she was late, but just thinking about it brought back memories of her mother being late to pick her up from school. She could remember sitting on the curb all alone, an hour or more after the bell had rung, feeling as if no one gave a shit.

God. If she did that to Hope . . . She popped open her cell phone and dialed Hope's while navigating the 134 east.

"Hey," came Hope's Southern drawl.

"Hey," Mia said quickly. "I'm on my way, I'll be there—"

"Sorry, I can't answer right now, but you all be sure to leave me a message and I'll get back to you."

Damn it! The kid's voice mail. What did a sixteen-year-old have going on that she couldn't answer her phone?

The possibilities, none of them good, goaded her into speeding as she called information for the teen center. She got directly connected, then waited impatiently while *that* phone rang.

And rang.

" 'Lo," came a low, annoyed voice of a male teen. "Teen center."

"Yes, this is Mia Appleby. I'd like to speak to Hope Appleby, please."

"Not here."

"What? What do you mean she's not there?"

"She's not here."

"Look, I thought you people aren't supposed to leave until your adult signs you out!"

No answer.

"Hello?"

"Hold on."

She grated her teeth and got stuck behind a truck. She tapped her fingers on the steering wheel while she thought of all the things that Hope could be doing: smoking, rewiring the entire teen center, cavorting with boys.

She really hated holding.

She hated waiting.

She hated—

"Mia."

Just the sound of Kevin's voice, low and a little rough, made her belly do a little quiver. Too much cookie dough, she told herself. "Yeah. Hi. I'm trying to get ahold of Hope."

"Ah."

She heard the quick flash of disappointment in his voice as he realized she wasn't calling for him, which brought a flash of shame to her cheeks, because she tended to show up in his world only when she needed him. When had she gotten so selfish? "I'm sorry, it's just that she didn't answer her cell—"

"I sent her on an errand to my classroom. She'll be right back."

"Oh. Okay, thank you."

"Want me to leave her a message?"

So formal. He'd been buried inside her to the hilt, holding her face for his deep, hot, wet kiss as he decimated her with achingly slow thrusts designed to drive her right out of her mind, and here they were saying please and thank you like strangers. She hated this. She opened her mouth to say so, to say she was sorry she was so stubborn in her ways, to say she didn't know how to be anything other than what she was but that she wanted him to like that woman. She really, really wanted that.

But the words stuck like straw in her throat. Damn pride. It wouldn't be the first time she'd choked on it. "No," she finally managed. "Thank you," she said again, inanely, and clicked off.

Drove.

Swore.

Yeah, the power had shifted, from herself to another.

To a *man*.

That was a first, an uncomfortable one, and she didn't like it. Not one bit.

Chapter Nineteen

A few minutes later, Mia came to a standstill in traffic and felt her brain matter begin to boil. *Never going to get there in time.*

Why hadn't she just told Kevin? Now she had to call again.

The same sullen teen answered the teen center as before, and she strove for casual. "Hi. Can I talk to Kevin again, please?"

She waited longer this time. Finally he picked up. "McKnight."

She let out a low breath and tried not to react to the way he said his name, as if he had all the confidence in the world, as if everything was as it should be, no doubts, no stress, nothing. "It's me."

He said nothing and she let out a breath. "Again." She winced. "I, um . . ." Lost in the desire to get him to soften toward her, she actually forgot what she'd wanted to say.

"You lose your nerve?" he asked.

"No. I just . . ."

"Just what? Why can't you say it? That you hated the way we got off the phone just now. That you care about what I think. That you want us to be more than fuck buddies."

"Actually, I called to tell you I'm running late." At his silence, she pressed the phone to her forehead, then brought it back to her ear. "Okay, yes. And I hated the way we got off the phone just now. All right? Happy?"

"Jumping for joy."

"Look, I really am going to be a few minutes late. I didn't know the protocol."

"I can take Hope home so you don't worry about it while you're navigating traffic."

"I can multitask. Worrying and navigating are no problem fine."

"Then multitask this—drive carefully while thinking about what I'm going to do to you tonight."

Her thighs quivered at the threat/promise, so silkily uttered she got goose bumps. "There's, uh, going to be a tonight?"

"Oh, there's going to be a tonight. My way."

She swallowed hard.

"Drive safe," he said again.

It wasn't often someone wanted to do something for her, and she squirmed for a moment, fighting with that age-old nemesis—her pride.

"This is where you say, 'Okay, Kevin, thanks.' "

In spite of herself, she had to smile. "Yeah. Thanks."

"Well, look at that," he said softly. "You didn't choke on it." Before she could process that, he said, "You can bring dinner. Pizza? The works would be great."

"I hadn't been planning on—" But she was talking to herself, because he'd disconnected. He had no idea, of course, that she didn't have time for that.

She had work to do, a teen to watch, a house to pack up, a hotel to find—

Ah, hell. She dialed information for the number of the local pizza joint.

And then did as he asked: drove while thinking about what he was going to do to her tonight.

* * *

Mia arrived at home half an hour later still wondering about what Kevin intended. She hadn't even gotten out of her car before she heard the wild cheering and screaming. Hoisting two pizzas and her briefcase, she followed the noise to the basketball court and stopped in surprise. From what she could gather, it was Kevin and Hope against Mike and Tess.

Tess, who'd never followed, much less played, a competitive game or sport in her life. Unlike the others, Tess wasn't wearing shorts, but a denim skirt, which made Mia laugh. Even she'd change out of her designer wear for a game.

Kevin was in a damp T-shirt stuck to his chest that read REPEAT AFTER ME: I WILL NOT SLEEP THROUGH MY EDUCATION and big, baggy basketball shorts hanging to his knees, with athletic shoes that should have been retired in the previous millennium.

He looked good enough to lap up with her tongue.

Mike snagged the ball from him, giving his brother a nice elbow to the gut as he did. Kevin bent over, and Mike tossed the ball to Tess.

Tess looked at the ball in her hands.

Mike waved his hands at her, gesturing that she should run and make a basket.

"Right!" Tess whirled and ran with the ball.

Without dribbling.

Mia rolled her eyes. "Tess, *dribble*!" she yelled from the sidelines.

Tess stopped and looked at her. "Huh?"

"Bounce the ball!"

Kevin straightened and started laughing out loud. "Travel!"

Mike elbowed him again, and Tess got to the basket before Hope caught up with her.

"Now what?" Tess called to Mia.

"You shoot!"

"Hope! You're supposed to stop her!" Kevin called

out, planting a hand in Mike's face, holding him off from delivering another elbow blow. "Grab the ball from her!"

But Hope didn't. She and Tess were talking.

"I'm not very good at this," Tess was saying.

"It's okay. Here." Hope showed her how to shoot with just one hand beneath the ball, the other merely a guide. "Keep your elbow in," she said. "I heard Kevin say that earlier."

Tess shot. The ball went too far to the left.

Hope grabbed it and handed it back to Tess. "Try again."

Kevin flopped to the floor dramatically and groaned. "This is not basketball." He turned his head and leveled that dark gaze right on Mia, still standing at the fence. "Do you see how she is? Completely disloyal."

Hope laughed.

Laughed.

Mia turned her head and stared at the girl, realizing she'd never heard the sound before. Hope jogged back to Kevin and sat at his side, Indian style. "Don't worry," she said and patted his shoulder. "We still totally won. I made sure of that before I stopped to help."

"Good girl." Weakly, he held up a high five.

She slapped it, then grinned, looking sweet, adorable, and very sixteen. "Did you see that last layup I pulled off?"

"Amazing." Groaning, he rolled over and got up, then offered her a hand up as well, which she took. "You should play high school basketball."

Hope blinked her black-lined eyes. "Really?"

"I'd recruit you. I coach the varsity team during the season."

Hope shot a quick glance at Mia, and her smile faded. "That's cool."

They all knew she'd be long gone by then. The

thought brought a pang to Mia, but she smiled and lifted the pizza.

Everyone perked up at that and headed off the court.

"Oh, and here's another adventure," Mia said as they gathered their things. "Hope and I are out of my place by six thirty for the exterminator. We'll have to hotel it for a week. Probably in downtown, though—nothing's available here. I'm thinking the Biltmore . . . I know, tough life, right?"

Kevin shook his head. "Don't do that. Stay with us."

Mia laughed.

"I'm serious."

Hope jumped up and down. "Yes!"

Mia shook her head. "No." *No way.* No way in hell. She couldn't even *look* at his house without wanting to strip down and jump his bones. She couldn't stay there. In such close quarters, it'd be . . . intensified. Maybe they'd have great sex, like always, and then what? She'd have nowhere to go afterward, nowhere—

"What's the matter?" Kevin asked. "Worried I'll hear you sing in the shower?"

"I'll have you know I have an excellent singing voice."

"Maybe you snore?"

She eyed his amused mug narrowly. "No."

"Ah. You have stinky feet."

"Not that it matters," she said through her teeth. "Since I'm not shacking up with you."

"I have a spare bedroom. You two can share it. That way Hope won't have to miss school. Plus, you'll be close to home so you can bully your terminators. We all know how you like to be in control of everything."

Mia eyed him. Is that how he saw her? Controlling? True, but not exactly flattering.

"Please, Aunt Mia?" Hope clasped her hands and batted her eyelashes.

"Maybe you missed the part where I said it's for a *week*," Mia said to Kevin.

"I heard."

Oh, God. "What if I get tired of you?"

He ran a finger over her jaw, an odd light in his eyes. "Is that what you're afraid of? Really? Because I think you're afraid you *won't* get tired of me."

She stared into his patient but amused eyes. *Damn it.* Damn him for always reading her mind. *Prove him wrong.* "I don't cook," she warned.

"I think we can manage."

He sounded amused, the ass. "When you regret this," she said, "you'll have no one but yourself to blame."

His smile, damn him, was slow and sure and took her breath.

Everyone came into Mia's house while she and Hope gathered what they needed for the week. When Mike, Tess, and Hope headed to Kevin's, Mia stood in her living room, taking one last look at her place.

Kevin held the pizzas and came toward her, all long, loose-legged stride. "Do we have the works in here?" he asked very seriously.

She nodded and he smiled, one of those really amazing smiles that said *The world is an awesome place*, that said *I'm always going to think so no matter what happens*, that said *If you let go just a little you could feel the same way*.

She didn't understand what it was about him, but even now she felt a funny tightness in her chest. There was also a flutter deep in her belly, and she'd begun to fear it wouldn't go away no matter how many times she got him naked.

"I'd give my entire bank account to know what you're thinking right now," he said softly.

"Sorry, but you can't afford my thoughts."

Instead of being insulted, he just let out another slow smile.

More than her belly quivered now. A little surprised to find herself reacting so strongly to a mere man, she backed up a step.

He arched a brow.

"Mia?" Hope called from outside. "You guys coming?"

Kevin didn't take his eyes off Mia. "*Are* you coming?" he asked very softly, silkily.

"God, I hope so," she murmured.

His eyes smoldered as he looked at her so directly, so deeply it also was too much. He touched her cheek. "Right behind you," he called out to Hope, then put his hand on the small of Mia's back to guide her out the door. "Bad day?"

"Yeah." She sighed. "Work sucked."

"Any more trash can fires?"

"No. But I almost strangled a coworker who thinks he's God's gift."

"The one who got Tess fired? The same guy who's trying to step on your toes and take your account?"

She looked at him in surprise.

He shrugged. "Tess told us. You should have seen Hope. She was pretty hot under the collar about your boss."

"Really?" Mia sighed and rubbed her forehead. "Maybe the kid likes me after all."

"You think?" He looked at her for a long moment. "You really do look beat."

"Gee, I want you, too."

"Oh, I want you."

She stared at him, disconcerted by the way he disarmed her. She swallowed hard. "Why do things seem so complicated right now?"

Another long, thoughtful look. "Maybe for tonight, over pizza and beer and laughs, things can get a little uncomplicated."

"Yeah. Maybe." But she didn't believe it. Then, before she knew it, they were in Kevin's kitchen, with Mike pressing a beer in her hand and Tess regaling them with the story of her adventures of getting Cookie Madness on the map. One of Mia's contacts called her after Mia had left her this afternoon—and ordered two hundred pounds.

Over more pizza, they all marveled at that. Then Kevin told them about his hopes of catching his pot-head, thanks to Hope's rigging his gas burners with an alarm. "Tomorrow," he said smiling, "is going to be fun."

Hope laughed again, and Mia looked at her, feeling her chest tighten again. God, she loved that sound, and she put her hand on Hope's arm.

"What?" Hope asked, still smiling.

Mia just shook her head. She'd just wanted to touch her, maybe hug her, but she wasn't sure how to do that. Tess moved around, cleaning up, touching Mike, pushing Kevin, kissing Hope, being so easy and free with her emotions that Mia felt a little lost. A little out of place.

"Hey."

She blinked, and Kevin was standing close, tipping her face up to look deep into her eyes. "Where did you go?"

"I'm right here."

Slowly he shook his head. Then he took her hand in his and led her to the door. "We're going to get more sodas," he told the room in general, grabbing the two helmets on the counter. "Be right back."

He didn't say anything on the walk to his bike or when he handed her a helmet. Or when he straddled the bike and waited for her to join him. She hadn't been prepared to press her body to his, but when she did, some of the odd tension left her.

And a new one gripped her.

He turned his head and looked at her, smiled, and

then, with a rev of the engine, they took off. Wind in their faces, the hills whipping by . . . *yeah*. This was just what she needed. All too soon, they were stopping at a convenience store for a six-pack of sodas, then heading back.

Dusk arrived and the heat lifted a bit. They parked on the street and sat there for a moment, not moving. Mia could smell the azaleas, could hear the buzz of a lone bee. From far down the street she could hear the normal sounds of traffic.

A world away from where she'd grown up. There the heat would still be thick, too thick to breathe. Dogs would be barking, growling, fighting. Kids screaming. Adults fighting. The smell of meat frying would be overwhelming. And above it all would be the sounds of her momma and Sugar, in their deep, Southern drawls, planning out their big catch at the rec center barbeque.

Mia's universe couldn't be more different. She'd carefully cultivated it to be.

So why wasn't she happy? She'd blame it on the kid, or work, but that wouldn't be honest.

She had the sexiest man on the planet looking at her, making her knees weak without even trying, causing her heart to pitter-patter like a kid's; a man who claimed to want her, a man who wouldn't accept her cool, calm façade she'd always given the world.

And yet she'd hidden herself for so long she didn't know how to reveal herself to him, or—even more unnerving—she didn't know who she really even was.

Kevin remained quiet as he got off the bike and reached for her hand. "Hey."

"Hey."

"Feel any better?"

"Is that what the ride was about?"

"It always works for me, so I hoped—"

"Yeah." She smiled. "It worked. I just got over-whelmed. You know . . . work, Hope, Tess."

"You mean Mike."

"Maybe him, too. Tess won't admit it, but she's been hurt, too much. Maybe you could tell him to move on now before it's too late. It won't be difficult. All he has to do is smile that smile and another woman will be falling all over herself to snag him."

Kevin smiled grimly. "I've had this conversation with him."

"And?"

"And he wants Tess."

"Damn it, Kevin."

"Look, I've seen him with her. They were here this afternoon with Hope, baking. My brother, the hound dog, measuring sugar and cracking eggs."

"So?" Mia shrugged, unimpressed. "A guy'll do anything to get laid."

Lifting a hand, he stroked a finger over her temple in the guise of tucking a stray strand of hair back. "Only guys?"

She slapped his hand away with a laugh. "Fine. Women do it, too."

"You're upset at all the changes."

"No, I'm—" She broke off, her eyes locked on his. "Okay, maybe. I don't like change."

"Of course you do. Look at your life and how you've changed it to suit yourself. Your job itself is a constant change. What you don't like is when you don't have the reins in your hands. When you're not sure of the outcome. You act all tough, but the truth is you're not much of a gambler if it's not a sure bet."

"You make me sound like a control freak. I'm not."

At that, he tossed back his head and laughed. "Yeah. Okay. You're also not in denial." He stroked a hand up her back and made her want to melt. "It's okay, I've got your number."

She hated how breathless his touch made her. "Think so?"

Leaning in, he kissed right beneath her ear. "Yeah," he said on a soft exhale and made her shiver. Smiling against her skin, he bit her lightly. "Now tell me what's really wrong, since you've danced around it."

Wrapping her hands around him, she cupped his butt and squeezed. "I've got a better idea."

He grabbed her hands in his. "I'm on board with that idea, trust me, but everyone is standing in my kitchen, probably watching us."

"Damn it. Why are there so many people in our lives?"

He laughed again. "I haven't a clue. Come on. Later we'll ditch 'em all and you can have your way with me."

"Promise?"

"If you promise to hang around long enough for me to get my heart rate back to normal afterward."

She stepped back in automatic defense, but he simply pulled her in anyway. "Is that elusive cuddle so terrifying? Really?"

"Is that why you asked us to stay with you?" she demanded.

"Well, all the possibilities did weigh in." He kissed her again, then straightened and smiled at her, and took away her breath. Her chest tightened, too, but she told herself that was just because her life suddenly seemed like it was a runaway train. She stared at him, then put her forehead to his chest. "God, you get to me."

"I'll take that as a compliment," he murmured, stroking a hand down her back. "I know things are changing fast right now. But work has been hard before."

"Not really. I've always loved it so much, it never

felt hard. But now with my boss out for blood and Ted out for my accounts, I'm not exactly feeling the love."

"Kick their asses." His thumbs stroked her jaw when she smiled. "Next time anyone's in your face, remember it's not about them, it's about the actual work and how much you enjoy it. Next problem."

"Tess. She's lost her job and she's about to get her heart stomped, and I can't help her with any of it."

"She doesn't seem too worried. She's a big girl, Mia. And she's got it together."

Mia blew out a breath, unable to concentrate with his hands on her. "Yeah."

"Next."

"Hope."

"A great kid."

"But she's not mine. She doesn't belong here with me."

"That explains why she's braced for the other foot to fall."

"Meaning?"

"She's just waiting for you to send her back."

Mia sighed. "Sugar doesn't want her back yet. Damn it. I can't send her back knowing that."

"Because you know how it feels?"

She lifted her head and looked into his eyes. "No, it wasn't like that for me. My mom wanted me around, I just didn't want to be there. I couldn't stand to be there. Pretty rotten of me, huh?"

He smiled and shook his head. "Is it rotten of Mike to want to hear? Is it rotten of me to wish I'd been good enough to play pro basketball? Is it rotten of Tess to dream about her cookie company? Or Hope to want to be you?"

"She doesn't want to be like me."

"Look again."

"Damn it, I am not a good role model. I'm not like you. I don't want to fix people."

He went still. "Is that what you think I do?"

"It *is* what you do. And I meant it as a compliment."

"Next," he whispered.

"You." This admission passed by her inner editor, and she lifted her head.

His eyes seemed to be deep and full and very warm. "I didn't realize I factored."

"Oh, you factor."

"That is very good to know."

She saw the light of intent in his eyes as he leaned in, and as much as she wanted to lose herself in his kiss, she planted a hand on his chest. "I have no idea what I'm doing here. You know that, right? I'm on this merry-go-round, and I don't know how to get off."

"Just follow your heart."

Could it really be that easy? She decided she'd never know unless she tried. So she slid her hands into his hair and tugged his face down for a kiss. He humored her for a beat, then tried to pull free, but she touched her tongue to his and dragged a low groan from him as he pulled her close and let her deepen the kiss.

Only when they were both breathless did he step back, still holding one of her hands, which he trailed down her arm, linking her fingers with his. He brought their joined hands up to his mouth and kissed her knuckles. Watching her over their fingers, he nodded. "You look better now. Less tense."

She felt her body humming. That kiss was far more potent than she'd expected. "I don't feel less tense."

"Yeah, you do." He ran a finger between her eyes, where there was usually a tight furrow. "You're not frowning. In fact, you're smiling at me. And your eyes are dreamy."

She leaned past him and looked at herself in the reflection of the side-view mirror of his bike. God. It was true.

He laughed. "Don't look so shocked."

She kept staring at herself. He hadn't mentioned the color of her cheeks and the almost giddy expression on her face. "Dessert," she decided.

"Sounds good."

What was good was him. She leaned against his body. "And then . . ." She pressed against his erection. "This."

"And then . . . ?"

She sighed. "Look, about that whole cuddle thing . . ."

He laughed and slung an arm around her. "You might like it, you know."

Yeah. She did know.

Chapter Twenty

Thanks to a certain night-owl teenager, Kevin and Mia's late-night rendezvous never materialized. Hope managed to stay up past Mia, who fell asleep in the queen bed with the teen next to her, rocking out to the iPod Tess had lent her.

Kevin stuck his head in to wave good night to Hope, smiling grimly to himself as he eyed the exhausted Mia. No doubt, she was going to wake up in the morning ready to kill Tess for giving Hope the iPod.

The next morning he found Mia with her head in his refrigerator, dressed to the hilt in some floaty sort of skirt that flirted with her legs and a top that played peekaboo with something lacy and made his blood race. She straightened, a scowl on her face.

"Nothing good magically appear?" he asked.

She whipped around, startled, and he realized it hadn't been the food making her frown, but her thoughts. "I'm late," she said in warning when he took a step toward her. She held up her hand to ward him off. "Very late."

"Just this then . . ." Pulling her close, the scent of her shampoo and sweet, soft woman tickling his nose, he kissed her.

She let out a low murmur and kissed him back

until his eyes crossed. Lifting his head, he eyed the pantry door with half a mind to drag her in there.

"No," she laughed breathlessly and blew out a frustrated breath. Looking sexy as hell, she moved out of his arms and into the kitchen, calling for Hope to "hurry her tush up" and leaving him behind, hot and bothered.

Nothing new, he'd been hot and bothered since he'd met her.

That evening was a repeat performance, but at least the next morning Mia softened enough to give Kevin a longer kiss. She'd just pressed him back against the refrigerator to feel him up—and down— murmuring, "If she stays up late tonight, I'll kill her," when Mike and Hope walked in.

Mike arched a brow.

Hope just stared.

Recovering quickly, Mia tossed Kevin half her bagel and commanded Hope to hurry, as if they hadn't just been going at it against the refrigerator.

Kevin took much longer to recover. Like all day . . .

On the third morning, Mia was feeling desperate, and shoved Kevin into the bathroom. "This is a ridiculous," she whispered. "How do married people ever have sex once they have kids? I can't wait any longer." She lifted her skirt.

No panties.

With a rough groan, he reached for her, but Mike banged on the door.

Mia thunked her head back against the shower. "I'm going to cry," she whispered. "I mean it."

But a few minutes later, in the kitchen, she gave him a whole bagel. Toasted and jellied.

Progress.

"You made this for me?" Kevin murmured, surprised.

"Maybe I'm staking my claim." Then she wrapped her arms around his neck and kissed him good-bye.

"Ew," Hope said, coming into the room, wrinkling her nose but looking secretly pleased. "Gross. Old people making out."

Old people wanting more than that, Kevin thought.

Late the next night, when Kevin had resigned himself to the fact that Mia was sabotaging their nights on purpose because she was freaked about "living" together, he heard someone in the hallway.

It was Mike, who smirked. *Still not getting laid?*

Kevin sighed.

Sucks for you, Mike signed, clearly dressed for going out.

Where are you off to?

To get what you can't.

With Tess?

Mike's smile fell, and he shook his head.

You saw her just last night. What happened?

During . . . an inopportune moment, Linda paged me. And then Shelly. They wanted me to go out with them.

Kevin shook his head. *Demanding harem you have there.*

Hey, I haven't seen any of them since I met Tess. But she doesn't know that.

And the calls look damning.

Mike nodded, a new expression on his face: shame. *It happened last week, too. She read one of the texts. It said* Come fuck me, big guy.

Ouch.

Mike let out an agreeing sound. *She dumped me. She cried when she did it, too.* Looking destroyed, he shrugged. *So I guess I'm going out with the gang.*

Why don't you stick around here instead? Kevin signed casually, trying to keep him from the need to go self-destruct. *I can put in a movie—*

Mike shook his head and brushed past him.

A moment later, the front door shut.

With a sigh, Kevin went to the kitchen, hoping his brother kept his brain turned on. He heard the pad of the bare feet a few seconds before Hope poked her head in. She wore a black T-shirt that fell to her knees and her hair in a ponytail. No makeup at all. She looked about twelve, and incredibly sweet. "Hey." He kicked out a chair. "You too old for milk and cookies?"

"Never."

He started to get up, but she waved him down and helped herself, serving him as well. He smiled and thanked her, and then waited.

It didn't take long.

"So this relationship thing . . ." She didn't look at him but into her milk as if it held the world's secrets. "How do you know when it's real?"

"What kind of relationship are we talking about?"

"There's different kinds?"

"Sure, there's the friendship relationship, the student/teacher relationship, the love relationship—"

"That kind."

"Ah." He nodded. "Well . . . there's the I-gotta-have-you-or-life-is-over love. That's usually a teenage thing, and lasts, oh, about a week."

She snorted and dipped her cookie in the milk.

"And then there's the I-love-you-if-you-change-into-the-person-I-really-want love. That usually doesn't last much longer than the teenage kind." He knew. He'd been there with Beth.

Another snort came from Hope as she shoved the cookie in her mouth, and he smiled. "And then there's the real thing. The I-can't-eat-can't-sleep love that snags you by the heart and won't let go. Only problem is, it's almost always fatal."

She went very still, then swallowed. "When you

spell it out, it's not really that hard to tell the difference at all, is it?"

"Are we talking about Adam?"

She looked away. "Actually . . . I was thinking about Aunt Mia. If she fell in love, the real kind, maybe she'd want kids. Maybe she'd want me to stay. And, you know, help."

God, she was killing him. "She'd be lucky to have you, Hope."

She played with another cookie for a minute. "Think she'd want to keep me?"

How to tell her Mia didn't want to "keep" anybody. "Your aunt has some things to work out in the keeping department," he said gently.

"And we can't work them out for her?"

"No, unfortunately."

She sighed. "Don't you hate it when you can't just fix stuff? And make it right?"

He absorbed the unexpected wisdom. He *couldn't* fix things. He *couldn't* make it right. Some things just had to go the course. The kids in his class. Mike, Mia . . . "Do you have any idea how smart you are, Hope?"

She met his gaze straight on. "Smart enough to know which kind of love it is you have for Mia." She smiled at his shock. "Don't worry. Maybe it won't be fatal this one time."

She left him after that, but there was no way he could sleep. He tried late-night TV and had just watched some stupid infomercial on exercise equipment and was contemplating a way to wake up Mia when his cell vibrated to life. He looked at it and knew.

Mike, in trouble again.

Don't you hate when you can't just fix stuff? Hope's words echoed in his head as he watched the cell shimmy and shake. He couldn't fix his students; they had to want to learn. He couldn't change Mia into wanting something she didn't.

And he couldn't rescue Mike by bailing him out over and over again. *Shouldn't.*

After a moment, the phone stopped vibrating, and with a sick, heavy pit in his gut, he got up and went to bed.

The next morning Mike slammed into the house, stalked down the hall, and went straight to his room. Kevin came out of his room and shouldered his way into Mike's before he was locked out. *What happened?* he demanded as his brother stripped out of his shirt.

Mike snorted. *Now you want to know? Fuck off.*

Tell me.

I was arrested for disorderly conduct for a bar fight which, by the way, I didn't start. You'd know that if you'd have picked up your phone. He started to brush past Kevin, who blocked him with a hand to his chest.

I told you I was done bailing you out.

Mike stared at him, then shoved him back a step. *Get your smug self-righteous face out of my room before I smash it.*

Mike—

Look, you're done saving my ass? Fine. No doubt I deserve it. But I sure as hell don't want to see or talk to you right now, so get out.

How did you get home?

Concern? Is that concern on your face? A little late, isn't it?

Mike—

I spent the night in jail and was picked up by Tess. Satisfied?

You called Tess?

For a ride home. She gladly gave it, unlike my own brother. Then she said I disappointed her, that she expects more from a man than I can give. Said I shouldn't call her again. Mike punched the wall, then rubbed his knuckles. *Look, just get the hell out.*

Mike—

But Mike turned and walked into his bathroom. The lock tumbling into place echoed into the silence.

Hope sat in science class, riveted by the lesson. They were learning about the effects of the moon's pull on the ocean, and she was taking notes, dreaming about swimming with the dolphins.

Kevin—Mr. McKnight here in class—was tense today. She knew something was going on when she'd entered his kitchen that morning because he and Mia had immediately stopped talking. They'd both looked extremely unhappy, which she assumed was Mia's doing. Why couldn't the woman get it together?

Adam touched his foot to hers, and Hope looked over in surprise. He passed her a note.

When are we getting together?

Though she'd been the one to say they could, she was avoiding actually doing so. She didn't know why. So she smiled but didn't answer, didn't know what to answer.

After class, he took her hand. "Walk with me to the teen center?"

She wasn't supposed to—they were supposed to walk in groups of three or more, and always with at least two girls—but he was pretty cute, and smiling at her with those eyes. " 'Kay."

But instead of going straight to the teen center, they veered off the path and entered the woods. There, with the trees all around them, the day dim from the low clouds, Adam kissed her.

"Um—" she began, but he thrust his tongue in her mouth.

Jeez. Still too much slobber. She tried to pull back,

but he held on tight, then stuck his clammy hand beneath her shirt. She jerked free.

"What?" he asked, lifting his hands.

"Um . . . wait a sec."

His eyes filled with impatience. "Jesus, it's always *wait* with you."

She knew she'd given him mixed signals, and she felt bad, but she *felt* like a walking mixed signal. "I'm sorry."

"If you're sorry, then kiss me," he whispered in that sexy voice and leaned in.

Okay, fine. *One* more. She let him stick his tongue back down her throat and put his hand back up her shirt, hoping he wouldn't unhook her bra. She tried to stand still to wait him out, but she just couldn't do it. She was about to shove him away when the twigs and branches on the path crackled beneath someone else's feet.

Adam jerked back.

And Hope looked up into Kevin's face. He looked pissed, and Hope wanted to crawl into a hole and die.

"We're not doing anything," Adam said.

Kevin uttered one very unteacherlike word, and Hope squeezed her eyes shut. *Please God, just kill me right now. Strike me dead with lightning.*

But God wasn't listening.

Kevin took a deep breath and looked at Adam. "You."

Hope shifted uncomfortably. "Kevin—"

"Zip it, Hope," Kevin said without looking at her. "You're next. Right now I'm talking to Adam."

Hope tried God again. *Please, I'm begging you. Kill me.*

"This is the—what?—the third time I've caught you out here this week playing tonsil hockey?" Kevin asked Adam.

Hope stopped talking to God and stared at Adam. "Wait. *Third* time?"

Adam backed up a step, eyes cool and hooded. "Kissing isn't against any rule."

"Being out here in the woods is," Kevin said. "You've been warned. You've been punished with extra assignments. Now you're going to be suspended."

Adam lost his smugness. "Hey, wait. I—"

"Too late," Kevin said firmly.

"But if you get suspended from summer school, you don't get credit for the class," Adam said. "I need the credit."

"Too bad."

Adam just stared at him. "I thought you were cool. I thought you cared about fixing us."

"Oh, I care, Adam," Kevin said quietly. "But I can't fix you. Only you can do that. You need to stop smoking pot and you need to get your act together while you're still a minor and these mistakes don't count against you permanently. If I can help you, I will."

"Funny way of showing it."

Kevin shrugged.

Adam glanced over at Hope, who was still stuck on the *third time* thing and looked away. Adam kicked the dirt and stalked off toward the teen center.

Hope couldn't help it, she let out a relieved little sigh. Kevin, unaware that he'd just saved her from having to tell Adam no, was now glaring at her. "You want to tell me how I've ruined your life, too?" he asked. "Because—what the hell—I'm on a roll. Let's hear it."

Hope shook her head.

Kevin sighed. Swore again.

And Hope worked up the nerve to ask her most pressing question. "Are you going to tell Mia?"

"No."

She sagged in relief that turned out to be short-lived.

"You are."

*   *   *

That night Kevin brought Hope home on his motorcycle, which she loved, but she couldn't fully absorb the joy of it because she was freaking out about facing Mia.

Mia came home a little bit later, looking tense, tossing her purse to the table as she held out a bag of Chinese takeout. "Moo shoo and pot stickers for everyone. Tell me you'll eat it," she said to Hope.

"Pot stickers?"

"I defy you not to moan with pleasure at the first taste."

Hope was used to feeding herself at home. Here it'd been a different story from the beginning. Having Mia even care brought a lump of guilt to her throat that she couldn't swallow away. "Um, I have to tell you something."

Mia had been looking at Kevin, doing that adult communicating thing without words. Again. Only for the first time since Hope had first seen them, it didn't seem sexual, it seemed like . . . concern.

Mia was concerned about Kevin.

Kevin just shrugged. "I'm going to take a shower."

Mia watched him go, then turned back to Hope. "What's up? And is it going to ruin my appetite?"

"I don't know. Today I . . . sorta broke a rule at school."

"Did it involve the police?"

"What? No. I . . . " Suddenly it all purged out of her in a painful rush: Adam, the walk to the teen center that ended up not going to the teen center at all, the woods, the kiss . . . "And really," she finished, "Kevin totally overreacted. It was just a stupid kiss."

Mia sighed and sank to a chair. "Oh, boy. Okay. First things first. There is never 'just a kiss.' Kisses lead to all sorts of . . . other stuff."

"Sex?"

"Well, yeah."

"But isn't that how all of us Applebys solve our problems?"

Utter silence followed this.

Hope clapped a hand over her mouth. She couldn't believe the words had come out of her mouth.

Mia sat there, stricken.

Remorse and regret and humiliation rose up and nearly choked Hope. She'd have to leave now, for sure. Mia would want her to. But she couldn't even speak to ask, because of the lump in her throat.

"Listen," Mia finally said, her disappointment weighing the room down. "Here's the thing. I'm an adult. That means I get to do what I want, when I want. I realize that sucks for you, but when you're grown up and done wearing Sharpie black ink as nail polish and eyeliner, then you get to do what you want. Get it?"

Hope looked at her fingernails and wished they were clear. She nodded.

"Do you? Do you really?" Mia asked. "Because it seems like we keep having this conversation. Whether you like it or not, I'm somehow responsible for you."

Hope nodded. She got that part. She'd come out here, uninvited, and put Mia in this position.

"Just eat," Mia said wearily.

Hope couldn't have swallowed to save her life. She hated knowing that she'd given Mia a reason to send her back home. "You could ground me."

"Can I ground you from talking ever again?"

"I don't think so. Are you going to send me home?"

Mia looked away, and Hope's heart clenched.

From somewhere in the depths of the house, the shower turned off. Mia cocked her head, listening. "We're not going to do anything right now. Listen, I'll . . . be back."

Telling herself she didn't care about the sudden

awkwardness between them, Hope grabbed her chopsticks. In her life, she'd pissed off a lot of people. She'd rather have Mia's anger any day over this clear disappointment, but she had no idea how to fix it.

Chapter Twenty-one

Mia let herself into Kevin's bedroom and shut and locked the door. She looked at the bed and ached. Instead of stripping and slipping beneath the soft brown and navy blue comforter like she really wanted, she sat on the edge and waited.

She already knew what had happened with Mike, and even if she hadn't, she'd get an earful from Tess. Mia's heart broke for all of them, but mostly for Kevin.

He'd looked so destroyed before she left for work that she cornered him in the pantry closet and did her best to take advantage of him.

That's when he told her what had happened. How he felt he'd failed Mike.

In truth, he'd probably never failed anyone a single day in his life. She sat on his bed, surrounded by his things and his scent, aching, and not just physically. She wanted to help him, soothe him, take away his problems.

Apparently his wanting-to-fix-people thing was contagious.

Finally he appeared, his long, lean body still wet, only a towel around his hips, and he arched a brow.

"Want to talk about it?" she asked.

"About what, the weather?"

"No."

"Hope?"

"About Mike," Mia said.

He dropped his towel and walked naked to his closet.

She eyed his very fine ass and shook her head. "Much as it pains me to say this, you can't distract me with your body."

"Well, damn," he said and shoved his legs into a pair of jeans.

Commando. God, she wanted him. Wanted to use that edge and temper she could see simmering just beneath his surface to her advantage. "Are you okay?"

"Sure."

"You don't seem okay."

"My brother hates my guts, did I tell you that? Oh, and I suspended a kid today, and he hates my guts, too. So does my boss, by the way, which he made clear when I was suspending said kid. Oh, and half the other kids hate me, too."

"Why, because you tell it like it is? Because you want them all to better themselves? Because you—"

"Butt in at every opportunity trying to make people be something they're not?"

Standing, she moved closer to him, feeling that heat of his carefully banked temper. "Then stop doing it. Worry about only yourself."

"That's your answer? That's what you came in here to tell me? Worry only about myself?"

"No, I came in here to jump your bones."

He stood there shirtless, shoeless, attitude-ridden, and gorgeous, and let out a sound that seemed to say *That works for me*.

She glanced back at the bed wondering if they could somehow—

He let out a harsh laugh. "Don't tempt me."

With a small smile, she slipped her arms out of her camisole dress and let it fall.

The breath whooshed out of his lungs, a satisfactory reaction indeed. Wearing only a demibra, a thong, and four-inch satin sandals, she put her hands on his chest and pushed him backward into the bathroom.

"Mia, we can't—"

She locked that door, too. Double protection, though she had no such help for her heart.

He made another rough sound. "This won't help—"

"Wanna bet?" Then she did as she'd promised. Jumped his bones.

The next morning, Hope didn't want to get up. It was their last morning at Kevin's, and Mia was in a snippy rush, snapping at Hope to hurry, hurry, hurry. Well Hope *was* hurrying, thank you very much, but she was also still feeling the heat of Mia's disappointment from the night before, and it made her snippy, too. Snippy enough that she felt the need to cause trouble.

It brewed inside her until she got to class and went up to Kevin's desk. "Mia wanted me to tell you that as our first night back in her house, she's cooking tonight to celebrate."

Surprised, Kevin looked up. "*Cooking?* Are you sure?"

"Very." Even as Hope said it, knowing Mia could burn water trying to make tea, she felt a grim sense of satisfaction.

Now *that* should bring Mia from disappointment mode straight to temper mode, no problem. Temper was something Hope understood and knew how to deal with. "She said to come over and have a home-made dinner with us tonight."

Pleased with herself, Hope went to her desk. Feeling someone looking at her, she turned around. The group of girls behind her, the popular girls, were glaring at her.

She smiled.

They glared harder.

Hope turned forward again, and a moment later felt something hit her in the head. It was a note, which read: *We know what you did.*

Too bad Hope didn't know.

At break, one of the guys explained it to her. The girls blamed her for two things: Adam being suspended, and that she'd "put out" for him in the woods before they'd gotten caught.

Put out? She hadn't put out, that rat-fink bastard!

Her neck was burning when class began again. She'd blown it in two out of two schools now. Nice record. She tried to concentrate on Kevin. He stood in the middle of the classroom holding a cylinder, head bent, boots unlaced, jeans looking as if maybe they'd been around for a few years, his T-shirt stretched taut over his shoulders and adorably frayed. Smiling.

He was usually smiling.

She loved that about him. She loved him. Not that she'd admit this upon threat of torture or even death, but sometimes, in the deep, dark of the night, she fantasized about him.

Fantasized that he was her dad.

It embarrassed her that she had that need, but it was there, burning in the pit of her belly.

He lifted his head and asked, "Okay, so if we use a vacuum on this cylinder and sucked out the oxygen, what's left?"

She knew the answer but bit her lip. She'd long ago learned to keep it to herself when she got things too quick, but especially here, now that everyone hated her, it would be worse.

"Cole?" Kevin asked.

Cole shook his head. He didn't know.

Kevin looked around. "Anyone?"

No one moved. No one appeared to even be breathing.

And Kevin let out a disappointed sigh.

Damn it. Hope raised her hand.

His eyes warmed. "Hope. I knew you'd know."

Her heart took a flying leap and hit her ribs. "Nothing. There's nothing in the cylinder."

His smile spread. "Correct."

The classroom was so utterly silent she could hear people breathing. Someone snorted, and someone else snickered. Heat flooded Hope's face. Then, from behind her, Cole shifted, leaning forward. "Cool."

In surprise, she craned her neck and looked at him.

At over six feet, he didn't fit into his desk so well, his long legs bent at a funny angle, his elbows hanging off the tabletop. He had dark hair on the wrong side of long, falling way over his collar and into his eyes. And he was so skinny she'd always thought of him as a scarecrow, but he had the kindest eyes she'd ever seen on a kid his age, and they'd drawn her that first day.

They drew her now, too.

All this time she hadn't spoken to him because the popular girls didn't like him. A thought that brought more shame. It just kept following her, starting from that time back at home when she'd been accused of stealing the lipstick.

At the end of class, she walked alone to the teen center, trailing a group of girls so as to follow the rules. Halfway there, she heard running steps come up behind her and whipped around.

It was Cole.

"Hey," he said, a little breathless but trying to be cool.

She didn't have it in her to come up with any smart-ass remark, so she just kept walking. He fell in besides her. She thought maybe he'd try to get her to talk, or even draw her into the woods like Adam, especially since everyone now thought she was that kind of girl, but they walked in companionable silence.

Out front of the teen center, he stopped and touched her arm. "You're too good for Adam" was all he said, and then he went inside, leaving her standing there, wishing she really *was* too good for Adam, wishing also that she hadn't invited Kevin over for Mia's home cooking. She really, really wished that.

Mia's morning was long, made even longer by the worrisome, underlying tension in the firm and the rumor of more layoffs coming. Damn it. She was in a staff meeting in a conference room when she had to leave to take a call from a client. She ran down the hall to her office and found her plant mysteriously tipped over. Only problem: the water from the container had spilled out, soaking the desk—and her laptop.

Her fried laptop.

Rumors flew at that. Some said she had enemies, some said it was karma. Her favorite was the one that said she'd done it herself to get attention. *Please.* As if she needed *that* kind of attention.

She actually thought about going to Margot, just for another female opinion, but the truth was, though Margot did not possess a penis, she would enjoy Mia's troubles.

But the bottom line was she couldn't even properly obsess about any of it, because she just didn't care the way she used to. Suddenly there were other things crowding her brain. She was worried about Hope, worried about Kevin, worried about Tess . . . Hell, she even worried about Mike. A new phenomenon, all this worry outside of work, but the list kept growing.

In an afternoon staff meeting, Ted came right out

and criticized her methods of getting accounts, which he claimed were too aggressive.

Bring it on, she thought grimly and sat back because surely someone would defend her.

The deafening silence around her spoke volumes.

Others felt the same way.

The joy in the job was fading, and that scared her because this job had always been everything to her. *Everything.* But the tension was too high to handle. Normally she solved that problem with a man. She looked around her and realized she didn't want just *any* man.

She wanted Kevin.

She checked her cell phone for the thousandth time, thinking maybe he left a message, something like *Now that you're back in your house, be sure to come knocking tonight.*

Or anything.

But nothing is what she got, and when she complained to Tess about it on the phone, Tess laughed at her.

"Let me get this straight," her supposedly best friend said. "You've told him you don't want a relationship, but you're mad because he doesn't call you?"

"Well, damn it, when you put it that way, I sound crazy."

"Honey, you *are* crazy. That is one fine, hot, sexy man. And I should know—his brother was just as fine, hot, and sexy."

Mia sighed. "I knew he was going to break your heart."

"He gave me my first man-made orgasm, you know."

Ah, hell. Tess had been in plenty of relationships, but she'd always had a hard time achieving full glory until Mia had bought her a vibrator a couple of Christmases back.

"He really did it for me," Tess said. "Without even trying, *bam*." She sighed dreamily. "I'd have married him for that alone." Her voice broke a little, and so did Mia's heart.

"I'm so sorry."

"Yeah, me, too. Did you know he thought I was sexy? *Me*."

"You *are* sexy."

"You aren't going to keep me warm at night."

"Damn it, I really want to kill him for screwing this up."

"I just want to hug him."

She sure as hell better not, Mia thought grimly. "He couldn't have supported you."

"Mia Appleby, queen of feminists everywhere, you did *not* just suggest I need a man to support me. I am woman, hear me roar."

"I heard you got some more orders," Mia said, executing a change of subject.

"Another thirty pounds a month. You were right, I need a bigger kitchen. I've applied for a business loan. Cross your fingers for me."

"I told you, let me loan you the start-up money."

"I can't take your money."

"Who said anything about take? It's a loan."

"No. But thank you."

"Tess—"

"You've helped me in other ways. Speaking of which, we need to go over marketing plans. How about tonight? Or tomorrow night? Doesn't matter really, I suddenly have a lot of free nights." Her voice got quiet and a whole lot less excited. "I don't know how you do it," she said softly, letting her pain be heard. "I loved feeling committed again."

"I'm perfectly happy alone."

Liar, liar.

"With no hold on Kevin? Really? Even knowing another woman could come along and snag him at any time? I'm just not built like that. I want a tie to a man. I want a diamond, damn it. I wanted that from Mike."

"Tess—"

"When you meet the right man, you'll understand."

"And how am I supposed to know when I meet the right guy?"

"Because it will hit you like a one-two punch," Tess answered softly. "You'll realize he makes you smile, he makes you laugh, he makes you think." She sighed. "And you don't think you can live without him."

"Jesus, Tess."

"I know, it sounds so dramatic, but it's the truth. You'll just know."

Mia supposed the problem wasn't the knowing, but whether or not she even had the gene to love like that. For so long it hadn't mattered. She'd had other things to obsess over, things like surviving, and her job. Meeting her goals.

But she'd done all that, and suddenly the life she'd always pictured herself with—the great job, great house, fat checkbook—all seemed just as Hope had told her . . .

Lonely. Everything.

And deep down an even scarier truth hit Mia—she no longer was satisfied by any of it.

Which meant she needed that elusive "more."

Chapter Twenty-two

Mia had her doubts about the day when she got a message that Dick needed to see her. In his office, he looked at her solemnly. "Have a seat, Mia."

She shifted on her heels, feeling suddenly extremely vulnerable. "Okay." She sat. "Let me be hopeful. You're going to tell me you're firing Ted for all his erratic behavior."

"No." Regret actually tweaked his features, and for a moment he looked almost human. "It's you I have to let go."

She stared at him as her world tilted off its axis. "What?"

"I'm sorry, Mia. We're having cutbacks, you know that. I have to lose three account execs. You're not meant to work in a place like this, as part of a team. You need to run your own ship, and helm it. It's nothing personal."

"Oh, it's personal," she bit out. "It's extremely personal. Ted—"

He was shaking his head. "Had nothing to do with it. This was a decision based on your inability to play as part of a team. I'm sorry, Mia, but I'm going to have to ask you to pack up your things and leave."

Mia's heart had been racing, but right then it seemed to screech to a shocking halt. As if in slow motion, she stood up and gathered her pride to shake his hand. "Don't be sorry. I'm going to be okay."

"I know it. I'm banking on you being extremely successful on your own. Good luck, Mia."

Somehow she walked out of there. *I'm going to be okay?* Had she really said that?

How? Her job was gone. She *was* her job!

Turning the corner she came face-to-face with Margot, who was smiling. "Hey, Mia, you should see the guys, they're—" She frowned. "What's the matter?"

"I—" She couldn't bring herself to say it. She'd lost her job, her identity, and, with it, apparently her bravado. "I have to go."

"You look pale. What's happened?" She looked back at the direction Mia had come from, Dick's office, and gasped. "Ohmigod! He let you go."

Mia narrowed her eyes at Margot. "Why would you think that?"

"He did, didn't he?" Margot couldn't quite keep her satisfaction in.

Mia stared at her, thoughts racing as she remembered all those times she'd been sure it had been Ted out for her blood.

But had it really been Ted?

Or Margot? How many times had Margot whined about Mia's accounts, her office, her everything? "You know what I think, Margot?" Mia asked softly. "That *you've* been the one messing with me. That you started that fire in my office. That you messed with my files."

"Don't be ridiculous." Margot crossed her arms, stepped back. "I didn't even know how to access that Runner account. And as for the Anderson—"

"Wait." Mia shook her head, then let out a laugh. And another. Because if she didn't laugh, she was going to strangle the woman in front of her. "No one knew about the Runner account except me and—"

"Margot." This from Dick, who'd opened his door

at some point. He was frowning, fiercely. "I'd like to see you. In my office."

"Um, I'm due in a meeting—"

"Now," he said.

"And I bet you poisoned my plant," Mia whispered as Margot moved past her.

Margot whipped around, all pretense gone, face furious. "No, that you killed all on your own."

Dick pointed at Mia. "Please wait right there."

Mia watched them vanish into his office, then felt an odd ping between her shoulder blades.

At least ten people had stopped working or walking or talking, and were staring at her.

She stared back and everyone galvanized into action, hustled to become busy again. She herself was nearly overcome with a need to look busy as well, but Dick had asked her to wait. Despite his faults, he was a man with ethics. When he discovered what Margot had done, he'd probably fire her instead and offer Mia back her job.

She went to her office and looked at her gorgeous desk. Damn, she was going to miss the desk. The plant sat on it, leaves all gone, dying, mocking her.

Lifting her chin, she picked up her purse and walked out, prepared to go as she'd arrived, with only the clothes on her back.

And yet at the last minute, she ran back in for her nearly dead plant. It would go well with the freshly fumigated house.

Mia's cell phone began ringing before she'd gotten on the freeway. Dick. She let him go visit her voice mail. Pride was a terrible thing but, damn it, at the moment it was all she had.

Traffic sucked, of course, but she looked at it as a silver lining. She wouldn't be dealing with it again, seeing as she no longer worked downtown.

Not a team player.

Maybe she was having a nightmare, and when she woke up she'd be standing in the middle of a single-wide next to a sewer plant, with eight kids and a husband in a wife-beater T-shirt with his beer gut hanging out, screaming for his pork chops.

The thought made her weak in the knees and she pinched herself to make sure she wasn't asleep.

Nope, she was wide awake, and this shocking reality was her life.

A little while later Mia picked up a suspiciously quiet Hope at the teen center. The kid hopped into the Audi, slapped on her seat belt, and stared straight ahead.

"How was your day?" Mia asked, as if things were normal.

"Can we just go?"

Mia looked at the teen center, then back at the antsy teen. "What, you rig the place to blow and you need a getaway car?"

"You think I have that much talent?"

"Honey, I know it." She pulled away from the curb. Silly to be wishing she'd caught even a little glimpse of Kevin. She didn't need a glimpse of the man.

But, God, she did. Today she really did, even if he was imprinted on her brain, the whole tall, lean, rangy length of him, with those smiling eyes and wicked smile . . . Yeah, probably a mind-blowing orgasm from him would be greatly beneficial in lowering her stress level. "The house should be cleaned and ready, I had a service come in today."

Hope nodded and said nothing.

They drove home in silence, with Hope not noticing—or caring—that Mia had an elephant of panic in the car with them. "Yeah, I had a great day, thanks," Mia said as Hope left the car and walked ahead of her into the house.

Mia just shook her head and felt her phone vibrating in her pocket. Tempted to answer it and agree to take her job back, pride be damned, she shut the thing off entirely. "You hungry?" she asked Hope as they went inside.

The girl had headed for the stairs, but went still. "Um . . . no." She looked down, her expression giving out a big warning to Mia.

"What?" Mia asked. "Look, are you sure you didn't blow up the teen center or something?"

"Okay, you caught me. I'm in cahoots with Satan, and occasionally I blow up entire teen centers just for fun."

"You know what? Go ahead, step on my last nerve, see if I care. My head is only about ready to blow off my shoulders at the moment."

"It's always ready to blow," Hope pointed out.

"Today I mean it."

Hope rolled her eyes.

"Now what did I tell you about doing that? Speaking of which, could you stop telling people I'm threatening you with physical violence? It makes the other parents a little anxious, and I wouldn't want you to lose out on friends on my account."

Hope's smile vanished. "I don't have any friends."

"Gee, really? With your warm, soft attitude? Imagine that."

Hope went taut as a bow, and Mia could have smacked herself upside the head. This was one of those tread-carefully moments that Tess had told her about, where bull-in-a-china-shop Mia wasn't needed, but a gentler, kinder Mia. "Okay, listen. I had a bad day. I'm sorry."

"No, you're right." Hope's face crumpled and she sat on the step, burying her face in her hands. "I got Adam suspended and now all the kids hate me. God, I hate boys! Every one of them are worthless and annoying."

Mia climbed the stairs and heavily sat down next to her. "Actually not all men are worthless and annoying. Some are dead."

Hope let out a sound that might have been a snort of agreement, or a sob.

Mia lifted a hand to touch her, then let it fall back at her side, but another sound came from Hope, a definite sob this time. "The hell with it," Mia muttered and scooted closer, wrapping an arm around Hope's skinny shoulders, feeling a little like crying herself. If there was a worse day since the one all those years ago when she'd driven herself west and never looked back, she couldn't remember it—and there'd been some pretty bad ones, especially in the beginning.

They sat that way for a long moment, silent, miserable, with Mia wishing things were different, that she could actually help make things better for Hope, or at least take away her misery. She cared about the kid, damn it, far more than she'd thought possible.

Her thoughts were interrupted by a knock at the door. Mia lifted her head hopefully, thinking maybe it was Kevin. He could fix this; he could fix anything. But the damn truth was she just wanted to see him. "Just a minute," she whispered to Hope and got up.

A tall, skinny, dark-haired kid stood on her doorstep. "Hi," he said, his Adam's apple bobbing. "Um, is Hope home?"

Mia looked over her shoulder. Still out of view on the stairs, Hope lifted her head, swiped quickly at her tears, and rose to her feet. "Cole?" she said, and came down the stairs.

He flashed her an uncertain grin that for some reason endeared him to Mia. "I just thought I'd see if you wanted to do tonight's science project with me."

Hope had black makeup smeared beneath her reddened eyes. Her hair had fallen out of its ponytail. She looked young, uncertain, and adorable, and right then and there, like the last piece of a puzzle falling into place, Mia fell the rest of the way in love with her.

"I don't know if we can," Hope said and jammed her hands into her pockets.

They both looked at Mia. "It's homework, right?" Hope nodded.

"Well, then what a perfect way to torture you."

Hope rolled her eyes but couldn't hide her pleasure. The two of them started to walk into the kitchen, but the doorbell rang again.

Mia opened the door and this time was caught utterly by surprise at the sight of Kevin. Wearing jeans and a white T-shirt, he looked so good she stood there for a startled second, just taking him in.

He didn't help the situation any by shooting her his smile, the one that always went straight to her throat. He lifted a bottle of wine. "So what's cooking?"

She couldn't have heard him right. "Cooking?"

"Uh oh," Hope said behind her.

Mia turned to look at her. "Uh oh *what*?"

Hope rolled her lips inward. "Can I, like, talk to you for a minute?" Without waiting for a reply, she came forward and pulled Mia into the hall, out of hearing range. "Okay, listen, this isn't going to go over well, but just remember, I was looking to piss you off."

Mia crossed her arms. "Keep talking."

Hope winced. "I sort of told him you were cooking him dinner."

"You *what*?"

"Shh." Hope put her hand over Mia's mouth. "I'm sorry," she said earnestly. "I was being a stupid teenager, okay? I was mad because everyone in the world was happy except me."

Mia pulled her hand from her mouth. "Oh, no,

you don't. You read that in my *Cosmo* mag. Ten Reasons Why Teens Act Out."

"Yeah, but it nearly worked on you, I could tell."

Mia paced the hall. "Damn it! This day was a total waste of makeup." Sighing, she looked at Hope. "You told him I'd cook him dinner, knowing that I'd rather have a root canal without drugs?"

Hope grimaced. Nodded. "See, you were all disappointed in me, and I decided I liked it better when you were mad."

"You know, that's just twisted enough that I believe you." Mia took a deep breath. "Okay, in the kitchen. Get started. I'll meet you there."

"Why don't I just tell him—"

"Oh, no! Are you kidding? Never admit your mistakes! Not to a man! Now move it—we have some major deception ahead of us. You know when you mentioned being in cahoots with Satan? You were just kidding, right?"

Kevin heard the frantic whispers and murmurs coming from the kitchen and glanced questioningly at Cole. The kid lifted his shoulder.

Kevin moved closer to the kitchen door.

"Canned soup isn't cooking," he heard Mia hiss. "You told him *homemade*."

"We don't have anything to homemake," came Hope's voice. "I keep telling you a growing teenager needs food in the fridge."

"Hey, I feed you."

"Yeah, takeout."

"Expensive takeout! And at least I'm making sure you're eating your veggies and fruit. Just this morning I bought you frozen yogurt."

"Hate to tell ya, but yogurt isn't a fruit or veggie."

"Yours had strawberries in it."

"You know," Hope said, "if you'd just be honest

and tell him you're not perfect, I wouldn't be able to get you in these situations."

Mia muttered an oath and Kevin grinned. So Mia wanted him to think she was perfect? Kinda cute, really. Cute and extremely revealing, especially since he already knew she was far from perfect.

"Look, this has been a bad day all around." This from Mia, sounding frazzled. "I just don't want to admit that I can't even put a meal together. It makes me seem pathetic."

"You've got other stuff going for you."

"Like what?"

"Like . . . um . . ."

"Yeah, don't hurt yourself, thanks." Mia sighed. "A real woman can cook. All right? I intended to learn, I just never got around to it." The sound of cabinets shutting drifted through the door. "Damn it, I don't even have a cookbook." More slamming of cupboards. "I ought to make you drive to Giapetti's and bring back takeout, which we could then claim as our own cooking, but making you drive the Audi isn't exactly a punishment."

"How about if I pretend to hate it?"

"Hope, I swear to God, if you don't try looking sorry that you got me into this mess, I'm going to ship you back to Sugar via UPS ground."

Kevin laughed—oh, yeah, this was what he'd needed; *she* was what he needed—and opened the kitchen door. He rattled his keys. "How about I drive us all to Giapetti's?"

With a squeak, Mia whipped around to face him. Her cheeks had two high spots of color and there was a strand of hair hanging in her eyes, but something else seemed off . . . Ah, she'd kicked off her heels, bringing her down to her own petite height. She fixed that by immediately slipping into them again.

Tell him you're not perfect.

The words had amused him a moment ago, but now he felt a hard tug on his heart. Didn't she get it? He didn't want perfection, he just wanted her.

She smoothed her hair in a calm, cool gesture he knew was faked. "Well," she said with a laugh. "I was going to cook something right here, but if you insist."

He smiled. "Oh, I insist."

He let her keep up the pretense all through dinner, which was excellent, but he could tell something else was seriously bugging her. He waited until they'd gotten back home and Hope had gone inside to do homework with Cole before he stopped her. "What is it?" he asked her.

Mia looked at him in surprise. "Is it all over my face then?"

"Maybe I just know you."

She studied him for a long moment, the evening breeze ruffling her hair. "Is it weak to admit I actually liked the sound of that? You knowing me?"

Her admission grabbed him by the throat, but he smiled and shook his head. "Not at all."

She leaned in as if to kiss him, and his engine revved, but her cell phone rang. She looked down at the ID and sighed. "It's Tess. I have to get it."

"I just heard," Tess said in Mia's ear. "Oh, honey. Dickhead didn't deserve you, either."

There on the sidewalk, Mia closed her eyes. "You heard? *How?*"

"The grapevine."

Absorbing the shock, Mia rubbed her forehead. "So the whole world knows I'm gone? Nice."

"What are you going to do?"

"I'll come up with something. I always do." Extremely aware of Kevin watching her, she turned away, not wanting to admit quite yet her public humiliation. "Listen, I'll call you tomorrow, okay?" She clicked off, plastered a smile on her face, and looked at Kevin.

He stood there, tall, lanky, gorgeous, making her heart hurt. She was holding on by a thread here, and the drama of the evening hadn't helped ease the drama of the day. She needed him with a shocking desperation. But she couldn't drag him upstairs; she had an impressionable teen in the house. She couldn't drag him to *his* house because of Mike. Damn it. She wanted him naked, hard, inside her, making her mindless how only he could.

Maybe they could go for a ride somewhere. Practically vibrating with need, she opened her purse to check for a condom.

"When were you going to admit you couldn't cook?"

She looked up. He was watching her. "Although, if you're wondering," he said, "I could care less if you can or not." He playfully tugged on a strand of her hair.

Her fingers wrapped around a condom. "Actually, I was thinking of another kind of cooking altogether . . ."

His hands stroked down her back as if he couldn't help himself, but then he stepped back, jamming his hands into his pockets. "Nice subject change."

She sighed. "If you don't care if I can cook, why bring it up?"

"Because you tried to hide it. Just like you hide everything that you think is too revealing."

"Like?"

"Like your past. Your weaknesses. Anything you think makes you less than who you want to be. You hide a lot, Mia."

"I don't—" But she did. They both knew it.

She'd never seen such a grim expression on his face as he backed a step from her. "You know what? I'm going in," he said.

The air felt charged as they stared at each other, and she knew the ball was in her court. "Don't," she whispered. "Don't go."

He let out a sound that managed to perfectly convey his disappointment in the fact she hadn't faced what he wanted her to face. That she hadn't talked to him: about herself, about her feelings, about them. When he turned and walked away, she felt her heart crack and give, but her heels felt as if they'd been stuck in wet concrete. She couldn't move.

"Wait," she whispered.

He looked back, saw the sheen of tears in her eyes, and closed his. "Mia." He came back to her and spoke in a quiet tone that broke her heart with each word. "I'm just tired of this, you know? Tired of digging for the real you. You hide at every turn, you close yourself off. I don't want to have to find out you've lost your job by overhearing a damn phone call."

Humiliation rose up and choked her. "I was going to tell you."

"When? When you had something else, when the situation was all fixed?"

"Well . . . yes."

"See that's just it. I want more. I want to be needed. I want to be a part of your life."

"I didn't keep it to myself to make you angry."

"I'm not angry, I'm hurt. I thought we were friends."

The panic that had been sitting in her chest since Dickhead's office rose up and grabbed her by the throat. "We are friends."

"How can we be, when you've never trusted me?"

"This isn't about trust."

"Bullshit."

She stood there staring at him, thinking it'd been a hell of a day. She'd lost her identity, she'd lost her sense of self, and now she was going to lose him.

"I've given you all I have to give. It has to be enough." *Please, God, let it be enough.*

He looked at her for another long moment. Then slowly shook his head.

"I'm sorry," she whispered.

"Me, too." Again he walked off.

And this time she let him go.

Chapter Twenty-three

Kevin took his bike over the canyons and hills of LA for several hours, but neither the cool breeze nor the scenery helped the hole in his chest. He had a feeling nothing would. When he got home, Mike was waiting for him. They hadn't spoken much since the arrest.

What's up? Kevin signed.

Mike shook his head. *Just waiting for you.*

Well there's a change.

Mike winced and Kevin felt like a jerk. *Look, I just broke if off with Mia and I'm not fit for company, all right?*

Mike looked stricken. *What happened?*

We don't agree on what a relationship should be. Story of my life.

I'm sorry. I know that's inadequate, but I am. Mike got in Kevin's way when he tried to move up the stairs. *Maybe we could hang out or something.*

I don't have any cash.

Mike's eyes reflected regret. *I don't want money. We could stay home.*

Kevin shrugged and turned away. *Nah.*

Mike shouldered his way in front of Kevin. *I know you don't believe me, but I just want to be here for you.*

I thought you were mad at me.

I got over it.

Kevin rolled his eyes.

I mean it. Come on, name a problem, let me try to fix it.

Kevin laughed. *You're going to fix my problems? You hate problems.*

Try me.

All right. Kevin crossed his arms and leaned back against the banister. *The teen center. I need a down payment to buy the building.*

How much?

About a hundred times what you've got.

I could accept Linda's marriage proposal.

Linda?

Remember that voice-over actress I dated last month? She's a daddy's little rich kid, and she wanted to marry me.

Kevin looked at him. *You'd actually get hitched? For me?*

Mike lifted a shoulder.

Kevin laughed. *You're allergic to commitment, much less marriage.*

I wouldn't be with Tess. Even Mike looked shocked at that. He staggered backward and sat down. *I can't believe that came out of my mouth.*

Kevin stared back. *You do know the definition of marriage, right? Till death do you part?*

Mike rubbed his heart, still looking staggered. *Shut up a minute.* He looked up at Kevin. *I'm having a moment. I just realized I'm in love with her.*

Ah, hell. Kevin sat heavily next to him and looked into Mike's stricken face. *She'd be crazy to have you. But damn lucky.*

That won't get you the teen center.

Yeah, but it'd make you happy. Happy would be good.

Mike nodded. *But I want you to be happy, too. You can fix this somehow, I know it.*

Kevin shook his head. *No more fixing. It's either right, or it's not.*

And at the moment, nothing seemed right, nothing at all.

Mia slept poorly, then got up at the crack of dawn like usual and checked her cell phone.

Not a single message.

Flopping back, she stared at the ceiling, trying not to panic. She was hugely successful. She'd have thought she'd wake to handfuls of offers.

But no one had contacted her.

She was undesirable. *"Shit."*

That the word came out sounding extremely Southern didn't improve her mood any. God, she missed Kevin already. One night, and she felt as if she'd lost an appendage.

But she'd given him every damn thing she had.

She had, she told herself again, shoving away the niggling doubt, because self-righteous indignation was much easier to deal with.

She'd given her all and had turned out to be lacking. A common problem, apparently.

Her phone rang. Her heart leapt, thinking that maybe . . . Kevin. She couldn't pounce on it fast enough.

"Hey, Apple, guess what? I'm missing the ol' kid."

Mia thunked her head down on the counter. *Sugar.* "I thought you were busy on your vacation from life."

"I was *recovering,*" Sugar said somewhat defensively. "But I'm done now. Send her home, damn it."

Suddenly suspicious, Mia lifted her head and frowned. "Let me guess. You've been dumped."

Sugar burst into tears. "Oh, Apple. And I thought he was the one this time. The real one."

Mia thought of Kevin and felt like crying, too. "Yeah."

"And the place is a mess. Only Hope can manage to keep it decent. I need her back."

Unreasonable panic hit Mia, because Sugar sounded like she meant it, and because . . . well, because, damn it, Mia had grown rather fond of the troublemaker.

"She's not the maid, she's a kid. And she's now enrolled in a science class that she needs. She wants to be a marine biologist. It's important to her."

"But she lives here. With me."

"Sugar." Why didn't she felt like dancing for joy? What was this irrational dread? "Things were bad between the two of you. She's getting herself straightened out, she's happy, she—"

"Have her call me," Sugar interrupted and hung up. The Appleby way.

When Hope rushed into the kitchen with one minute to spare, Mia used that as an excuse to not mention Sugar's call. She dropped Hope off at school and drove straight to Tess's.

"I've thought about this. I don't want to get another job working for some other Dickhead. I want to work for myself. For us. I want in," she said.

"In what?"

"In Cookie Madness."

"You're already in."

"I want to be a partner. You interested?"

"I am *not* taking your money."

"Take? No. Invest. Yes. And believe me, we'll use it wisely."

Tess looked torn between joy and caution. "I'm not letting you take a chance on your money."

"Are you kidding me? We're not taking a chance on anything. We're going to succeed."

Tess gnawed on her lower lip. "Mia. Friends shouldn't do this, combine funds."

"You're not my friend. You're my sister."

Tess's eyes filled and Mia shook her head, pointing at her.

"No. Don't do that—"

Too late. Tess threw her arms around Mia, making her stagger back a step, hugging her hard so that Mia's eyes burned, too, damn it.

"Besides," Mia whispered. "We both know how good I am at selling. I'm going to sell us all the way to the bank."

Tess choked out a laugh and Mia took her first real breath of the day. She had a purpose again, a direction to concentrate her efforts, which meant she was going to be okay.

That night Cole came over for Hope. The two of them sat at the kitchen table, heads bent over their science final projects, looking so happy Mia could hardly breathe.

She'd worked hard all her life, always thinking that the *next* step would be the one to bring her happiness, but, damn it, she was tired of waiting for that elusive feeling to materialize.

Especially when the truth was, the only time she'd come close had been in the company of a man.

One man.

Kevin McKnight.

In a moment of weakness, she waited for Cole to leave, then downed three cups of caffeinated coffee to guarantee staying awake longer than the kid. It wasn't easy, but adrenaline—and caffeine—fueled her, and when Hope was asleep, Mia sneaked out her back door into the warm, sticky, lightly raining summer night.

God, to have someone to stare up at all those stars with . . . But there was only one someone that interested her. Her heels sank into the damp grass as she crossed her yard, and then her neighbor's, and came to Kevin's.

She stood there alone in the dark, raining night, aching for the sound of his voice, his smile, his arms to come around her.

But his house was dark.
Just like her heart.

Kevin paced the house like a caged tiger. The weather was too bad to go for a long ride on the bike, and nothing else appealed.

In the end, he sat in the darkened kitchen nursing a beer, listening to a late-summer storm pound the windows. Lightning flashed like a strobe, and he got up to look out the windows as the storm raged. On the next crashing boom, the sky lit up, the landscape imprinted on his brain like a picture. The low-riding hills, the bush-lined trail to his door . . . and a woman standing at the end of the trail.

Mia, standing there in the rain and wind, staring at his house. He couldn't see her expression, but he wanted to think she was filled with the same pain and longing that filled him.

But in the next flash of lightning, she was gone.

After zero sleep, Mia rose at dawn and dressed for a run. Despite the light drizzle, she was determined to run off some tension. After one block she was joined by familiar battered athletic shoes, topped by a mouthwatering body.

Kevin McKnight.

Mia soaked up the sight of him, so relieved she was speechless. His hair was spiked with rain, his tank top and shorts equally splattered, and he looked, well, vibrantly masculine.

"Hey," he said in a voice that made her yearn, and adapted his stride to hers.

She knew she was strong, but she couldn't help herself. "I, um, missed you."

He tripped, then caught himself. "Excuse me?"

"You heard me."

"I suppose I did." He let out a smile. "I just wanted to hear it again."

He looked at her and she looked right back, drinking in all the details, the sheen of his several-day-old stubble, the shadows beneath his eyes that said he wasn't as laid-back and happy as he seemed, the planes and angles of his face, the sexy line of his jaw.

The piercing eyes that saw right to her soul. "If you missed me," he said, "you knew how to fix that."

"One would think. But apparently, smart as I am in some areas, I'm a little slow in others."

He didn't correct that, and they jogged along.

He wanted more from her, and she struggled to give it. "Sugar wants Hope back."

"Does she?"

"Yeah. Best news I've had in weeks," she quipped, then could have bit her tongue. *Why did she do that?*

Seeing right through her, he slanted her a long look but didn't speak. They ran in silence past the park on the right and onto a trail leading into the woods, where there was no development, just trees and wild growth on either side of them. The rain was coming down harder now, cooling her overheated body.

"I'm sorry," she said, gasping for breath. "That back there, about Hope. I lied. I'm going to miss her like hell. Kevin . . . I'm sorry I hurt you."

"Me, too."

She nodded, not liking the terrifyingly final tone to his voice. She took them off the trail, into the woods.

"Hey," he called, following her. "Where are you going?"

She kept running. Hoping he followed.

"Mia, I have to get to work . . ."

She kept running. *Please follow me.*

"Well, as long as it fits into your schedule, Ms. Gotta Do Everything Her Way or the Highway," he muttered.

Finally she stopped and, huffing for air, turned to

face him. "See, now this is why you shouldn't pour your heart out to people. They'll use your personality traits against you."

He made a sound that might have been a laugh or a snort of agreement, but it was cut off when she pushed him back against a tree. "You're going to ruin your shoes," he warned. "Isn't that a crime in Mia-land?"

"Ha ha." She knew they were surrounded by suburbia, and yet it was hard to believe it in here. Craggy rocks and tall pines and oaks were interspersed with patches of high bush and crevasses. They were isolated enough, with no one else around for what felt like miles.

"Mia—"

She held him to the tree, her palms slapping up against the tough, damp sinew of his chest. It shouldn't have turned her on but it did. He did. She had a feeling he could just stand there breathing and he would arouse her. "Listen to me."

"I've been listening to you for weeks," he said. "Want to know what you've been saying? 'Do me, Kevin.' 'Do me and then walk away, Kevin.' 'Don't get attached.' 'Don't try to get to know more.' 'Don't love me.' Well, fuck it, Mia. Whether you like it or not, I've done all those things, and I'm done. Cooked. DOA."

She stared up at him in shock. "You . . . *love* me?"

"Have you been paying attention at all?"

Spots swam in her vision, and from far away she heard him swear as he reversed their positions so that he pressed *her* back against the tree, holding her there with his body. Rain plastered his hair to his head, dripped off his nose, his chin.

"That night at the restaurant . . . I convinced myself you didn't really, that you couldn't . . ." She gulped in air, held it.

"Breathe, damn it."

"Hold me. Please—just hold me."

He swore; then his hand skimmed down to the backs of her legs, where he lifted her up. His erection pressed into her, and despite the wet, she sighed in pleasure. "Oh," she breathed, her head falling back against the tree so that the raindrops fell on her face.

"Yeah, oh." He did not look or sound nearly as soft and relieved as she felt, and she lifted her head. His eyes were dark, his face taut, his mouth grim. Angry, frustrated. *Turned on.*

"Here," she gasped. "Please, here."

"I'm more than this," he ground out. "I have to be more than this to you."

"Yes—God!" She gasped when his fingers dipped between her legs, beneath the edge of her panties. He stroked one long finger right over her while she thunked her head back against the tree.

"We're back where I promised myself I wouldn't go."

With effort, she lifted her head and blinked past the now heavy rain to focus his face. "Kevin—"

"Yeah. You know what I think? I think sex with me is safe for you. Short, fast, and damn good." Another stroke and she arched into him. "But when it comes to more, no can do. Wonder why that is, wonder what you're afraid of? That I'll see the real you?" His gaze swept down her body, flushed and damp with perspiration, with rain. "News flash, Mia. I've seen the real you. I've always seen the real you."

Unbelievably touched, Mia closed her eyes.

"You're passionate, smart, sharp as hell, and damn funny when you want to be. You'd give a perfect stranger a room in your home, even when you don't open yourself easily. Yes," he said when she began to shake her head in denial. "You'd give a friend your entire savings account."

He knew about that? She'd kill Tess later.

"And yet you'd go to great lengths to hide what

you think are your faults so that someone who means something to you won't turn away. Goddamn, Mia, do you think I don't know your faults?''

"Well—''

"You're bullheaded, opinionated, and you swear like a sailor.''

She squirmed, braced for more, but he shook his head and murmured, "I don't give a shit about any of that. I love you anyway.''

The words, uttered with frustration, with anger and heat, with utter bare-soul honesty, made her gasp.

"Yeah,'' he growled. "And I know that thrills the hell out of you.''

She clutched at him, rain falling on her face, his hands in her shorts, still stroking her. "Kevin . . . I don't know what you want from me.''

"You. *You*, Mia, without me pushing, goading, prodding to find that you beneath your protective layer. Let me in, goddamnit.''

"In?'' she cried, overwhelmed by the emotion she'd been holding at bay since . . . since forever. "No one wants in. They want me to be strong, be in charge, they want me to be a team player. But I'm not! Do you hear me? I'm not any of those things really, I'm just me. Plain Mia Appleby, who can put a spin on anything, including a damn fine façade. Don't you get it? I don't know *how* to let you in.'' She sank her fingers into his hair and tightened her grip, nose-to-nose with him, furious, upset, and far too close to tears. "I'm giving you all I can, but it's not enough! I should have never brought you cookies that first night—''

"Damn right you shouldn't have,'' he growled, hands clasped on her bottom to hold her in place. "Or come knocking on my door the next night, and the one after that, looking like sin personified, promising all sorts of things with those gorgeous, wounded eyes, things that had nothing to do with what we give each other in the deep, dark of the night."

The skies let loose then, dumping buckets down on them. It didn't matter; Mia for one was so hot that the rain felt good on her steaming skin. "I want to be enough for you," she whispered. "Just as I am." She arched up, gliding the wettest part of her over the hardest part of him. "*Please*, Kevin. Let me be enough."

He swore at that, and in the next instant slammed his mouth over hers as he tugged down her shorts and panties, shoved his shorts to his thighs, then lifted her back up to wrap her legs around him. "Hold on to me then," he demanded. "Damn it, hold on."

"I am." She hung there, suspended by time, by his body, by the storm, lost in his possession, in his ragged breathing and the rain pummeling her heated flesh, in the feel of his muscled body, the scrape of his beard, the scent of him, and the wet trees and earth all around.

He slid into her with one powerful thrust, making her cry out. She had no idea how it was always like this between them, a match to dry timber, a moth to flame, every single time. She would die if she didn't have it. *Him.* No one but him. "Kevin . . ."

A low, rough, gravely sound of tortured pleasure escaped him, and with the rain pelting down on them, he surged into her, again and again, until with a gasping sob she exploded. She was still in the throes when he followed her over, her name on his lips.

Still quivering, she closed her eyes and just held on, loving the way he had his face plastered to her neck, panting for breath, his arms crisscrossed against her back, protecting her from the bark of the tree, bowed over her body so that the majority of the rain fell on him instead of her.

Even when frustrated, hurt, and furious, he was the best man she'd ever known, and from nowhere the emotions reared up and battered her. She tightened her arms on him, preventing him from stepping free, but he didn't even try. He stayed still with her a long moment, his muscles still quaking, until finally he lifted his head. His eyes were dark and shadowed. "You okay?"

She closed her eyes and pulled his face close, touching her forehead to his. "Yes," she whispered.

"Sure? It was kind of rough." He eased her shaky legs down until her feet touched the ground, and helped her right her clothes. "I'm sorry."

She couldn't speak past the lump the size of a regulation basketball in her throat, so she just shook her head. She didn't want him to be sorry, she wanted— *God.* What she wanted.

They walked back in the pouring rain, their fingers entwined. Outside his house, he brought her fingers up to his mouth. "I have to go to work."

And she did not. The wince came out of her before she could stop herself. He squeezed her fingers. "Mia—"

"I'm a big girl, I can handle it," she said. "Besides, I have tons of stuff lined up—" She broke off, looked away, and then back into his eyes. "No, that was an embellishment. I have nothing. No leads, no interviews, nothing. I am unemployed. Completely. All I have is a part of a cookie dough company that looks good in theory but has yet to prove itself. How's that for letting you in to see the real me?"

His smile was slow, and no less sexy for the sympathy in his eyes. "A damn good start. I was getting tired of being a piece of flypaper for the obnoxiously bullheaded and obstinate."

She felt her own reluctant smile. "Obnoxiously bullheaded?"

"Hey, if the shoe fits . . ."

She laughed, and, God, that felt good.

"So what now, Mia?"

"I don't know."

He looked at her for a long moment. "Let me just lay it out there for you. I want you more than I've ever wanted anything or anyone else in my whole life."

Once again the breath backed up in her throat.

"You either feel that way back, or you don't."

Since she couldn't breathe, she just stood there. Brilliant.

"What's the worst that could happen, Mia, if you go for it?"

"I could screw it all up. I could—"

"Snore?" he asked ironically. "Have stinky feet? Be bad in bed?"

"This is not funny."

"No," he agreed, his smile gone. "It's not. But if we're going to just do this, I want all of it."

"Define 'all.' "

He just looked at her, and she swallowed. "You mean—" She swallowed again. "The whole white lace dress, tacky white tiered cake, complete with a lease on a double-wide?"

"I'm not trying to freak you out, I'm just telling you how I feel."

"Kevin."

Something in her face must have given him her answer, and he stared down at his feet. Nodded. "Yeah." He looked at her then. "Good-bye, Mia."

A sob welled up and she bit it back. If this was really how he felt, it was the end.

The end.

Oh, my God. Through blurry eyes she watched him walk away, a profound sorrow working its way through her as she realized she'd never see him smile at her, never feel the touch of his kiss, hear the timbre of his voice all directed at her in that special way he had of making her feel like the only woman on the planet.

Not ever again.

She waited until he was gone to sink to the ground, curl up in a ball, and watch the rain fall.

Alone.

Chapter Twenty-four

When Mia got home, she was surprised to find the world still spinning. The refrigerator hummed, music emitted from Hope's alarm that she was ignoring . . . Yep, everything looked and sounded completely normal. Chilled, she took a long shower. By the time she got out, she was warmed and dry again. She surveyed her closet. Prada or . . . Target?

Target. Sweats and bunny slippers, to be precise. Dressed, she headed for the kitchen and any alcohol. Only problem, it was still morning. Settling for caffeine, she dumped three teaspoons of sugar into the coffee to add a desperately needed sugar rush. Then she glanced at a box of small chocolate donuts on the counter. Hope's. Screw watching calories, this was a mental-health emergency. She ate one, then five more.

At seven thirty, Hope staggered into the kitchen, went straight to the refrigerator, and pulled out the OJ container. She shook it and drank straight from the jug. "I'm going to finish it," she said when Mia just looked on.

"Fine."

Hope eyed her more closely. "You look like crapola. What's wrong?"

"Nothing." Gee, unless you count the fact my life is in the toilet. "Why?"

"Are you wearing . . ." Hope squinted in disbelief. "The *Target* clothes?"

That the girl recognized the difference of designer versus plain brand gave her a proud-aunt moment.

"Are you?" Hope pressed.

"Tell anyone and die."

Hope laughed.

"Hey, I'm not kidding. And just so you know, I wasn't always a clothes snob."

"You know it sounds like English coming out of your mouth, but I just can't quite make it out," Hope told her.

"Great. A comedienne."

Hope set down the juice. "Okay, what's wrong really? Tell me the truth, because you're not harping on my clothes or makeup, you're not harping on what I'm not eating—"

"Does this train of thought have a caboose?"

"What did you do, call my mom and get me booked on a bus or something?"

Ah, shit. Sugar. She needed to find a way to tell Hope her mom wanted her back. "No. No bus riding."

Hope put the dishes from the sink into the dishwasher. Got to hand it to the kid; she knew how to pick up after herself. She'd probably been doing it for years. Mia took another long look into Hope's face and felt a squeeze on her heart. There were purple smudges beneath her eyes that had nothing to do with her baffling choice of makeup. And her face seemed drawn. "Clearly, I'm not the only one in a pathetic mood," Mia said.

Hope looked up in surprise. Lifted a shoulder.

Oh, boy. A fishing expedition in the expanse of a teenage mind. "So . . . Cole seems nice."

Bingo. Hope plopped into the chair across from Mia. "Yeah. But just a few days ago I was gaga over Adam. I'm not sure how I'm supposed to trust my feelings now. It seems so . . . comforting." She looked at Mia. "Any maternal urges coming to you? Any advice at all?"

"In case you haven't noticed, I'm not so good with feelings in general, so I'm probably not one to ask."

"You're with Kevin. You have feelings for him."

"Well, no to the first, but yes on the second."

Hope's mouth trembled open. "I thought he loved you."

"Maybe love isn't always enough."

Hope looked vastly disappointed by that, but Mia told herself she was young, she'd learn.

"I think what I feel for Cole is more . . . *real* than what I felt for Adam. Does that make sense?"

Mia thought of Kevin and compared him to every guy she'd ever been with. There was no comparison. "Perfect sense."

"He kissed me."

Mia cut her eyes to Hope.

"Don't worry. No sex."

Mia nodded and ate another donut.

"You know, my mom would be spouting stuff like, 'Marry a trucker, they have good insurance.' Nothing I'd want to hear. You don't do that. If you don't know something, you don't pretend to. You just tell it to me like it is."

"I guess I wish I'd had someone do that for me when I was your age."

"Were you scared? When you left?"

"Terrified. Still am." *Now that I'm back to square one.*

"You never seem scared. You always seem like you know exactly what you're doing."

Mia laughed. "Well, trust me, I don't. I'm all screwed up. I lost my job yesterday."

Hope's eyes widened. "Are you going to be out on the street?"

Mia's smile faded. She'd nearly forgotten what it was like to be sixteen and living seriously day to day. In Hope's world, no job meant no food and a manager banging on the door demanding rent, or else. "We're going to be okay for a while."

"You said we."

"So I did."

Hope smiled, but it faded. "How long is a while?"

"Long enough that you don't need to worry about it. Longer if Tess and I make Cookie Madness work."

"I can work for Tess. I can even quit the science class and work full-time."

"No. No way. You're staying in school. Wherever that might be."

Hope blinked. "What does that mean?"

Mia sighed. "It means your momma wants you back."

Hope was quiet a moment. "And what do you want?"

"I want what's best for you."

"Oh." Hope looked down at her clasped fingers. "I guess I actually miss her sometimes. You know, a little."

A knife to the chest. "That's good." Trying not to lose it right there, Mia got up and grabbed her keys. "Time for school."

They were in the car before Hope spoke again. "I want to be just like you when I get to be as old as you are. What is that, forty?"

"Do you want to see your next birthday?"

Hope actually smiled. "Twenty-five?"

"See, *now* you're talking." So she'd turned the big three-oh last year. She could handle that. Yeah, her life sucked at the moment, but she could handle that, too.

For a long moment after Hope left the car, Mia sat there absorbing the morning sun. Hope wanted to be like her.

God help the both of them.

*   *   *

That afternoon Hope sat on a swing in the park. The early-evening sun beat down on her head as she idly kicked her foot in the sand, rocking back and forth, eyeing the lazy blue sky. At home she'd have been lying on her bed, wondering why she had no friends, why no one wanted to get to know her.

It should have disturbed her that she was still alone, but somehow it didn't. She didn't feel sick and sad all the time, she didn't feel like her chest was too tight. She didn't feel like she wanted to hurt something.

And—and this was the biggee—she didn't feel like wearing black all the time. For one thing, it was freaking hot. And for another, she liked Mia's clothes.

She liked it here.

She hadn't talked to her mother yet. Sugar had needed a break, which Hope understood, because she'd needed the break, too. But now that break was over.

Still, it would have been nice to hear from her momma, even once, to know she'd been missed, worried about. Even though that wasn't really her way. Hope would have bet that wasn't Mia's way, either, but Mia always wanted to know where Hope was and when she was coming back. At first, Hope had thought it was because Mia needed a break, too, but now she knew differently.

Mia worried about her.

And though that knowledge should have felt weird, should have been suffocating, it wasn't.

She heard the footsteps and knew it was Cole. He'd said he'd come hang out. He always did what he said he was going to, and the sheer comfort in that warmed her from the inside out. Lifting her head, she watched him walk toward her. He wore baggy cargo pants, a Zeppelin T-shirt, and a tight expression that said his mother had been yelling at him again.

But then his gaze caught hers and the shadows in his eyes went away. He smiled.

She smiled back.

"You look really pretty when you do that," he said.

She felt the heat settle in her cheeks. "You don't have to say stuff like that."

"I know." Moving behind her, he gave her a push.

Laughing as the swing began to move, she closed her eyes and let the warm wind blow over her face. It felt so good. He pushed her for a few minutes, then sat on the swing next to her.

"Adam broke up with Amber," he said.

She opened her eyes and caught the worry in his. "I don't care about Adam," she said.

He didn't say anything.

"I don't," she repeated, wanting him to believe her. "I don't care about any of them."

"What do you care about?"

"My aunt Mia. Kevin, and Tess, and Mike. I care about school. About . . ."

"Yeah?"

"You," she whispered, holding on to his swing when he would have backed up. "Cole, I mean it."

He looked like he desperately wanted to believe her but didn't.

"Adam was stupid," she said. "Being with him was *me* being stupid. I'm done with that. And I'm done with trying to hurt people to get attention. I just want to be." She leaned in close, her heart in her throat. "And I just want to be . . . with you."

He just stared at her as if she was speaking a foreign language, and it gave her the courage to admit the rest. "Cole, I've never . . ." With a grimace, she looked down at her toes. "I've never really felt . . . excited by a guy. I mean, I pretended to, but it's always pretty much been an act." Never having made the first move before, she wasn't sure how to make it count, but she lifted her head and stared into his eyes, then shifted even closer, their mouths a breath apart. "But when I'm with you, it feels different."

He stared at her, not moving a muscle. "Different like I'm-going-to-puke different, or different good?"

"The truth?" She shook her head and stared at his mouth. "I'm not sure yet. I want to find out, though. I have to find out. But you also need to know . . . I have to go back to Tennessee."

"When?"

"Soon, probably."

He paused. "That's going to suck."

"Yeah. Big-time." Her heart was going to barrel right out of her ribs, but she had to do this, wanted to do this. "Cole."

He was still as stone, not even breathing, as far as she could tell, his fingers white-knuckled on the steel line. Then his Adam's apple bounced once, hard.

For some reason, that little motion of vulnerability boosted the fledgling courage she felt inside and she touched his mouth with hers.

He groaned, a sound that did things to her belly and made her legs feel rubbery, all good stuff, so she kept her mouth on his.

He made the sound again, and then slid his arms around her. His nose bumped hers, hard, and she pulled back.

"Sorry," he whispered.

She clutched at his shirt and stared at him. "No, it was good. I don't feel like throwing up," she said, her voice all strange and breathy. "I feel like . . . *wow*."

He let out a long breath. "Yeah. *Wow*."

She bit her lip and looked at his mouth again, a little surprised to find her body sort of quivery, wanting more. "I want to say one more thing about me. And Adam."

Some of his smile faded. "You don't have to. It's okay."

"I didn't—"

"None of my business—"

"—have sex. I've never—" She managed to look him in the eyes. "—had sex. I just wanted you to know."

He looked at her. Then smiled.

"What's so funny?"

"I haven't either."

Was it possible to actually die of happiness? Hope thought maybe it was.

Over the next few days, Kevin managed to teach without losing it, managed to avoid Mike's probing, thoughtful gaze whenever possible, but he hadn't managed to avoid Hope. He just couldn't do it to her, so when she came up to him at lunch and whispered, "I know," squeezing his hand, he could hardly speak.

But he opened his desk drawer and pulled out her car keys.

Hope stared at them. "You mean—"

"Finished." He'd stayed up late putting in the new alternator and water pump for something to do other than obsess. "All yours."

Her smile was worth every moment. "Thank you," she whispered.

"I don't know what your rules are, so check with Mia before you drive anywhere."

"I will."

"And no more driving across the country until you're thirty."

"I won't." She hugged the keys to her chest. "You are the best man on the planet."

He nodded, but he didn't feel like the best man on the planet. He felt like the emptiest man on the planet.

Basketball had always been Kevin's drug of choice, and he needed to self-medicate, bad. Luckily, after work he had a basketball game scheduled at the court near his house. He headed toward the gate with more than enough pent-up aggression, and hoped the guys he was playing this week could handle it.

They could. The other team consisted of all twenty- and thirty-year-olds, and by the time the game was over, Mike bled from his lip and one knee and Kevin thought maybe he'd cracked a rib or two. Plus, he could hardly put weight on his ankle, which he'd twisted twice in his college days and apparently reinjured today in one of his fan-fucking-tastic layups, if he said so himself.

You're getting old, Mike signed when Kevin winced as they walked/limped/whimpered off the court.

Kevin straightened and ignored the screaming in his ribs. *Speak for yourself.*

I might be bleeding, and possibly getting old, but at least I'm heading for a woman who's going to feed me and then tuck me into bed, clucking over my injuries, kissing me allllllll better. He waggled his eyebrows as he backed from Kevin, jingling his keys.

Who?

Tess.

I thought she dumped you.

Mike's smile faded. *She did. I'm slowly working my way back into favor.*

And he would, too. Mike was the most charming, funny, easy-to-love guy he'd ever met. *Let her go*, Kevin signed. *Pick someone else.*

Mike shook his head. *There's not going to be anyone else. Ever. And I know that's a helluva long time, but that's how I feel.* Mike looked down at his battered athletic shoes, then back up. *I'm going to prove myself to her. And you. I realize it might take a while, but I'm okay with that.*

You have nothing to prove to me.

The hell I don't. You've been saving my sorry ass for too long, and I've let you because, well, I guess I liked you feeling guilty. But I can't get my own life together if you're the one running it, and I want my life together. I want Tess.

Kevin stared at him, saw the real regret and honesty and frustration in his brother's eyes, and for the first time felt a true surge of hope. *What are you going to tell her?*

The truth, for a change. That I've been working my way through any woman I could get my hands on, trying to feel better about myself and my screwed up life. That until she came along I never felt whole.

Kevin nodded, thinking how much he'd love to hear such things from Mia. *You might have to be patient.*

I'm willing to put the time in. Mike smiled, then walked off the court, leaving Kevin to wonder if he'd really get his happily-ever-after.

Or, for that matter, if Kevin would. He grabbed his bag, and when he turned around, his gaze locked on Mia.

She stood on the other side of the fence, on the path that would take her to her house, wearing some knockout business suitdress that made his tongue waggle and his heart hurt.

She looked like a million bucks, even as her eyes narrowed on him, her mouth opening in a little O of distress as she came through the gate. "What the hell have you done to yourself?"

He touched his lip and his fingers came away bloody. "Just a little cut." He bent to pick up his duffle bag and then whimpered unmanly when the pain stabbed into his ribs.

"What's the matter?" she demanded and put a hand on his arm.

"Nothing." He managed a smile, and sweating all

over again—and not entirely because of his injuries—
he headed out the gate, dragging his bag instead of
picking it up.

Dragging his ass, too.

Her heels clicked on the asphalt as she followed at
his side. "You're hurt."

"Part of the game." She smelled like heaven. He
wanted her, of course; he always wanted her. But
oddly enough, while dragging her into the woods
and shoving up that hot, short skirt had plenty of
appeal, he wanted other things, too. Her smiling, for
one. Her happy, talking, laughing. Just being. With
him.

Idiot. *You can't fix . . .* "You're dressed up."

"I worked a new job today."

"That's great," he said and meant it. "What—" He
broke off when he tried to shoulder his bag, because
the sharp pain stabbing into his ribs made it impossible to do anything else.

She made a soft sound of distress as she reached
for him, but he gritted his teeth and shook his head.
"I'm fine," he managed, not wanting her hands on
him. That would only make things worse. "Nothing
a shower can't cure." He lengthened his stride ahead
of her, gritting his teeth as he took the three stairs
toward his front door, each jarring his ribs.

"Kevin—"

"Yeah, I gotta go. I'll see you, okay?" He shut the
door, dropped the bag and the pretense, and sagged
back against the wood.

Chapter Twenty-five

Mia stared at Kevin's front door. He'd dismissed her. *Unbelievable.* Well, guess what? She was done with being dismissed. She'd spent the afternoon working Cookie Madness for all it was worth, and she'd kicked some serious ass. She had big news and—other than Tess, who already knew—no one to share it with.

At least no one to get naked and share it with.

That's when she'd had her epiphany—and better late than sorry, right? She'd been wrong to hold back, wrong to let her past and fears stand in her way, and she wanted Kevin to know it.

Damn it.

She lifted her fist to knock, but decided the hell with that. They were way past knocking, so instead she turned the handle and pushed. She felt a resistance, then heard a pained "Oomph."

"Hello?" She pushed again, then realized Kevin himself must be leaning on the door. "Kevin?"

"Yeah."

Slipping inside the crack, she found him sitting against the wood, pale and sweaty. "Damn it." She put her hands on her hips rather than hover over him like the worried hen a small part of her wanted to be. "Let's go. *Now.*"

"Sorry, honey." Brow damp, he shot her a weak

smile. "I don't think I can do you right now. I've got to—"

"Doctor," she said through her teeth. "I meant I'm taking you to a doctor."

"Not necessary." Getting up *very* carefully, he moved to the base of the stairs, then just stared up at them in dismay.

"Oh, for God's sake." She dropped her briefcase and moved forward, slipping a hand around his waist. His skin felt hot to the touch, and damp. "Did you break a rib?"

"Nah."

He was holding his breath as they took the stairs, she noticed with concern, and now looked a little bit green. "I still think we should—"

"Wow, I must have hit my head, because I thought you just said we."

"Kevin—"

But he just walked through his bedroom and into his bathroom, slowly pulling off his shirt. "Start the shower?" he asked her.

She cranked it to what she knew was his personal favorite—scalding.

He kicked off his shoes with the slow, purposeful movements of the very drunk or the very injured, and she got mad again because mad was easier. "Damn it, Kevin, you need a doctor."

"Shh," he said, then toed off his socks.

"Look, I'm dragging your ass straight to the ER."

He shoved off his shorts, then stood in front of the mirror inspecting his lip.

Because she was human, her gaze took a tour of his rock hard body. Long, powerful legs. Fantastic ass. Lean hips. Smooth, sleek back.

Coming up behind him, she put her hands on his already bruising ribs. Beneath her hands, his muscles leapt. He hissed out a breath.

She met his gaze in the mirror. "Sit." Gently pushing him onto the closed commode, she grabbed a towel, wet it, then dabbed at his lip.

He winced.

She scowled, and dabbed some more. Damn it, she was not good at this coddling shit. She dabbed again and his hand came up and caught her wrist.

"I'm fine," he said.

She tossed the towel aside in frustration and glared at him. "Great. You're fine."

Slowly, holding his breath, he stood again and put his hands on her arms. "And you're not."

Hey, she was perfectly great, just because apparently she couldn't even show him how she felt. *What was wrong with her?* How was it she'd not gotten the gene to do this—to love?

She tried to turn away and he stopped her. "What's wrong?"

"What's wrong?" She tossed up her hands and let out a laugh that didn't fool either of them. "Are you kidding? Nothing's wrong. I'm damn perfect." With a rough sound she pushed him into the shower. Then she left the bathroom. She felt the urge to fix him something, something to eat or drink . . . something.

She loved him.

She loved him, and she was afraid even that wouldn't be enough and she'd be left with this huge gaping hole in her chest. She was going to break an ankle on his stairs, but she didn't care as she rushed down them and into the kitchen, then looked around her wildly. What could she make him? She looked at the counter, at the table.

He'd taken her there.

The counter, too, and on the floor, in that amazing storm.

"Oh, damn," she whispered, throat thick, and sat right there on the floor, folding into herself, putting her forehead to her knees as she did the grown-up thing.

She burst into tears.

The house cracked, and she lifted her head, gasping at the two feet right in front of her. Long legs hunkered, and then Kevin's face appeared. Reaching out, he touched her wet cheek. "What's this?"

Sniffing, she wiped her nose on her arm. "Allergies."

He gave her a long look. He'd pulled on fresh basketball shorts but was still wet. Lip still bleeding, his eyes were warm and concerned and filled with things that caught her breath. "Mia."

She closed her eyes. "Something blew in my eye."

"Why can't you admit it? That maybe you need to lean on someone else for comfort once in a damn while?"

She lifted her chin at that. "The only comfort I need is the occasional orgasm."

"I hate to break it to you, but you like it more than occasionally. As studly as I like to think I am, I can hardly keep up."

She snorted and swiped at her nose again. "You keep it up better than any other—" She broke that thought off, thinking that had probably been 5-1-1. Too much information.

But he went down to his knees, a motion that made him wince, then slid his fingers into her hair and not so lightly tugged her head back so he could look into her eyes. "Better than anyone else? Is that what you were going to say?"

"No."

"God, you are such a liar."

The back door of the kitchen opened, and suddenly people poured in. Tess, Mike, Hope, all carrying grocery sacks.

"I need help," Tess said, actually sounding close to tears herself as she took over the kitchen without taking a good look at Mia. "I have to come up with one hundred pounds of dough tonight—"

"Tess," Mia managed. "We're in the middle of—"

"I'm sorry, Mia, but you got me into this mess and I can't screw it up now!" Tess helped herself to the kitchen cabinets, barking out directions. "Grab bowls and start mixing! The sooner we do this, the sooner we can all get back to our regularly programmed evening."

Hope dug right in.

Mike dug right in.

Mia stood there, watching Kevin. *Damn it!* She had so much to say . . .

"Get busy!" Tess demanded.

Mike set the bowl down and signed something.

"Slave driver," Kevin translated for him, looking fine with the interruption, of course, because he *was* fine. He didn't have an epiphany to share!

Tess waggled her brows at Mike. "That's right, baby, and keep it moving. I'll reward *you* later." She planted one quick smacking kiss on his lips.

"Hey," Kevin protested when she passed him, no kiss.

"Sorry." Grinning, she backed up and gave him a smacking kiss just to the right of his cut lip.

Mia knew it was silly and irrational and childish, but the green monster bit her on the ass.

"Now *that's* what I'm talking about," Kevin said with a smile.

Mike shoved his shoulder, leaving a white flour handprint on Kevin's bare skin.

Kevin eyed it, but Tess quickly stepped in between them, laughing. "No wrestling in here. I mean it! You can fight over me later."

Mike nodded. Worked for him.

Kevin began cracking eggs.

Mia tried to be just as cavalier, but casual and cavalier weren't her strong suits, and she'd never been so aware of another person in her life. Every move Kevin made she caught. Every smile, every egg he cracked with those long, talented fingers . . . He still had that flour handprint on him, which should have looked ridiculous but didn't. He had at least a day's growth of beard on his jaw, and she wanted to rub hers to it. She wanted to feel his mouth on hers.

She wanted him to hold her, tight, so that she could feel the steady, secure beat of his heart beneath her ear. But more than anything, she just wanted to be with him.

God, she had it bad. Bad, bad, bad.

Behind her Hope had gotten serious about the measuring, pointing out to Mike that he had enough flour.

"You're hired," Tess said. "Seriously."

Hope blinked. "Really? I can work for you?" She looked at Mia. "Can I?"

Mia looked into her eager eyes and felt another tug. *Damn it!* All these strings on her heart! Somehow she smiled past the lump in her throat. "For as long as you—"

"Stay." Hope looked down at her flour-covered hands. "Yeah."

Mia's gaze caught on Kevin's.

He was looking at her with understanding and empathy, and she had to turn away rather than lose it. *God.* She couldn't take it, she just couldn't. She was losing everything, and everyone.

Hope touched her finger to Mia's nose and left a flour print. "Pretty."

Mia narrowed her eyes. "You didn't just do that."

Hope arched a cocky brow.

Mia dipped her fingers into the flour and took a step toward the kid, but Tess stepped in between them as she had Mike and Kevin. "I swear it, I'm going to start cracking the whip!"

Behind Tess's back, Hope stuck her tongue out at Mia. "Out of my way, Tess," Mia said.

"No! Now I have to create four hundred more orders by the weekend. I don't have staff. I don't have space. You goaded me into this, Mia Appleby, and our new place isn't ready yet. I'm a half inch from a spectacular breakdown that, believe me, you don't want to see, so—"

"New place?" Kevin asked.

Tess looked at Mia. "We invested in a building. Mia didn't tell you?"

Mia shook her head. Not yet, she hadn't.

Tess sighed. "We're leasing part of the building to Cookie Madness. The other part—"

"Later," Mia said and begged Tess with her eyes. "I'll tell you all later." It was important she tell Kevin herself, alone. Important that she do it right this time, preferably no audience. "After I cover Hope in flour—"

"Oh, no," Tess said. "Kiss and makeup right now or I'll make you do dishes."

"I don't do dishes," Mia said.

Tess didn't look like she cared if Mia wanted to do dishes or not, and Mia sighed. "Okay, fine. *Sorry*," she said to Hope.

"And I'm sorry about how ridiculous you look with flour on your nose," Hope said, tilting up her chin.

"*Kiss*," Tess demanded.

"Can't," Hope said. "She's not big on PDA."

"That's true." Kevin cracked an egg with more force than necessary, and shame filled Mia. And sadness.

And more regret than she could have put words to.

Hope was looking at her with a daring expression, and that was it. Mia grabbed the little monster and kissed her noisily first on one cheek, then the other, then ruffled her hair with her flour-covered hands. "There. I've covered some of the black."

"When I leave, you'll not have to ever see black again."

"Thank God," Mia said with a fervor she didn't come close to feeling.

"Yeah, no kidding," Hope seconded toughly. "I can't wait to get out of here. No one complaining about my music or my favorite color."

"No one leaving entire boxes of donuts in the house."

"No one harping on my curfew."

"No one cramping my style."

Mia looked at her.

Hope looked back.

Mia thought if she had to come up with one more thing, she was going to burst into tears right there. "Actually, I take back the donuts part."

"I knew it. You *did* eat them."

"Every last one," Mia said and heard the catch in her own voice. *Ah, hell.* "And I guess I should tell you . . . rap is growing on me."

"No."

"I think 50 Cent is a hottie."

Hope clapped a hand over her mouth, but the giggle escaped anyway, along with a tear. "I like it when you harp on my curfew. It means you care."

"Well, then I must care a helluva lot. I know you have to go, but I was hoping next summer—"

"Yes! And Christmas?"

"And Thanksgiving. I'll send plane tickets for every holiday."

Hope let out another laughing sob. "My mom—"

"I'll handle Sugar. I'll do whatever it takes."

Hope nodded and hugged Mia hard, streaking her black mascara and eyeliner mixed with the flour on her Dolce & Gabbana, and Mia didn't even care.

"I'm sorry," Tess said softly, hugging them both. "This is good. But we *have* to finish. I *have* to deliver."

Kevin's gaze touched over Mia's features, soft and

warm for that one moment, as if he was happy for her. And proud of her for sharing her feelings.

Her throat burned, her heart ached. She wanted to tell him to sit down for this one, because there was more, much more that she wanted to share, but Tess the drill sergeant was standing over her.

"Resume duties!"

Grinding her teeth, Mia took a bowl from Tess and began mixing.

"Yikes." Tess looked into the bowl. "Honey, you have to commit to mixing—you can't just go halfway."

"She's not that great at committing," Hope said, smiling at her own quip. "It takes her a while."

Kevin shot Mia a look that said he most definitely agreed.

Tess worked on fixing the mixture. "You should have just told me you were bad at this and just walked away."

"Yeah, now that she is good at." This from Kevin's corner.

Tess went still. Everyone went still.

Hope glanced at Mia, waiting for her reaction.

Her reaction? That she couldn't do this. She couldn't even *joke* about what had been the best thing to ever happen to her, before she'd walked away, as Kevin so helpfully pointed out. She reached for her keys.

"Oh, no," Tess said. "You're not going anywhere."

"I've got to—" Fall apart. Cry. Kick my tires . . .

"*I'll* go." Kevin shouldered his way to the door, but Mike slapped a hand on it, keeping it closed, pointing to Tess.

"Oh, my God, oh, my God!" she cried.

"What?" Mia demanded, whipping back around. "Honey, what is it?"

Tess had been holding a bowl in the crook of her arm, whipping the contents with a whisk, which she'd lifted above the bowl and was peering at intensely. Specifically, between the steel twines, all covered in cookie dough, something sparkled.

Mike, watching Tess very carefully, set down his own bowl and dropped to his knees. Reaching up, he took the bowl from her hands.

Tess stared down at him as she reached into the whisk and pulled out the diamond ring.

A drop of cookie dough landed on Mike's nose.

"A ring," Hope whispered, stating the obvious. "A diamond ring!"

Tess dropped the whisk and brought the ring up to her mouth, sucking off the cookie dough. Then she looked down at Mike, letting out a laughing sob, and dropped to her knees too, leaning in to kiss the drop of cookie dough off his nose.

Mike signed something with his hands.

"Will you marry me," Hope whispered.

"How do you know what he's saying?" Mia whispered, her heart in her throat.

Hope beamed. "He's been teaching me."

Tess signed something back, and with his eyes suspiciously bright, Mike slid the ring on her finger.

They signed back and forth to each other.

"I didn't know—" Hope translated. "I thought we were going to wait— No, I don't want to wait, I don't want to ever wait. You're the love of my life. There's no one else, there will never be anyone else. I love you—" Hope broke off as they kissed. "That part is sort of self-explanatory."

Mia stared at Hope. "She said yes."

"Actually, I think she said, 'Oh, hell yes, yes, *yes*.' "

Tess laughed as she rose to her feet, swiping at her tears. "No more distractions! We have to get this done! You"—she pointed to Hope—"measure. You"—she pointed to Kevin—"mix! And you—" This was for Mia.

Mia lifted her hands and backed to the sink. "I'm on it. But, God, Tess."

Tess welled up again. "I know." She wrapped her arms around Mike, kissed him once and then shoved him away. "Later. We all celebrate later."

It was hours and hours before they finished, and in the end they all sat on the kitchen floor, covered in various ingredients, exhausted.

Except Hope. She looked at her watch. "I'm going to go meet Cole. 'Kay?" she asked Mia.

"'Kay," Mia said. She had her eyes closed, head back against the cupboard. "Where at?"

"Dairy Queen. He's working there."

"Put out the word that Tess is hiring. She'll pay good for hard-working teens to work a couple of hours every afternoon."

"I don't know about good," Tess said. "But I'm a kind, patient boss."

Everyone snorted.

Hope left.

Mike rose and pulled Tess to her feet, kissed her, then pulled her out of the room, waving good-bye at Mia and Kevin, neither of whom had moved.

Finally, they were alone. "Kevin."

He opened his eyes but didn't move a muscle. His hair stood straight up; he had flour on one cheek and nose and across his chest. He looked like the sexiest, baddest, most adorable man she'd ever seen.

And she had to do this, had to do it right. "I wanted to talk to you."

He didn't move, didn't speak, but his eyes were on hers, dark and intense.

She shifted up to her knees and crawled over to him, hunkering back on her heels at his side, wishing he'd reach for her, touch her, smile. Anything. "First things first. About the new property for Cookie Madness. I bought the old drive-through restaurant."

"The what?"

"The building you house the teen center in. Tess and I wanted the huge kitchen. But as you know, there's another seven thousand square feet that I thought . . . you might want to . . . *damn it*. I want you to have it for the teen center. You can lease it if you'd like, or owe me, or don't pay at all, for all I care, but it's a done deal." She took a breath, and then another. "Are you going to say anything?"

He blinked once. "I'm not sure."

"Okay." *Fair enough*, she thought, as she hadn't ever said much. Or enough. "Second, about what I said to you the morning after we first, um . . ."

"Fucked?"

"Made love."

He arched a brow.

"I know, look at me maturing right before your very eyes."

His lips quirked, but that was all. No warmth, no affection . . . just a bone-deep terrifying nothing. She closed her eyes, then opened them. "That morning, I was scared."

She would have sworn that caused a flicker in his gaze, and warmed by that, she sped up. "You reached into a part of me and made me feel things I didn't know I could feel anymore. See, I thought I had it all closed off. So I pushed you away, thinking it would be easiest. I said you were bad in bed. You . . . uh, weren't."

"I know."

She stared at him, absorbed the cocky words, and had to laugh. Hope might be the one taking classes this summer, but the truth was, Mia was the one getting several life lessons. One, there was something a little terrifying and a lot arousing about a man so damn sure of himself. Two, keeping a man like that would never be boring.

And three, she'd missed him with all she had,

heart and soul. She missed him so damn much she didn't want to be alone tonight. Or any night. She wanted him in the same bed, in the same house.

Day in and day out. "And then you kept wanting more," she said. "And even though in theory it sounded exciting and right and good, I wasn't ready."

"I tried to give you the time you needed. I even understood your need to have it. I just couldn't take it anymore."

"So were you always on to me?" she asked. "From the beginning?"

He nodded.

"See," she said with a catch in her throat. "That's what gets me, right there. You saw right through me and my neurosis, and you still liked me."

That brought out a smile. "How do you know I like you?"

"You—you said."

"That's right." His voice was low and so achingly familiar she wanted to crawl into his lap, but he still hadn't touched her. "I said. I always say what I mean, Mia. What I feel. No pretense. No hidden meaning. No games."

"I know." Oh, God, her voice cracked now. Her eyes burned. "That's new for me. But, Kevin, it's very, very welcome."

"So welcome you walked away."

"Actually, technically, I believe it was you who walked," she said much lighter than she felt.

"Whatever lets you sleep at night," he said wearily and closed his eyes again.

She looked into his face, rugged, rangy, tough, and yet kind. The kindest face she'd ever known. He gave and gave and gave, to his family, to his students, to anyone who was in need.

Who gave to him?

She sure as hell hadn't, and the shame of that

nearly choked her. "I'm not. Sleeping at night," she added.

His eyes opened again.

Slowly she shook her head. "It's my own fault. I screwed up with you so badly. I mean, for someone so determined to be careful, to do everything perfectly, could I have done worse?"

He winced. "Mia—"

"No, you've got to hear me out on this one. I was so busy keeping you in a certain area of my life—"

"Which is to say the naked area."

Now it was her turn to wince. "Yeah, I sure did my best to keep you naked. To keep it just sex. I managed to do that for approximately five seconds."

That got his attention. He looked right at her, and she rushed to keep going, for once in her life to get it right. "You see, I always knew," she said, her voice pitchy and uneven.

"Knew what?"

"That I loved you." The words felt rusty in her mouth, assuring her that she had not said them enough. "I do love you," she whispered. "So much."

His eyes darkened. "While those are very welcome words, I've learned love isn't always enough."

"No. Not when one of us is holding back, trying to keep herself from sinking in too deep. But I've finally realized, I'm not drowning at all, because no matter how deep or hard I fall, you're there with me."

He stared at her for a beat, then snagged her hips and tugged so that she fell over the top of him.

She put her hands on his chest and smiled up into his face. "See? You broke my fall."

He let out a low laugh, shook his head as if to clear it. "Spell this out for me, Mia. What are you saying?"

"I'm saying that maybe you're not the only one who can make changes."

Though his eyes remained serious, his lips curved. "You're going to stop folding your underwear?"

"Okay, smart-ass. I'm trying to say something here."

"Then spit it out."

"I made you feel as if there wasn't room in my life for you, but there is." Sliding her fingers into his hair, she tightened her grip just a little, and kissed him. "I want to take the next step. I want to be with you, only you. And hold on to something, Ace, because here comes the biggie. I think I might someday actually want that whole white dress, white cake thing."

His eyes widened. His fingers tightened on her hips. No doubt he was leaving more flour stains on the Dolce & Gabbana, but she couldn't care less. "You mean—"

"I know you didn't ask me, but since I'm doing everything upside down and ass backward, I thought it'd be fitting if I asked you." The waterworks were threatening again, but she blinked them back. "Will you have me, Kevin? Through thick and thin and cookie dough parties? Through better or worse, or worse-est?"

"Mia—"

"Wait," she said quickly, not wanting him to say no yet. "You're probably having doubts that I mean all this, doubts that I could let go enough to love you as much as you love me. But I can, Kevin. I—"

"Mia," he said again, with such tenderness it blindsided her. He framed her face with his hands. "I don't have any doubts. You just take my breath, is all."

She stared into his eyes and felt herself smile, at peace for the first time in . . . *ever*. Sliding down, she snuggled in close and pressed her face into his throat, breathing him in, holding him tight enough that their hearts beat in unison. "I don't either anymore. Not a single one . . ."

National bestselling author
JILL SHALVIS
is turning up the heat.

BLUE FLAME
0-451-41168-4

When San Diego firefighter Jake Rawlins is injured in a
fire, he retreats to the Blue Flame, the Arizona guesthouse
he inherited from his father. There he finds
Callie Hayes, the ranch's tempestuous manager, and
his life is changed forever.

WHITE HEAT
0-451-41142-0

Bush pilot Lyndie Anderson lives only for her plane and
the open sky, until she's hired to fly firefighter
Griffin Moore into the heart of a raging inferno—and
the sparks of desire begin to fly...

SEEING RED
0-451-21502-8

Summer Abrams nearly died trying to save her father from
the warehouse fire that took his life. Consumed by guilt,
she flees the town where her world fell apart—and into
the arms of the wildly sexy fire marshal who's
able to ignite her deepest desires.

Available wherever books are sold or at penguin.com